"And what brings that smile to your face, Nora?"

Nora turned to find the sheriff at her elbow. "Just thinking about how weddings bring out the romantic in even the most unexpected of hearts."

She realized how that must have sounded and her cheeks warmed. She quickly changed the subject. "Is there something I can do for you?"

"Just the opposite," he said. "Thought I'd offer you a ride back to your place."

How thoughtful of him.

"I promised your brother-in-law I'd keep an eye on you in his absence," he added.

Well, so much for his romantic i‌ ‌‌‌hought. "Thank you, I would be m‌ ‌‌‌t your offer of a ride. Would ‌ ‌‌‌while I fetch her things?"

He backed up a‌ ‌‌‌on't I fetch her things for yo‌

She'd never met a ‌ ‌‌‌ndoffish when it came to little kids.

She wanted to know *why*.

IRISH BRIDES: Adventure and love await these Irish sisters on the way to America…
The Wedding Journey—Cheryl St.John, April 2012
Mistaken Bride—Renee Ryan, May 2012
A Baby Between Them—Winnie Griggs, June 2012

Books by Winnie Griggs

Love Inspired Historical

The Hand-Me-Down Family
The Christmas Journey
The Proper Wife
Second Chance Family
A Baby Between Them

Love Inspired

The Heart's Song

WINNIE GRIGGS

is a city girl born and raised in southeast Louisiana's Cajun Country who grew up to marry a country boy from the hills of northwest Louisiana. Though her Prince Charming (who often wears the guise of a cattle rancher) is more comfortable riding a tractor than a white steed, the two of them have been living their own happily-ever-after for more than thirty years. During that time they raised four proud-to-call-them-mine children and a too-numerous-to-count assortment of dogs, cats, fish, hamsters, turtles and 4-H sheep.

Winnie has held a job at a utility company since she graduated from college. She saw her first novel hit bookstores in 2001. In addition to her day job and writing career, Winnie serves on committees within her church and on the executive boards and committees of several writing organizations, and she is active in local civic organizations—she truly believes the adage that you reap in proportion to what you sow.

In addition to writing and reading, Winnie enjoys spending time with her family, cooking and exploring flea markets. Readers can contact Winnie at P.O. Box 14, Plain Dealing, LA 71064, or email her at winnie@winniegriggs.com.

It is of the Lord's mercies that we are not consumed,
because his compassions fail not.
They are new every morning:
great is thy faithfulness.
—*Lamentations* 3:22, 23

To my fabulous agent, Michelle Grajkowski, who remains my biggest cheerleader. And to my fellow authors in this continuity series, Renee and Cheryl, who made this experience such a great one.

Chapter One

❧

Faith Glen, Massachusetts, August 1850

Nora Murphy looked at her two younger sisters across the room and tamped down the pinprick of jealousy that tried to intrude on her joy at their good fortune.

After all, this was her sister Bridget's wedding day to Will Black, a good and honorable man who loved her dearly. Everyone in town was gathered to celebrate here at Will's home—Bridget's home now, too. It was a joyous occasion and it would be selfish to put her own feelings above her sister's.

So what if just a scant month ago Maeve, the youngest, had also married a wonderful man? No matter how it felt, Nora assured herself, it wasn't *truly* pitiable to be the oldest and the only one still single and with no marriage prospects. After all, at twenty-five she had a few years left to her before she'd have to don her spinster cap.

Strange how in just a little over two months—a seeming eyeblink of time—her whole world had changed. Back then they'd lived in Ireland amidst the terrible burdens of the potato famine and the sickness that had taken so many of their friends and neighbors, and finally their beloved da. Suddenly orphaned and facing eviction, they'd been left all but destitute and desperate. The startling discovery of a possible inheritance across the ocean in America from an old suitor of their mother's had been an answered prayer. She, Bridget and Maeve had left their homeland, headed for the land of promise with only their faith and the hope of finding a new home in the small town of Faith Glen, Massachusetts, to keep their spirits up.

They'd all taken jobs aboard the ship the *Annie McGee* to replenish their drained savings after purchasing their passage. Maeve, the youngest, had fallen in love with and married the ship's well-to-do doctor, Flynn Gallagher, before they'd even set foot in America.

And now Bridget, the middle sister, had married Will Black, a mill owner and Faith Glen's wealthiest citizen.

How wonderful that her sisters had found good, honorable men who loved them deeply and who could care for them extravagantly. It was surely a blessing from the Good Lord Himself. And she was certain the Good Lord had plans for her, as well. Whether or not those plans included marriage was another question altogether.

Father Almighty, I really do want to be obedient to You and to patiently await Your will for my life. But please be patient with me when I try to get ahead of You. I am prideful and too often try to control my circumstances.

"I brought you a glass of punch."

Pulled out of her musings, Nora found Sheriff Cameron Long, the man who employed her as housekeeper and cook, standing in front of her. He had a cup in each hand and was holding one out to her. His always-ready, lopsided smile was in evidence, giving him a boyish look despite his imposing size. Really, the sheriff could be so considerate.

When he wasn't being so maddeningly stubborn.

She looked up, meeting his gaze. Unlike her sisters, she had more of her father than her mother in her and had been the tallest of the three siblings. But Sheriff Long still towered over her, which was an uncommon but not entirely unpleasant experience.

"Thank you." She accepted the cup and took a quick sip. "'Twas kind of you to bring it to me."

He took a drink from his own cup. "If you don't mind my asking, what are you doing over here by yourself? As a sister of the bride I would think you'd want to be in the thick of things."

Nora waved toward the cradle that held her infant ward. "I'll rejoin them shortly. I just put Grace down for her nap."

She still found it hard to believe that no one had come forward to claim the newborn foundling who'd been abandoned during their voyage. Perhaps, for some reason, the child's family members couldn't reveal themselves. But whatever the case, Nora was guiltily glad they hadn't. The idea of giving Grace up now was too painful to consider.

As usual, the sheriff avoided more than a quick look Grace's way and merely nodded, then changed the subject. "I understand you made most of the cakes for this little gathering."

"It was my gift to Bridget and Will."

His smile broadened and his heather-blue eyes regarded her in that teasing way he had. Didn't he realize there should be a certain formality between an employer and his hired help?

"And a mighty tasty gift it was," he said, saluting her with his cup. "That was as fine a use of the Huntley-Black chocolate as I can remember. Most everyone is saying how good the desserts are and I saw several guests sneak back around for seconds."

Bridget's new husband owned and operated the Huntley-Black Chocolate Mill, a business that employed a large number of the town's citizens. It had given Nora a great deal of satisfaction to devise a recipe using Will's product for this reception. "I enjoy cooking and baking. I'm just pleased others take pleasure in the results of my efforts."

"And I'm pleased I get to enjoy them on a regular basis."

Her cheeks warmed at the more personal compliment. "Thank you. As I said, I enjoy cooking."

He finished his punch and she expected him to drift away, but instead he nodded toward the other side of the room. "They make a fine picture, don't they?"

Bridget had stooped down to say something to Will's three-year-old twins—her new stepchildren—and the youngsters were giggling. Will stood next to his bride, looking on with a besotted smile.

Nora nodded. "They do indeed. They are all blessed to have found each other."

"Do your Maeve and Flynn plan to stay here for a while?"

She followed his glance toward her other sister and brother-in-law. "No, I'm sorry to say. They'll be returning to Boston as soon as they see Bridget and Will off. Flynn has some patients to look in on tomorrow."

"Well, they can't get their new home built soon enough. The folks in these parts are really looking forward to having their own doctor right here in Faith Glen." Cam turned back to her. "And I'm sure you'll be glad to have your other sister close by."

"It *will* be good to have the three of us close together again." Maeve and Flynn were having a home built here in Faith Glen but it wasn't finished yet so they were currently living in Flynn's family home in Boston.

Nora cast a quick glance back over her shoulder to make certain Grace was all right. She smiled at the sweet picture the babe made as she slept.

"Speaking of your sisters," Sheriff Long said, "it looks as if they're headed this way."

Nora turned back around and sure enough, Bridget and Maeve were crossing the room toward her, arms linked and skirts swishing as they walked.

"Ladies." The sheriff gave a short bow as Nora's sisters halted in front of them. He smiled at Bridget. "I've already told Will more than once what a mighty lucky fellow he is."

Bridget smiled in return. "Thank you, but I feel like I'm the one who's been blessed."

Cam widened his gaze to include all three of them. "I must say, all of the Murphy sisters are looking especially fetching today."

Did his gaze linger on her just a heartbeat longer than her sisters? Nora pushed that ridiculous thought away. While she was honest enough to know she wasn't plain, she also knew she couldn't hold a candle to her sisters. Maeve was petite with beautiful curly red hair and the exquisite features of a porcelain doll. And Bridget was delicate, soft and dreamy-eyed with untamable hair that always gave her an ethereal look. Nora knew herself to be tall and rather thin, with hair that was plain brown and features that were pleasant enough but nothing out of the ordinary.

The sheriff held his hand out toward her and it took her a moment to realize he was offering to take her now-empty cup. Feeling her cheeks warm, she thrust the cup at him with a bit more force than necessary.

He raised a brow, but accepted the cup graciously enough. "I'll take care of putting this away for you and let you ladies talk."

"Must be nice having him pick up after you for a change."

Nora frowned at Maeve's words. "The sheriff is a good man and a fair employer."

Maeve raised her hand, palm out. "I didn't mean to imply otherwise. I just meant that after cleaning up after him all week I would imagine it would be a pleasant change to have him return the favor."

Nora merely nodded, then turned to her other sister. "Will you and your new husband be off soon then?"

Bridget's cheeks pinkened becomingly as she reached for her sisters' hands. "Yes. But before we leave for Boston, I wanted to thank both of you again for all you did to help make my wedding day so special."

Maeve, who'd supplied the beautiful gown Bridget wore, gave their sister a hug. "It was my pleasure. But, to be sure, your smile is the most beautiful thing you're wearing today."

Nora nodded her agreement before hugging her, as well. "And your joy is sweeter than my baking." She stepped back, taking both of Bridget's hands in hers. "I only wish Mother and Da could've been here to see you today."

Romantically minded Bridget gave her a watery

smile. "I do, too. Though I felt very close to them all through the ceremony."

Maeve patted her arm. "They would have been very proud of you."

Nora was certain of that, as well. She hoped their parents would also be proud of her. She'd done her best to hold their household together after their dear mother passed on ten years ago. But with Maeve and Bridget married now, the caretaker part of her life was over, at least as far as her sisters were concerned. She'd always thought she'd feel freer when this day came, not consumed by this sense of loneliness.

Of course she wasn't completely alone. While her sisters had new husbands and lives apart from hers now, the Good Lord had provided her with companionship of a different sort. Nora glanced back toward the cradle and smiled. Her sisters had husbands but she had this sweet, sweet babe.

"I see Grace is taking a nap."

At Maeve's comment, Nora refocused on her sisters. They had linked arms again and were facing her with identical determined looks on their faces. What were they up to? "Yes. Poor wee babe is worn out from being around so many people today. I should be getting her home soon."

Home. Such a small word for such a wonderful, wonderful thing. For the first time in her life, she finally had a place to call her own that no landlord could remove her from.

Bridget cleared her throat. "We have something to say to you before Will and I leave for Boston. And we want you to hear us out before you say anything."

Nora's curiosity—as well as her concern—climbed.

Something told her she wasn't going to be pleased with what they had to say.

"You've done a lot for us over the years," Bridget continued. "So now it's our turn to take care of you."

Take care of her? Did they think her incapable of handling things on her own? Nora felt a protest form, but before she could say anything, Maeve chimed in.

"That's right. I know you are working on making the cottage into a cozy home, but the new house Flynn and I are building here will have plenty of room. You and Grace could settle in with us easily enough. And Flynn would be as pleased as I to have you there."

"Or you can move in right here with me and Will," Bridget added quickly. "It would be nice to have you and Grace so close."

Something inside Nora tightened. She was grateful, of course, but at the same time she had to swallow a feeling of annoyance. "Thank you," she said, choosing her words carefully, "those are generous offers. But you're both newlyweds with new households. Bridget, in addition to your new husband, you have two precious children and a mother-in-law to care for now. And Maeve, you and Flynn are building a new home and starting up a new medical practice here. Neither of you need to be burdened with additional responsibilities right now." Besides, even if none of that were true, Nora would be uncomfortable living on what amounted to their charity.

Bridget drew herself up. "Nora Kayleigh Murphy, I'll have none of that talk. You're no burden, you're our sister."

As if the ground had shifted beneath her, Nora felt a sudden change in her relationship with her sisters. Ever since their dear mother had passed on ten years ago, she'd done her best to look out for her sisters. And when their da had passed on just a few months ago, she'd felt the mantle of responsibility for their little family wrap even more tightly around her. But now the roles seem to have reversed. In their new elevated positions as married women, her sisters were now trying to take on responsibility for her.

"I meant no insult," she said, trying to smooth their ruffled feathers. "But that cottage was a gift to our mother. Remember how the mere idea of it gave us the courage to come to this country in the first place? The dream of having a home of our own gave us much-needed purpose through the long voyage." She looked from Bridget to Maeve and back again. "It just seems wrong somehow to abandon it now that we finally have it."

Bridget shook her head. "We wouldn't be abandoning the place altogether, Nora. The Coulters would still live there." James and Agnes Coulter were the elderly couple who'd been caretakers of the cottage for many years before the Murphy sisters even knew of its existence.

"Exactly." Nora pounced on Bridget's statement. "If it's sound enough for the Coulters to live in, then it's sound enough for me to live in, as well. Besides, the repairs are coming along nicely. Before you know it, it'll be a fine, snug little home."

"Perhaps it's fine now while it's still summer, but autumn will be upon us soon and with it colder, damper weather." Maeve's expression was unusually sober.

Keep your tone calm and reasonable, Nora told herself. "No more so than what we faced back in Ireland. In fact, I hear the weather is milder here."

"If you won't think of yourself, think of Grace,"

Bridget insisted. "Shouldn't she have the best accommodations possible?"

That set Nora back a moment. Was she being selfish and prideful? "I—" She rubbed a hand over the side of her face as she gathered her thoughts. "Of course Grace deserves the very best we can give her. But I'm not so sure what that is." She dropped her arm and drew her shoulders back. "This is not something to worry over today. Let us see how things fare when autumn gets here."

Bridget opened her mouth to speak, but Maeve placed a hand on her arm, shooting her a quick warning look. Turning back to Nora, she smiled. "Then we'll not say more until then." She wagged a finger Nora's way. "But don't think for a minute we've given up on this."

Nora was quite certain they hadn't.

Cameron Long set the two empty cups on the small side table that had been reserved for just that purpose. The three Murphy sisters stood together, pretty as butterflies in a spring meadow.

But to his way of thinking, Nora was the most compelling of the trio. He supposed it was the contradictions he sensed in her that intrigued him most. From the moment he'd first set eyes on her—tall and willowy with her hair pulled back in that tight little bun and her posture perfectly straight—she seemed to exude a no-nonsense air of practicality and discipline. But a moment later the infant she held had made some noise or movement that commanded her attention and her expression suddenly softened and she'd cooed some nonsense or other to calm the baby, and he'd glimpsed another side of her entirely. From that day forward he'd made a point of trying to get to the truth of who the real Nora Murphy was beneath her prim facade. He'd found her by turns amusing, irritating and admirable.

Looking at her today, he saw something new. Her dress wasn't as frilly and fussy as the getups her sisters wore, but for once she'd worn something besides those serviceable homespun dresses she generally favored. The bright blue color and simple lines suited her perfectly. And while her sisters seemed somewhat softer and more relaxed than Nora, that touch of steel in her appealed to him.

Of course, she was a smidge on the bossy side, too, but he figured he could give as good as he got in that area. Truth to tell, it was a bit fun to watch her hackles rise and her finger start wagging and poking when she got riled.

All in all he was quite pleased that he'd ended up hiring Nora as his housekeeper instead of her sister. In fact, if he were the marrying kind, he'd probably set his sights on someone just like her. Not that that was either here or there. He'd decided long ago that he most certainly *wasn't* the marrying kind, and never would be. A man with a history like his had no business raising kids. It's why he never let himself get too close to any of the women he'd encountered over the years.

Shaking off those gloomy thoughts, Cam focused on the Murphy sisters again, then frowned. Something seemed to have upset his no-nonsense housekeeper. Not that she was making a big show of it, but he could tell by the appearance of that little wrinkle that furrowed above her nose whenever she was fretting over something. What could have put that crease there on what should be a happy day for her?

Before he could decide whether or not to saunter

back over, the air seemed to clear and the sisters were hugging again. A tiny wail from the vicinity of the cradle diverted all three women's attention and Nora bustled over to tend to Grace. But he could sense the eldest Murphy sister still fretted over something.

Perhaps he'd find out just what was bothering her when he offered her a ride home after the reception.

Chapter Two

Nora swayed and rubbed Grace's back, trying to soothe the fussy infant as she watched Bridget and Will ride off in their carriage, followed closely by Maeve and Flynn in their own vehicle. The two couples would travel together on the road to Boston and separate once they reached the city—Maeve and Flynn to their home, Bridget and Will to the fancy hotel where they would spend their two-day honeymoon.

Grace finally settled down again, her head lolling against Nora's shoulder. The last of the guests were dispersing.

Well, all except Mrs. Fitzwilliam and the McCorkle boys. The Murphy sisters had met the starchy, well-to-do widow on the voyage over here from Ireland. She'd seemed quite patronizing and standoffish at first, but in time she and the sisters had become friends. Learning that the dowager was traveling to America on a quest to find her prodigal stepgranddaughter, her only living relation, had endeared her further to Nora and her sisters.

Though Mrs. Fitzwilliam had yet to find the runaway, she was no longer alone. She had, in fact, become guardian to the three orphaned McCorkle brothers who had also traveled aboard the *Annie McGee.* Mrs. Fitzwilliam and the two younger boys had settled in Boston. The oldest boy, eighteen-year-old Gavin, had yearned for a bit of adventure and had wheedled his way, in the most engaging manner possible, into the role of Sheriff Long's deputy-in-training.

Bridget had invited Mrs. Fitzwilliam and the two youngest McCorkles to spend the night at their home so Gavin would have an opportunity for a nice visit with them.

Esther Black, Will's mother, stood near the gate, re-assuring her twin grandchildren that yes, their father and new stepmother would most definitely be return-ing in just a few days. Ben MacDuff, the sheriff's more seasoned deputy and former mentor, was hovering near Esther in a way that raised Nora's brow. Was some-thing brewing between the two, something deeper than friendship? Wouldn't that be lovely for them?

"And what brings that smile to your face?"

Nora turned to find the sheriff at her elbow. "Just thinking about how weddings bring out the romantic in even the most unexpected of hearts."

Seeing his quirked brow she realized how that must have sounded and her cheeks warmed. Trying to cover the moment, she quickly changed the subject. "Is there something I can do for you?"

"Just the opposite. Thought I'd offer you a ride back to your place."

How thoughtful of him. But Nora needed some time alone to think over that conversation with her sisters and the half-mile walk back to the cottage would be just the thing. "Thank you but that's really not necessary."

"Sure it is. I promised Will I'd keep an eye on you in his absence."

Well, so much for his personal interest in her well-being. "Both my brothers-in-law worry overmuch."

His look chided her for her tone. "They don't just feel a responsibility for you, you know. They care about you, as well. Is that such a bad thing?"

He was right—she was being too touchy about her new status. She took a deep breath and smiled. "You're right. Thank you, I would be most pleased to accept your offer of a ride."

He nodded his approval. "You can say your good-byes to Esther and the twins while I get the wagon."

A few minutes later, the sheriff had set the brake and hopped down to help her up. Since everyone else had either gone back inside or were on their way home, Nora stepped toward him. "Would you mind holding Grace while I fetch her things?"

He backed up a step. "Better yet, why don't I fetch her things for you? Just tell me where to find them."

She'd never met a man so standoffish when it came to babies. "Everything is in a canvas bag next to the cradle."

"Easy enough. I'll be right back."

True to his word, Cam was in and out of the house in just a few minutes. Swinging the bag with an easy rhythm, he deposited it in the back of his flatbed wagon then turned back to her. She noted the instant he realized he'd have to hold Grace in order for her to climb up into the wagon. His smile faltered and he darted a quick look around as if searching for someone to take his place.

But when she held Grace out to him, he swallowed hard, raked his hand through his hair and took the child, holding her as if she would bite him if he pulled her too close.

Nora climbed up quickly then reached down to take Grace from him. Looking as if he'd just survived a face-off with a bear, Cam quickly moved to the other side of the wagon and climbed up beside her. With a flick of the reins and a click of his tongue he set the horse in motion.

As the horse slowly plodded through town, Nora mulled over what the future might hold for her. How much time did she have to get things in order? "What are autumns like here in Faith Glen?"

He cut her a curious glance. "Well, now, the nights will start getting cooler come mid-September but the days will usually remain passably mild through October. You'll start to see more rain along about October or November, too."

The summer here in Massachusetts had been much warmer than what they'd experienced back in Ireland— it seemed that would work to her advantage when they moved into fall. She and Grace would be fine right where they were for another couple of months at least.

"If you're worried about how you'll fare at the cottage once the weather turns colder," he continued, "I promise I'll do my best to get the biggest of the cracks in the roof and walls fixed before the worst of it sets in."

He, Will and Flynn had already spent one entire day making repairs around the place when Bridget and Nora had first moved into the cottage a few weeks ago. Since then, all three had come by to advance the repairs as often as they could, but then Will had proposed to Bridget and wedding plans had superseded everything else. "That's kind of you. But actually, both Bridget and

Maeve have invited me to live with them." She tried to maintain a neutral tone. "All I have to do is choose between them."

From the too-even tone of her voice, Cam could tell Nora was not at all pleased with the idea. Is that what had upset her earlier? If so, was it the choosing between her sisters or the moving from the cottage that bothered her? "And what did you tell them?"

"That I'd think about it."

"And have you?"

She cut him a guarded look. "I haven't had much time. They only brought this up when they were preparing to leave earlier."

"But you're not overly pleased with the idea." Didn't her sisters know how their offer would strike their independent-minded sister?

She sighed. "I like having my own home." She frowned, as if just thinking of something. "Of course, Bridget and Maeve do each own a third of the cottage, as well."

The sisters had shown him the deed when they first arrived in town, so he was familiar with it. "That they do."

"But then there's Grace to consider." She seemed to be talking more to herself than to him. "A few windy drafts won't bother me, but if the repairs aren't all done in time…" She glanced his way. "No offense meant, but there's a lot of work to be done and you do have your sheriffing to do. I don't expect you to take on the role of my full-time handyman."

Cam could think of worse ways to spend his free time than in Nora's company. "Not full-time, but I *do* have two deputies, now." He let that sink in a moment since he'd hired Gavin McCorkle, a youth she'd met on her voyage over, at her insistence. "That gives me a lot more free time on my hands."

She worried at her lip. "But if you are going to spend more time working on the cottage, I'd want to pay you." She sat up straighter. "I suppose you could hold a portion out of my salary to cover it."

He knew good and well she needed every bit of that money to support her household, especially now that Bridget's wages wouldn't be helping supplement it. But he also knew better than to argue the point. "I'm certain we can work something out along those lines."

She fussed a moment with Grace's blanket and he could see the wheels turning in her mind. "Do you think I'm being selfish by denying Grace the opportunity to grow up in a fine home like the ones Bridget and Maeve could offer her?"

Nora Murphy was lots of things—obstinate, bossy, opinionated—but she was also the least selfish person he knew. "I think, as long as her needs are met and she feels truly loved, it doesn't much matter where she grows up."

He was rewarded with one of her rare approving smiles.

Looking considerably lighter of spirit, she lifted her head and changed the subject. "Any luck yet finding out who that girl was who nearly ran Gavin over?"

Cam flicked the reins, frustrated that he hadn't been able to resolve that particular matter to his satisfaction. The female thief had stolen his horse while he was helping with the repairs at the Murphy sisters' cottage a few weeks ago and had almost gotten away with it. Gavin's quick action had slowed her down and allowed Cam to recover his horse but she'd managed to elude capture.

That didn't sit well with him, not at all. It was his job to keep the peace in these parts and it was the one thing he was good at. Or at least he'd thought so until that wily slip of a girl had outfoxed him.

More worrisome than his injured pride, though, was the question of what she'd been doing near the cottage that day. The place was a half mile from town out near the shoreline and had nothing about it to tempt a thief.

Not only had he been there that day, but Will, Flynn and Maeve had been visiting, as well. Not to mention Mrs. Fitzwilliam and Gavin's two brothers who'd all come in from Boston to see the cottage the Murphy sisters had crossed an ocean to claim.

Had the little thief followed one of the guests there hoping to find an easy mark? Or had she been there for some other reason?

He didn't want to worry Nora with any of his as yet unfounded suspicions, though. "No, and no sign of where she's holed up yet either."

Nora's free hand fluttered then dropped back to rest against Grace. "I know she's a criminal, but I'm worried about her. She looked so young. The girl must be truly desperate to have turned to a life of crime." Nora shivered. "I hate to think of what might have happened to me and my sisters if we hadn't had this place to turn to."

Intrigued by the hint at what her past might have been like, he tried to learn more. "Were things so bad for you back in Ireland?"

She shot him an abashed look, as if sorry she'd said as much as she had. "There were some who had it worse. At least, thanks to the unexpected inheritance of the cottage, we were able to come here and find a home waiting for us."

She shifted Grace to her other shoulder. "Maybe Gavin's thief has left Faith Glen by now."

That was a very deliberate changing of the subject if he'd ever heard one. There was a lot she was leaving unsaid when it came to her former life. Was it so painful to talk about? Or did she just feel it was none of his business?

As for her question… "Maybe," he temporized. Because he doubted it, now more than ever. Just yesterday Ellen Kenny had mentioned that something had gotten into her root cellar and made off with some dried apples. Cam was inclined to believe it was a "someone" not a "something."

But again, there was no sense worrying Nora with that. He returned to the subject of her former life. "You never did say how you three came to possess the deed to Laird O'Malley's place. Was he a relative of yours?"

His question seemed to make her uncomfortable. She shifted in her seat and fussed with the baby for a moment. "Actually, he was a suitor of our mother's before she married our da. When she turned down his proposal, Mr. O'Malley left Ireland and came here. Apparently he never forgot her. He sent her the deed to the cottage and said it was for her and her heirs if she or they should ever need a place to call their own."

Cam remembered the deed had been dated twenty-six years past. "Pined for her all that time, did he?" If the late Mrs. Murphy was anything like her three daughters he could see where such a thing would be possible.

Nora nodded. "So it seems. But we didn't know anything about him or about the deed. We only found it by chance when we were packing up our things to leave."

Interesting. "So you were planning to leave your home *before* you knew about this place?"

She cut him another of those I've-said-too-much looks. But this time she didn't immediately change the subject. "The stone cottage where we'd lived all our lives did not actually belong to us, nor did the land. When our da passed, Mr. Bantry, the landlord, told us he'd decided to lease it to a relative of his instead. We had no choice but to leave."

Cam's brow lowered. "Are you telling me this Bantry fellow kicked you out of your home while you were still in mourning?"

"It was his right," she said with a shrug.

But he could tell the memory still stung. His hands tightened on the reins as he thought of what fate could have befallen them if they hadn't had Laird O'Malley's cottage to fall back on. It was a good thing an ocean separated him from this blackguard Bantry, otherwise he'd be sorely tempted to teach the man a lesson or two about looking out for those in his care. "So this bully Bantry kicks you three out of your home, you find a twenty-six-year-old deed to a cottage an ocean away, and decided, just like that, to come to America all on your own." He shook his head. "That took a lot of courage."

Her lips pinched into a prim line. "It wasn't as if we had many other choices."

She could downplay it all she wanted, he still thought it a brave thing to do.

Then Nora's expression softened into a smile. "Isn't it a wondrous thing how, twenty-six years ago, the Almighty was already laying the groundwork so that me and my sisters would be taken care of in our time of need?"

Her comment caught Cam off guard. A lesser person would be grumbling to God for putting them through all that Nora and her sisters had obviously endured. Yet here she was, praising Him instead for the good that had come out the other side of that valley.

"How long have Will's mother and Ben known each other?"

She was obviously ready to turn the subject to a less personal topic. "Quite a while I'd guess. Certainly since before I wound up in Faith Glen, back when Ben was sheriff himself instead of stepping back to be deputy."

That expressive brow of hers rose. "Oh, I didn't realize you weren't raised here. Where are you from?"

Now it was his turn to shift uncomfortably. Trust his sharp-witted housekeeper to pick up on that. "I was born in Boston. I didn't move here until I was nearly sixteen." And that was all he was going to say on *that* subject. "So why the interest in Ben and Esther?"

"Oh, just something I noticed today that made me wonder if they were more than just casual friends."

"Ben and Esther?" He grinned at the thought. "Now wouldn't that beat all?"

She waved a hand. "Oh, I'm probably wrong. Weddings just tend to bring out the romantic in folks."

"Speaking of Ben," Cam added, "he and Gavin pounced on that last slice of the pie you left for me Friday. Thought I was going to have to wade in and referee when they started arguing over who got the biggest piece. They said to tell you it was the best they'd ever tasted."

He saw her cheeks pinken and her blue eyes light up at the praise. Delight looked good on her.

"That was nice of them to say. Maybe I should stick an extra pie in the oven come baking day. Wouldn't want Faith Glen's fine, upstanding lawmen to be found squabbling over a bit of pastry."

Was no-nonsense Nora making a joke? "You won't get an argument on that score from me. Just add the ingredients to my tab at the general store when you do the marketing."

They rounded the last bend and the cottage came into view. Just as he had every time he'd been here since the incident with the horse thief, Cam carefully studied the area around the cottage for anything that might look suspicious or out of place. But, just as before, nothing seemed amiss.

Still, he'd make his rounds before he left, same as always.

He didn't intend to take any chances. As sheriff, it was his duty to protect Nora Murphy, whether she wanted that protection or not. The memory of another time, of another young mother he'd let down intruded, but he determinedly pushed it aside.

There was no way he'd ever allow such a thing to happen again on his watch. He didn't think he could survive such a tragedy a second time.

Chapter Three

Nora leaned back and inhaled a breath of in-this-moment contentment. The sight of the cottage as they rounded that final bend always filled her with such joy and pride. Already this felt like home to her. How could her sisters believe she would ever want to leave it?

She glanced down at Grace and made a silent pledge. *I promise you that, whatever else shall be, in this home you shall never want for love.*

"You know, I was thinking," her companion said slowly, "most of the urgent repairs are done on the place. Before you spend all your money on additional repairs, you might want to look into getting yourself a horse and wagon of your own."

Nora's cheeks heated in embarrassment. Had she overstepped on his kindness somehow? Since the day she'd moved into the cottage a few weeks ago, he'd insisted on bringing his wagon around to pick her up in the mornings and bring her back in the evenings. She'd protested at first, but as usual he'd ignored her. He'd said at the time that it was no trouble, but she wondered now if perhaps he'd changed his mind.

"Of course," she said quickly. "I didn't intend to take advantage of your kindness. You're a busy man and it's an easy walk into town from here—"

"Hold on," he said, interrupting her. "That's not what I meant. I don't mind one bit giving you a lift into town on workdays. In fact, it gives me an opportunity to start my rounds by checking things out on this side of town."

She wasn't entirely convinced that he was being completely honest. "Then was there some other reason you brought this up?"

"What I was thinking was that if there's ever any kind of emergency out here it would be handy for you to have your own transportation."

"Emergency?"

"You know, like if one of the Coulters or Grace got hurt or took ill."

"Oh, I see. I hadn't really thought of that." But she was thinking of it now. The Coulters *were* quite frail. And if something should happen to Grace…

"I can find you a good deal," the sheriff assured her. "I'll even loan you the money and you can pay me back a little at a time."

Seemed he was always doing that—loaning those in need the means to get by. Well, she wasn't one of his charity cases. "That's very kind of you but we've managed to make do this long, we can get by a bit longer until I can save up the funds."

"No offense, and I know you have your pride and all, but I really think we should go ahead and take care of this now."

Of all the high-handed— "Sheriff Long, I appreciate your concern, but this is really not your decision to make."

Her not-so-veiled reprimand failed to have the desired effect. "Now don't go getting all prickly on me." His tone contained the barest hint of amusement, setting her teeth on edge.

"Because," he continued, "as a matter of fact, this *does* concern me. I've worried about Agnes and James out here on their own for years now, but haven't been able to do much more than check on them regularly. If you had a vehicle—"

"Well, they're not on their own any longer," she interrupted. "I'm here to keep an eye on things."

"Yes you are, and that does relieve my mind a bit. But that doesn't change the fact that James and Agnes are getting on in years and you have an infant to take care of which limits your ability to just take off and go for help if help's needed. So, being the conscientious lawman that I am, I'd still feel obligated to come out here on a regular basis to check in on things. Now, if I knew you had a means to go for help if something... *unexpected* happened, then I wouldn't feel as if I had to come out here and check on things so often."

She clamped her lips shut and glared at him. He was trying to manipulate her but it wouldn't work. "I apologize," she said stiffly. "I had no idea you were inconveniencing yourself on our account."

She brushed at her skirt with her free hand. "Well, you can set your mind at ease. James and Agnes may be unable to get around very well, but I'm perfectly capable of running to town for help if an emergency should arise." She lifted her chin. "So there's no need for you to continue to check in on us any more than you do any other citizen of Faith Glen."

"But that's my job. You wouldn't want me to shirk my duties, would you?"

She held back her retort, settling for merely glaring

at him. Not that he seemed at all appreciative of her restraint.

"Tell me," he asked equably, "how would you feel if James or Agnes got hurt or took ill while you were in town and they were alone out here with no way to go for help? I know I certainly wouldn't want something like that on my conscience. Especially if it was just a bit of pride that kept me from providing them with the means."

She felt her resolve fade, but glared at him resentfully. "You, sir, do not play fair."

The sheriff's little-boy grin reappeared, signaling that he knew he'd won.

But she wasn't going to let him have his way altogether. "I don't want anything fancy mind you. A serviceable cart and pony will do just fine."

He swept his hand out to indicate the rickety wagon they were currently riding in. "As you can see, my tastes don't usually run to fancy." He pulled the vehicle to a stop near the front of the cottage. "I should be able to find something for you to take a look at on Monday."

He hopped down and strode over to her side of the wagon. This time he didn't hesitate to take the baby from her, though he still held Grace with more trepidation than enthusiasm.

Once she was back on the ground and he'd returned Grace to her, the sheriff snatched the bag with Grace's things from the bed of the wagon and escorted Nora inside without waiting for an invitation.

They found the Coulters in the kitchen. Ben had driven them home earlier, and the older couple had already changed out of the clothes they'd worn to Bridget's wedding and were back in their everyday work clothes. Agnes sat at the table, darning a nearly threadbare sock with knobby fingers that had lost much of their nimbleness. James sat nearby, reading silently from a well-worn Bible.

Both looked up when they entered. Cam set the bag on the table and turned to James. "Good news. Nora here has decided to get a cart and a pony to pull it."

Nora shook her head as she set Grace in the cradle that sat next to the table. Leave it to the stubborn lawman to make it sound like it had been all her idea.

James, however, seemed to approve. "Good thinking," he said, smiling in her direction. "Now, make sure you let Cam here help you pick it out. He knows a thing are two about livestock and wagons."

Nora nodded dutifully, refusing to look the sheriff's way.

"That's high praise coming from you, James," Cam said. Then he turned back to Nora. "James worked with horses and carriages for years before he moved here to Faith Glen."

Interesting. She was ashamed to say she hadn't given much thought to what Agnes and James's lives had been like before she met them. "It's reassuring to know I have such talent under my roof."

But James just waved off their praise. "That's all in the past now. But I should go out to the barn and make sure it and the barnyard are in good enough shape to house your horse and wagon when they get here."

The sheriff nodded. "You're right. Why don't the two of us go look things over and see if there's anything that might need immediate attention?"

James pushed himself up from the table. "It's been a while since anything other than the cow and a few cats sheltered in that old barn. And the fence around the barnyard couldn't hold in a spindly foal, much less a full-grown horse."

"Pony," Nora corrected.

James's brow went up and he glanced toward Cam.

The sheriff merely shrugged and smiled that infuriating humor-her smile of his.

Rubbing the back of his neck, James turned to face Nora. "Well, if that's what you think best, I won't speak against it." He nodded toward the counter. "There's fresh milk for Grace. I milked Daisy after we got in from the wedding."

"Thank you." Nora moved toward the milk pail. "I'm sure Grace will be fussing for her bottle any minute now."

James waved Cam forward. "Come along, boy. I'll show you what I think needs tending to first."

"Lead the way."

Much as the sheriff could irritate her with his highhanded ways, at times like this Nora couldn't help but admire Cameron Long for the way he deferred to the older man. He had a way of helping people without robbing them of their dignity in the process.

James, who walked with a limp he'd acquired before she ever met him, led the way, talking to Cam about spare timbers to brace up the barn's north wall.

"Cameron is a good man." Agnes made the pronouncement as if she thought Nora might argue with her.

Instead Nora merely nodded and proceeded to get Grace's bottle ready. When she finally spoke, she deliberately changed the subject. "It's a pity you and James couldn't stay for the reception," she said over her shoulder.

Grace started fussing and Agnes set down her darning and rocked the cradle with her foot. "When you get to be our age," the older woman answered, "you don't spend much time away from home. But the ceremony was lovely and Bridget was beautiful."

"That she was."

Agnes gave her a knowing look. "You're going to miss having her under the same roof with you, aren't you?"

Nora thought about that a moment. It would certainly be strange not having either of her sisters living in the same house with her. They'd never been all separated like this before. No more shared bedrooms and late-night whispers, no more working side by side at their chores, spinning stories for each other and dreaming together of their futures. She would miss that special closeness. But it wasn't as if she'd never see them again. Soon they would all be living in the same town and there would be opportunities aplenty to visit with each other.

She smiled at Agnes as she moved back to the table. "I suppose I will a wee bit. But it's the natural order of things for siblings to grow up and start separate families of their own." She lifted Grace from the cradle. "And I still have Grace, and you and James, here with me. That's plenty of family to keep a body from feeling lonely."

Agnes, her eyes a touch misty, reached over and patted Nora's hand. "You're a good girl, you are, Nora Murphy, to be adding James and me to your family. And we feel the same about you and that sweet little lamb you're holding, as well."

And right then, Nora knew with certainty that she could not abandon this place, this life, no matter how much Bridget and Maeve tried to convince her otherwise.

Almighty Father, surely You didn't bring me to this place just to have me leave it. Help me to make the right choices to build a good life here for all of us. But always, according to Your will.

Agnes spoke up, reclaiming Nora's attention. "Do you mind if I ask you a question of a personal nature?"

Nora smiled. "You know you can ask me anything. What is it?"

"When you and Bridget first arrived here you mentioned that you discovered the deed to this cottage only a couple of months ago, and that none of you girls knew anything about Mr. O'Malley before then. I've been waiting ever since then for one of you to ask about him and I confess to being a bit puzzled that you haven't. Are you not the least bit curious?"

Nora shifted Grace in her arms, giving herself time to think about her response. Truth to tell, she'd been a bit afraid of what might come to light if she learned too much. Laird O'Malley had obviously loved her mother a great deal in his youth, and had continued to love her until he died. But had her mother returned that love? Had she secretly pined for this man who had traveled to America and never returned? And if so, what had she felt for their da?

No, Nora wasn't at all sure she wanted to know the answer to that question.

But Agnes was waiting for her response. "I already know that he was a generous man who loved my mother very much," she said carefully. "I'm not sure I need to know more."

Agnes studied her closely for a moment and Nora tried not to squirm under that discerning gaze. Finally the woman resumed her darning. "I see. Do you mind if I tell you something of him? I think he deserves that much."

Nora knew it would be churlish to refuse, so she gave in graciously. "Of course."

"Mr. O'Malley was a good employer, fair and not overly demanding. He loved this place, especially the garden, which he tended to personally." She smiled reminiscently. "There was even a rumor that he had buried a treasure out there, but of course that's nonsense. Even so, after he died we would sometimes find an occasional youth sneaking out here and digging around, trying to find it."

Nora was relieved she hadn't gone down a more personal road. "So he was happy here."

"Ah, no, I wouldn't say happy." Agnes continued to focus on her stitches. "There was a sadness about him, a sort of lost emptiness that seemed to weigh him down. Many's a day he would spend walking along the beach and staring out over the ocean as if looking for a ship that never came."

Had he been yearning for her mother all that time? Better not to dwell on that. "Did he have many friends here?"

"He kept to himself for the most part. He wasn't shunned or outcast, mind you, he just never made much of an effort to get close to anyone, more's the pity."

Nora's curiosity got the better of her. "Did he ever speak of his life back in Ireland?"

"Not to me or James. But then, he was a very private person and never spoke about much of anything." Agnes sighed. "I always sensed the man had a good heart—he never uttered a harsh word in my hearing and he could be generous if he became aware of a need. It's such a sadness that he spent so much time dwelling on his past rather than enjoying his present."

She knotted and snipped her thread, then began putting away her sewing things. "Anyway, in his own way, Mr. O'Malley provided for all of us in this household and I just thought you ought to know the sort of man he was."

Grace had finished her bottle by this time, and Nora lifted her to her shoulder. "Thank you for sharing that with me. It sounds as if he was a very lonely man." How sad to have loved someone so deeply and not have had that love returned.

She remembered how dejected and hurt Bridget had been when it looked as if Will would be honor bound to marry another woman. Thankfully, it had worked out happily for them in the end, but what if it hadn't? Would her sister have recovered from that blow, especially after she'd already suffered being left at the altar once before?

Giving your heart so completely to someone else was a dangerous thing, especially if one had no assurance that the feelings were returned. She had made that mistake once. Back in Castleville, there'd been a young man, Braydan Rourke, who'd lived in the village near their cottage. Braydan was handsome and strong and had a winning smile and generous heart, much like Cam. He'd been kind to the Murphy family, helping them out when Nora's father had injured his foot and couldn't tend to his crops for a few weeks.

As she always had for their da, Nora had carried Braydan's noonday meal and flasks of water out to the fields, and during those breaks they had shared many a conversation. She'd been sixteen at the time and was enthralled when Braydan had confided his dreams of a better life to her. It embarrassed her now to remember how quickly and completely she'd fallen for him. At least she could take some small comfort in knowing that no one had suspected what a love-struck fool she'd been. Because when her da returned to the fields three weeks later, Braydan had not only left their farm but left Castleville itself without a backward glance and she'd never heard from him again.

It had been a painful lesson, but she'd learned it well. She would not so easily give her heart to a man again. Perhaps she was better off focusing her love on Grace.

James and Cam entered the kitchen just then, pulling Nora from her somber thoughts. The two men were sharing a laugh and Nora was caught again by how caring the sheriff was toward the Coulters, how boyish he looked when he was in a good humor and how his laugh could draw you in and make you want to smile along.

It would be so easy to develop stronger feelings for such a man. In fact, if she was honest with herself, she would admit that she already felt that little telling tug of attraction when he was around. His gaze snagged on hers and she could almost convince herself that his eyes took on a warmer glow. Almost without thought, she found herself responding in kind.

But then she dropped her gaze. That way lay heartache. She would not become another Laird O'Malley. Sheriff Long was her employer, nothing more. And if at times he seemed to treat her with special warmness, she needed to remind herself that that was just his way. Despite his nonchalant manner, she'd seen over and again how caring and protective he was of those around him. It was what made him such a good lawman. But she wasn't in need of his charity or his protection. Her life had been hard, but it had taught her how to take care of herself. And that was exactly what she would do.

As she fussed with Grace, Nora heard Agnes invite the sheriff to stay for dinner. She mentally held her breath while she waited on his response. When he refused, she wasn't certain if it was relief or disappointment that whooshed through her.

Later that evening as she lay in her bed, Nora found herself restless and unable to sleep. Not that this vague sense of discontent had anything to do with her earlier realizations about her relationship with the sheriff. No, it was most likely due to knowing Bridget was no longer part of the household—nothing more.

After all, it wasn't as if her heart was in any real danger since she'd come to her senses in time. And she was perfectly content to settle for Cam's friendship.

Turning over on her side, she steadfastly ignored the little voice in her head that wanted to argue the matter with her.

Chapter Four

On Monday morning, Nora patted Grace's back as she stared out the kitchen window at the gloomy weather. The rain had slacked off to a drizzle but it was still falling steadily. If it didn't let up soon it would make for an unpleasant ride into town this morning.

Not that she was one to let a bit of weather get in her way. There were four mouths to feed in this household, and, as her sisters had pointed out on Saturday, there was still lots of work to be done on the cottage itself before the cooler weather of autumn settled in. Work that required funds for supplies.

And there were more immediate needs cropping up every day. She'd awakened this morning to the sound of water dripping from the ceiling onto her bedchamber floor. Two hand spans over and those drips would have landed right on Grace. That had been a sobering sight.

But there was reason to be optimistic, as well. Just last night she'd had an idea for a way to bring in some extra money. She hadn't worked out all the details in her mind yet, but that was another reason she was eager to get to town today despite the weather—she'd really like to get Sheriff Long's opinion on this scheme of hers. After all, he had much more knowledge of Faith Glen and its people than she did.

Grace hiccupped and Nora patted her back. Then she frowned as she came back to this morning's weather. She didn't mind getting wet herself, but it wouldn't be right to take an infant out on such a day if it wasn't truly necessary.

But what other choice did she have?

"Surely you're not going to take that little lamb out in this rain." Agnes Coulter crossed the room, a soft smile on her face.

Nora shook her head. "I don't really want to." She glanced out the window once more. "Then again, perhaps if I wrap her really well…"

Agnes tsked. "You have another choice. You can leave Grace with me and James."

Nora immediately thought of a half-dozen reasons why she couldn't do that. The Coulters were elderly and frail. And they'd never had children of their own. Did they even know how to take care of an infant? And what about Grace's favorite lullaby—could either of them sing it to her when she got fussy?

She gave Agnes what she hoped was a convincing smile. "That's very kind, but I wouldn't want to impose on you that way. It's not raining very hard. Perhaps it will let up—"

"Don't be silly. I know you're as attached to that baby as a turtle is to its shell, but you can't keep her by your side all day, every day. You both need a break from each other occasionally."

Both women turned as the back door opened and

James limped in carrying a covered pail that no doubt contained fresh milk.

Agnes immediately started back across the room, her finger wagging like a gossipmonger's tongue. "James Barnabas Coulter, stop right there. Don't you dare go tromping water and mud across my clean floor." She made shooing motions with her hands. "Set that pail down and take yourself back out on the stoop and make use of the bootjack and dry off with that feed sack before you come back in."

"No need to yell at me, woman," James grumbled. "I was just trying to get the milk inside before Grace started wailing for her breakfast." But despite his aggrieved tone, James did as he was told.

Nora lay Grace down in the blanket-lined cradle and hurried over to retrieve the pail before Agnes tried to carry it herself. The older woman nodded her thanks and moved back toward the table, while Nora moved to the counter to strain the milk through a cheesecloth.

"This kind of weather is hard on his hip," Agnes said as the door closed behind her husband. "He doesn't like me to make a fuss over him, though."

Nora could hear the affection in the older woman's voice. The couple had been married for over fifty years she'd learned. Would she ever find that kind of love for herself?

An image of the sheriff, with his smoky blue eyes and straw-colored hair, floated through her mind at that thought. Realizing where her mind had drifted, Nora pulled herself up short, reminding herself of what she'd resolved just two days ago. There would be none of that. Better to remember that the man was not only her employer but more often than not she found herself at odds with him.

She watched Agnes's expression soften as Grace latched on to one of the woman's gnarled fingers, and Nora wrestled with the idea of leaving Grace in her and James's care. She'd barely been separated from Grace for more than a few hours since she'd first laid eyes on the squalling babe aboard the *Annie McGee.* The few time that they *had* been separated, Grace had been with one of her sisters. The Coulters, for all their kindness and good intentions, seemed hardly up to the job of caring for a baby. And she didn't want to put them to the the test when she wasn't at least nearby to observe.

Nora set the bowl of milk aside and moved back toward the table. She resisted the urge to pick Grace up, instead letting Agnes continue to play with the child.

"See, Grace and I will get along just fine." Agnes smiled up at Nora, and then, as if she read something in Nora's face, her own expression changed to resignation. She reached over and patted Nora's hand. "It's okay, Nora girl. I understand."

Rather than making Nora feel better, Agnes's words shifted Nora's perception of the elderly couple. Yes, the Coulters still wore the frailness of their advanced years, but both Agnes and James had come a long way since she'd first met them. They moved with new purpose now, and the pinched, resigned looks they'd worn when she'd first met them were gone.

Besides, Grace was very little trouble and was still of an age where she stayed wherever she was placed. It wasn't as if they would have to chase after her.

As Agnes had said, she needed to accept that she couldn't have Grace with her every minute of every day, and this was an ideal time to see how both she and Grace would handle being apart.

Nora had a feeling that Grace would handle it much better than she would.

Taking a deep breath she smiled at her friend. "Actually, you're right, it would be irresponsible of me to take Grace out in this weather simply because I like the pleasure of her company. If you're certain you don't mind, I'd be most grateful to have you and James watch over Grace for me today."

Agnes's face split in a wide grin and she tapped Grace's chin. "Did you hear that, sweetling? You're going to spend the day right here with me and James."

Nora studied the woman's awkward movement and gnarled fingers and wondered if she'd made a mistake. But it would be too cruel to tell her she'd changed her mind now.

As Nora placed a clean apron and half-dozen fresh baked biscuits into a hamper to take with her, she thought that maybe she'd see if the sheriff would mind if she only worked a half day today. She mentally grimaced. One thing was for certain, he'd no doubt be glad she was leaving Grace with the Coulters for a change. She still hadn't figured out why Grace made him so uncomfortable, but there was no denying that she did. Would it be prying if she asked Ben if he had some insights into why?

Fifteen minutes later, Nora stood in the cottage doorway, tying the ribbon of her wool cape. She winced as she spotted droplets trickling down the wall near the parlor chimney. They were making progress on repairs but there was still so much to be done around here.

As she stared out at the lane, she wondered if perhaps she was assuming too much by expecting the sheriff to come out to fetch her in this weather. After all, he was under no obligation—

Right on time, she spied his wagon lumbering up the drive. Despite his sometimes lackadaisical demeanor, she had to admit the man was *always* punctual. He was wearing a long brown coat similar to what the fishermen back in Ireland wore, and what the sailors aboard the *Annie McGee* had worn. She thought wistfully about how nice it would be to have something to wear on a day like today that shed water so nicely. Perhaps she would add that to her growing list of necessary purchases.

As soon as the wagon drew near, she pulled the hood of her cape up over her bonnet and grabbed the hamper that rested at her feet.

No point standing on ceremony on a day like today.

And with that thought, she took a deep breath and prepared to dash out to meet him.

Chapter Five

By the time Cam had set the brake and hopped down from the wagon, Nora was already out the door. Fool woman, why couldn't she let a body help her every once in a while?

He waved her back to the house and she stopped short. Frowning at him, she turned and dashed back to shelter.

He reached under the wagon seat and grabbed the oilskin coat he'd brought with him, then marched over to meet her. "Here, Ben sent this for you to use. It'll keep you drier than that bit of wool you're wearing."

Her eyes widened and her lips pinched into a straight line. No doubt she was unhappy with his tone. But there was a hint of appreciation in her eyes, as well. "That was very thoughtful of *Ben*." She didn't sound convinced that it had been his deputy's idea. Then she motioned him inside. "Come in off the stoop while I put this on."

He shook his head. "I don't want to track inside your house. Besides, I won't get much wetter than I already am."

She sighed, as if she were dealing with a stubborn

child. But she didn't comment. Instead, she reached for the coat.

But Cam was having none of that. Instead he shook out the folds, stepped a little closer and held it up to assist her into it. After only the slightest of hesitations she allowed him to do so.

He was just being polite, he told himself. And if he happened to enjoy the fact that the action brought him close enough to brush a hand against her neck, to inhale the scent of cinnamon and flowers that seemed a part of her, well, that was just incidental.

Once the coat was wrapped around her, Nora turned to offer him a smile. "Thank you."

He cleared his throat. "Here." He handed her a fair-sized square of the oilcloth. "I didn't think you'd want to wear one of Ben's hats, but this will work almost as well. Just tie it over your headgear."

She took it without protest, quickly folded it into a triangle and covered her head, bonnet and all, tying it firmly under her chin.

That was one thing he liked about Nora, she didn't put on airs or complain. Good qualities to have in a housekeeper. And a friend.

He was relieved to note Grace wasn't anywhere in sight. It saved him the trouble of convincing her that the baby should stay inside on a day like today. "Glad to see you had enough sense not to take Grace out in this."

She nodded and he saw her worry at her lip a moment. "Agnes offered to take care of her and I couldn't turn her down."

He gave her an approving smile. "No reason why you should. It's about time you let Grace out of your sight for a bit."

She immediately stiffened and crossed her arms over her chest. "Of *course* I'm protective of her. That poor child was abandoned once already in her short life. I want to do all I can to make certain she feels loved and secure with me."

It seemed he'd gotten her back up yet again. He raised his hands, palms out. "I wasn't criticizing. It's obvious how much you love that little girl and I'm sure you're doing a fine job caring for her. It's just rare that I see you without Grace nearby."

Nora's feathers seemed a little less ruffled at that. "It's just for today." She glanced back over her shoulder. "You don't think watching Grace will be too much for them, do you?" She'd lowered her voice so that it didn't carry back to the kitchen.

He smiled. "They'll be fine." Then, wanting to reassure her further, he added, "And if it makes you feel better, Agnes worked as a nanny for some very prominent families in Boston for a number of years. I hear she was quite good at her job."

Some of the tenseness left her shoulders. "That's good to know." She gave a sheepish smile. "I suppose you think I'm being foolish."

"I'd never dare think such a thing," he said with mock seriousness. He was pleased when his teasing added a little spark to her expression.

Cam took the hamper from her and offered her his arm. "The ground is slippery," he said by way of explanation. "Ready?"

She nodded and took his arm. He could almost believe the no-nonsense Miss Murphy was suddenly shy. Almost.

They crossed to the wagon quickly, dodging puddles

along the way. Cam made note of a number of maintenance issues that would need seeing to in the coming days.

He helped her climb onto the wagon and, once she was settled, handed up the hamper and then sprinted to the other side. As he took his own seat he saw her pull the coat more tightly around her. The sudden urge to draw her closer—to protect against the elements of course—surprised him.

He cleared his throat. "Sorry there's no cover on this wagon. I'm afraid even with the coat you'll be damp by the time we get to town."

She didn't seem concerned. "It appears to be letting up now. And a bit of soft weather won't hurt me."

"Soft weather?"

"Back in Ireland, when the weather turned all misty and damp, which was quite often, we'd say we were having a soft day."

There was a faraway look in her eyes, as if she were seeing her homeland in her mind. He flicked the reins, wordlessly directing the horse to turn the wagon back toward town. "Do you miss it much? Ireland I mean?" He kept his tone casual but he found himself tensing as he waited for her answer.

She seemed to consider his question a moment before speaking. "It's my birthplace and I have a lot of fond memories of growing up there." She grasped the seat on either side of her and leaned slightly forward. "Ireland will always be a part of who I am. But near the end of our time there, there was so much sorrow and pain, so much loss and uncertainty, that I'm grateful to be here and have this chance for a fresh start."

She flashed him a smile so full of hope and promise that it took his breath away. "Only yesterday I was thinking how nice it was that this place—both Faith Glen and the cottage itself—already feels like home to me."

Her words warmed him, made him sit up taller.

Not that he read anything special into them. He was merely glad to know his housekeeper was happy here.

Cam brushed that thought aside and changed the subject. "Oscar Platt over at the livery has a wagon and horse for sale that I think might be just right for you. He'll have it ready for you to look at after lunch if that's agreeable."

Her brows drew down. "I thought I'd said to find me a pony and a cart."

Was she going to be stubborn about this? "I think the horse and wagon will work out better for you in the long run," he said patiently.

But she wasn't appeased. "Sheriff Long, I understand that you think you always know what's best, but I'll have you know I have been making my own decisions for quite some time now."

He shook his head. No matter how many times he asked her to call him Cam, she insisted on using the more formal title of his office. But he did admire her spirit. "I'm sure you have, but that's not the point. Oscar owes me a favor and he's offering a good deal on the animal, which I am willing to pass on to you. You won't find a better value for your money anywhere." He raised a brow. "Unless you're so set on a pony and cart that you're willing to do without while you search for one? I suppose I can continue to worry about the Coulters for another few days."

She clamped her lips shut at that and they rode along in silence for a little while. When she finally spoke again, she surprised him by changing the subject. "I'd like to ask your opinion on a matter I've been mulling over the past few days."

So, she wanted his opinion on something, did she? And from her tone it was something of import to her. Best not to read anything into that, though. No doubt she turned to him because he was her boss and the town sheriff—an authority figure of sorts. Still, she deserved his full attention.

He sat up a bit straighter. "Ask away."

"It's a matter related to finances."

Was she worried about owing him for the horse and wagon? Or the repairs that were still needed on the cottage? The woman did have more than her fair share of pride. "Go on."

"I mentioned to you on Saturday that my sisters would like me to move in with one of them. Well, I've decided, much as I love my sisters, that I would definitely prefer to stay right where I am."

That didn't surprise him at all. In fact it was the decision he would have predicted she'd make.

"The thing is," she said carefully, "in order to do so, I must prove to them, and to myself, that I can handle such a responsibility, both temperamentally and financially."

"Do you doubt that you can?"

"I believe I have the temperament and skill to do it, of course. But I spent some time after services yesterday figuring out what monies I'll need to provide for the basic needs of the four of us."

So, she considered the Coulters part of her responsibility, did she? Nora might have an excess of pride but she also had an excess of heart to match. "Perhaps you won't need quite as much as you think."

She gave him that prim spinster-aunt look. "Oh, no,

I'm quite good at figures. After Mother passed on, Da left me to handle the household finances."

Another responsibility she'd shouldered. How old had she been when she'd taken that one on?

"Anyway, even being conservative," she continued, "the figures were daunting. And I know that there's not just food and everyday supplies to think about. I need to consider the repairs that still need to be done to the house and now to the barn." She raised a hand. "Whatever you were planning to say, please don't. I simply cannot let you continue to work at the cottage without pay."

She shifted in her seat. "There will be the added expense of the—" she paused a moment and eyed him primly "—the *wagon animal* to see to."

Still smarting over his insistence on a horse, was she?

"And while I am quite good at stretching provisions if I do say so myself," she sat up straighter, a proud lift to her shoulders, "I need to make certain there is sufficient food on the table each and every day for four people."

No doubt about it, in spite of her prickly exterior, Nora Murphy had a nurturing streak a mile wide. But where was she going with all of this? "If you don't think I'm paying you enough—"

She shook her head vehemently. "Oh, no, I've no complaints on that account. The wage you pay me is more than generous, and, the Good Lord willing, I truly think I can make it stretch to cover most of our expenses."

"So what is it that's worrying you?"

"There's something else I need to do to make the

cottage truly a home for me and Grace as well as the Coulters."

"And that is?"

She clasped her hands in her lap, squeezing them tightly together. "As Colleen Murphy's daughters and heirs, the cottage belongs to all three of us. Since my sisters now have homes of their own, I would like to purchase their portions from them."

Now that *did* surprise him. Not the idea that she wanted to stake her claim to independence, that was absolutely in character. But that she thought her sisters would require, or even accept, payment from her. He didn't know Bridget and Maeve well, but he knew them well enough to know they'd be affronted at even the suggestion. "You really think they'd expect you to buy it from them?"

"Oh, I'm absolutely certain that they would simply give it to me if I asked them to, but that's not what *I* want. I won't feel like it is truly mine unless I do what's right and proper."

"And what's to say that them giving you their portions is not exactly what is right and proper?"

"My conscience. So, I need to find another way to earn money in addition to the work I do for you."

Stubborn woman. "I see. Then you want to cut down on the hours you spend working for me—is that it?"

"Not exactly. Actually, I think I have the perfect solution, but I wanted to get your thoughts on it."

He was both intrigued and a bit flattered by her request for his counsel. "I'm listening."

"I'd like to make pies and cakes to sell here in town." She announced her plan as if it was the answer to all her problems. Then she looked at him expectantly.

He tried to wrap his mind around what she'd just said. "Start a bakery business you mean?"

"Yes, but on a very small scale." She seemed less certain now. "You did say that folks seem to like my cakes and pies."

"Absolutely. I can't say as I ever tasted better."

His answer seemed to buoy her confidence once more. She smiled up at him with the raindrops glistening on her long dark lashes, vividly brightening her blue eyes, and he had to blink to clear his suddenly muddled thoughts.

"And Will has asked me to consult with his chocolatiers on how to improve his chocolates," she continued, "so perhaps I could somehow combine the two things."

Did she really understand the amount of work that would be involved in such an undertaking? "You'd have to make an awful lot of baked goods to make any sort of profit at it."

"I know. And I'm not afraid of hard work. But I would need your help."

She'd managed to surprise him yet again. "You want me to help you do your baking?" His only foray into baking was biscuits and he wouldn't exactly be bragging on his results.

But his question earned him a grin. "Nothing so challenging. I would, of course, do a lot of my baking at home. But I'd like to do some of it during the day, as well. Only, well, that would mean using your oven." She fluttered a hand in an uncharacteristically nervous gesture. "I promise not to do any less work for you than I already am." The words were rushed, as if she was trying to forestall an objection. "I can continue to clean and wash and cook your meals while my baked goods are in the oven."

He didn't for a minute doubt that she would be conscientious about her work. "Where do you plan to sell these delicacies?"

The look she shot him let him know she realized he hadn't answered her question. But she followed his lead. "I thought perhaps Mrs. James at the general store might be willing to sell some goods on commission for me and perhaps Rosie over at the boardinghouse would take some to serve to her boarders, as well." She stared at him expectantly. "What do you think?"

She really had given this some serious thought. "I think it's certainly worth a try. I might be able to drum up a few other customers for you, as well." That earned him a grateful look. "In fact," he added, "the workers over at the mill might be a good group to talk to."

"Oh, I hadn't thought about that. I'll speak to Will when he and Bridget get back into town." She eyed him uncertainly. "So you're agreeable to my baking while I work for you?"

"On one condition."

"And that is?"

"That you start small and don't work yourself to exhaustion."

She nodded. "I understand. I wouldn't be very useful as a housekeeper if I didn't have the energy to do my job."

Cam didn't comment. If she thought that was his reason then far be it from him to say otherwise.

Chapter Six

Nora shook her head over Cam's insistence that he drop her off at the door to his office, but she was grateful nevertheless. As he handed her down, she noticed that where the ends of his hair had gotten wet, the straw color had darkened to chocolate brown and had started to curl just the tiniest bit. She found her thoughts straying to what it might feel like to test the spring of that curl against her fingers.

Shaking off that totally inappropriate thought, she said a quick thank-you and bustled into the sheriff's office. She greeted Ben and Gavin, both of whom were sipping cups of the thick liquid that passed for coffee inside these walls when she wasn't around.

"Well, aren't you a pretty sight on a dreary morning." Ben's smile changed to a frown. "Where's Gracie? Nothing's happened to her I hope."

"No, no, Grace is just fine. But I didn't think it would be wise to take her out in this weather so I left her with the Coulters today."

He nodded. "I suppose that was the right thing to do. I'm sure going to miss having that little girl around today, though."

Ben and Gavin had both warmed up to Grace quickly enough. They even helped watch her when Nora was particularly busy with some chore or other.

Nora turned back to Gavin. "Did you have a nice visit with your brothers and Mrs. Fitzwilliam after the wedding?"

Gavin nodded. "I sure did." Then he grimaced. "If only Mrs. F would quit trying to talk me into returning to Boston with them."

Nora raised a sympathetic brow. "She means well."

He shrugged. "I know. And I'm grateful that she's seeing that my brothers go to school. But that's not for me—this is where I want to be."

"Give her time. She'll come around." Nora untied her makeshift rain hat. "How goes her search for her granddaughter?"

Gavin shook his head. "No sign of her yet. I think Mrs. F is beginning to feel a bit discouraged."

Nora's heart ached for the older woman. "I will continue to pray for the two of them."

As she hung the hat on a peg, Ben rejoined the conversation. "You'll find a pair of freshly cleaned rabbits in there." He nodded toward the kitchen. "Andy Dubberly brought me those yesterday evening in exchange for a favor I did for him. Thought they might be good for lunch."

"How wonderful." Nora was genuinely delighted. This being a coastal town, fish was plentiful and inexpensive, so that was what she usually purchased when she did the sheriff's shopping. But red meat was a welcome change. "And I know just how to cook them." She was already going over the list of supplies she'd need to make her da's favorite rabbit stew. *Carrots, onions, turnips*—

"I have the stove already warmed up for you, Miss Nora."

Nora smiled at Gavin's not too subtle hint that he was ready for the morning meal. "Thank you. I'll have breakfast ready quick as can be."

She shook herself out of the borrowed raincoat. "And thank *you* for the use of your coat," she said to Ben. "It was most welcome on the ride in this morning." She hung it next to the hat. "It certainly kept me drier than I would have been without it."

Ben shook his head. "It's Cameron you should be thanking. The boy let himself into my place before dawn and grabbed my coat without so much as a knock or a may-I." Then the older man smiled. "But I'm very pleased to see he put it to such good use."

So it had been Cam's idea, not Ben's as he'd led her to believe. "Well, thank you anyway." She moved toward the kitchen. "Now, I believe this is a three-egg morning for the lot of you." She wagged a finger at the two deputies. "And no snatching the biscuits while my back is turned."

Nora found herself humming as she moved to the room she had nicknamed her "galley."

The sheriff and Ben had living quarters in a small two-story building behind the jailhouse. Ben lived on the lower floor and the sheriff on the upper. Both homes, if one could call them that, were quite small. They each had three very small rooms—a kitchen, a parlor and a bedroom.

Gavin, the newest member of the peacekeeping team, slept in one of the two cells at the jailhouse. He couldn't afford to stay at the boardinghouse and there was nowhere else.

She'd decided almost from the outset to do the cooking in Ben's quarters instead of the sheriff's since it was on the ground floor and meant easier access for everyone. She also insisted on feeding them at the same time so neither had to eat their meals cold. But when Gavin came on the scene it really made Ben's tiny place seemed cramped and uncomfortable.

Especially since Cam wouldn't hear of her excusing herself to work elsewhere while they ate. Instead, he insisted she share their meals with them and would not even listen to her very reasonable arguments on why it was inappropriate for the hired help to sit down to dine with her employer.

I need to make sure you're keeping your strength up so you can handle these chores I hired you to take care of, he'd said. And, on another occasion he'd made the outrageous statement that *I can't have a cook who won't eat her own cooking in front of me.* So she'd finally given in.

Which meant four people sat down to eat two meals a day in Ben's cramped quarters.

But when she'd returned to work the Monday after Gavin became a permanent resident, the men had had a surprise for her. She'd arrived at the sheriff's office to find that they'd cleared out the jailhouse storeroom and set up a makeshift kitchen in its place. The sheriff had *said* it was so he could eat in the office where there was more room, but she suspected it was as much for her benefit as anything else.

Whatever the reason, Nora had been delighted with the new arrangement. There was a brand-new stove already stoked and ready for her to put to use. One wall was lined with shelves that now contained foodstuffs, cooking implements and rudimentary serving dishes. A small but sturdy table stood near the opposite wall.

And the room even had a window that not only let in the sunlight but provided her with a view of Ben and Cam's living quarters.

Water had to be hauled in, of course, but there was a small water barrel in the corner and Gavin, bless him, usually took care of keeping it filled for her.

She'd nicknamed the storage room-turned-kitchen her "galley" because it reminded her of the kitchen aboard the *Annie McGee* where she'd spent a good deal of her time on their voyage from Ireland. She'd worked as a helper to the ship's cook.

So now she started her days in here, fixing up a hearty breakfast for everyone.

Nora continued humming as she cracked three eggs for each of the men and one for herself. The more she thought about her baking venture, the more excited she became. And now that she knew the sheriff wouldn't be opposed to her combining her job here with her new business, the way seemed clear for her to give it a try. It was certainly a generous concession from him, and she was determined to make certain he didn't regret it.

He was right about starting small, of course. Maybe two pies and a cake of some sort each day this week. Hopefully it would grow from there. And if things worked out well, perhaps one day she could have her own little bakery right here in Faith Glen.

By the time Cam came back in, Nora had the morning meal almost ready. "There's a fresh pot of coffee here on the stove," she called out to him. "You have just enough time to grab a cup before I serve breakfast."

Cam joined her in the galley, his large presence filling the small space. "Something sure does smell delicious. That's the kind of aroma a man likes to be greeted with on a day like today. I should have set up a kitchen in here ages ago."

Just as she turned to retrieve a platter, he reached around her to grab the coffeepot from the warmer. The minor collision that ensued caught Nora completely by surprise.

His arms reflexively closed around her to keep her from falling and she pressed her hands on his chest in an effort to maintain her balance. For a frozen moment of time they were locked in an embrace that took her breath away and pushed everything else aside. She couldn't move, couldn't think straight. All she could do was feel—feel his arms around her, feel his heartbeat beneath her palms, feel the warmth of his breath on her forehead.

Then everything came rushing back in, including her wits. Flustered, she took a hurried step back and he released her, dropping his hands to his sides. Unable to look at him directly, she cast a sideways glance his way, trying to figure out what he was thinking. But his expression was unreadable.

"I'm so sorry." She was appalled by the stammer in her voice and swallowed, trying to get herself back under control. Where was that resolve she'd counted on?

Before she could say more, he spoke up. "My fault entirely. I shouldn't crowd you here in what is indisputably your domain." If his tone was any gauge, he'd been entirely unaffected by the momentary contact.

She mentally cringed at the implication behind that betraying thought. Of course he'd been unaffected. It had been nothing more than a little everyday mishap. Her own reaction was no doubt due to the fact that she'd been caught off guard. She wouldn't allow it to be anything more.

His expression changed to one of concern. "I hope I didn't hurt you."

Mercy, did she look as rattled as all that? Nora attempted a reassuring smile. "No, no, I'm fine. Don't think anything of it." *Please* don't think of it.

"Well, then, I'll just leave you to your cooking. I can get that cup of coffee later."

"Nonsense." Glad of an excuse to turn away, Nora quickly poured him up a cup. She turned and handed it to him, careful to keep their hands from touching. Then she made shooing motions with her hands. "Now, if you'll leave me to finish up in here, I'll have breakfast ready to serve in just a moment."

Raising the cup in a friendly salute, he left the galley and joined Ben and Gavin.

Nora turned back to the stove but had to force herself to concentrate on the task at hand.

Because she could still feel the beat of his heart under her palms. And she didn't understand why that should make her feel so flustered.

Cam sipped his coffee without tasting it. Hang it all, what had just happened in there? It had been a simple accident, a reflexive response to a minor collision, nothing more. Yet it had affected him more than it should have, and from the expression on Nora's face just now, it had affected her, as well.

Only he wasn't sure in just what way. As far as that went, he wasn't sure exactly what *he* was thinking or feeling about it either.

Truth to tell, he was having trouble getting his thoughts clear from the warm feel of her hands against his chest, the sight of her suddenly wide blue eyes and the sound of her quickly inhaled breath that inexplicably seemed to suck all the air from the room.

This was definitely *not* a good development. He liked Nora well enough. To be honest, maybe a sliver more than "well enough." But it wouldn't do for him to start having stronger feelings. And not just because she was his housekeeper.

"Hey, sheriff."

Gavin's hail brought a welcome break from Cam's muddled thoughts. "I'm listening."

"I almost forgot to tell you—Mr. Lafferty stopped by while you were out fetching Miss Nora. He said someone's been raiding his garden and he wants you to do something about it." Gavin shook his head. "He sure was mighty angry."

Ben snorted. "Amos Lafferty's not happy unless he's got something to complain about. Why, if someone walked up and handed him a fistful of coins he'd likely complain because it wasn't in a shiny leather pouch."

Cam grinned at Ben's very apt description of the town's most cantankerous citizen.

Ben leaned back in his chair. "It was likely just a deer or fox or some such deciding to take a midnight graze through his place."

Ben was probably right. Still… "All the same, I think I'll go have a look around after breakfast. If there *is* somebody raiding his garden I want to put a stop to it."

Ben shrugged. "Suit yourself. If you want to go tromping through a muddy garden in the rain on a wild goose chase, that's your business."

"I don't mind a bit of rain," Gavin piped up. "Can I go with you?"

Cam eyed his overeager deputy, then nodded. "Sure. You can ride Ben's horse since he plans to stay in out of the rain."

He moved to his desk and gathered the few papers that had accumulated since yesterday and stashed them in the top drawer. That effectively turned his desk into a dining table at mealtime, with each of the four of them taking a side.

Right on cue, Nora bustled across the room carrying a large tray. He knew better than to offer to help since prior experience had taught him that she'd only lecture him on how he should get out of the way and let her do her job. Still he watched her, looking for signs that she was at all rattled by their earlier encounter. But she seemed as efficient and unflappable as ever. She didn't once make eye contact with him, but that could be nothing more than her being distracted by planning for her new venture.

Five minutes later she had everything laid out before them and all four took their seats. After they said grace, Cam nodded to Nora. "Did you tell Ben and Gavin about your idea for a new business?"

Ben paused in the act of spreading jam on his biscuit. "A business venture? Are you going to be a woman of means soon?"

Nora laughed. It seemed there was no lingering nervousness on her part.

"Nothing so spectacular," she said. "I'm thinking about baking a few extra pies and cakes to sell around town."

"Well, now, I'm guessing you're going to have people lining up to buy them." Ben pointed his fork her way. "And if you need someone to do your tasting for you, I hereby volunteer."

"That's a mighty generous offer," she said dryly, "but I don't think I'll need to impose on you."

Cam noticed the way her eyes brightened when she was in a teasing mood. Not that he saw this side of her often. Which was really too bad.

Gavin, however, didn't seem to find the subject a teasing matter. "You mean you're going to be baking all kinds of desserts in here and we aren't going to be able to eat any of them?" The boy looked absolutely crestfallen.

Nora laughed. "Don't worry, Gavin, I'll still make sure you gentlemen have something fresh for dessert every day."

"Well, I for one think it's a dandy idea." Ben scooped up a forkful of egg. "And now that the folks in town have had a chance to sample your baking talents at your sister's wedding reception, I don't think you'll be wanting for customers."

Her cheeks pinkened. "Why, thank you, Ben. I certainly hope you're right."

Cam ate his breakfast in silence while Nora continued to banter with Ben and Gavin. Why was she so relaxed and easy with the other two, calling them by their first names and even lapsing into this teasing banter, yet at the same time she insisted on being formal with him? The whole thing got under his skin more than it should.

After all, they'd known each other a month and had gotten to know each other well. Was it too much to ask for her to treat him as more of a friend than a boss?

And being friends was all he wanted from her, all he would *allow* himself to want from her. Because he'd decided long ago he couldn't have a family of his own, especially not one that included a child. There were too many inherent dangers for a man like him in a relationship like that.

Yes, sir, he'd accepted his own limitations in that area and moved on a long time ago. So why was he feeling so restless about the whole matter lately?

Nora absently pushed the broom across the floor of Ben's kitchen. Cleaning this place and the one upstairs was no hardship—they were so small and both men were fairly neat. It was no wonder, though, that the two men spent most of their time over at the sheriff's office. It must be lonely in their very separate, very small spaces. Not that either of them would ever admit to such a thing.

She'd made good progress this morning and was well ahead of schedule. Since Ben had provided rabbits for today's meal and the pantry was well stocked she hadn't had to go to the market. And without Grace to tend to, her work had gone much faster. And been much lonelier.

It was quiet in here today. Too quiet. Even the patter of the rain had faded away about thirty minutes ago. No doubt about it, she missed having Grace with her. Listening to the baby coo and gurgle and even fuss always provided welcome company during her workday.

Nora wasn't normally a talkative person, preferring to keep her own counsel. But her life had undergone so much change in the last few months that she'd found herself longing for someone to discuss things with, as much to sort it out in her own mind as to seek advice.

And it turned out that Grace was a very good listener. During those times when it was just her and Grace, she'd gotten into the habit of talking to her while she worked, holding entire conversations, as if Grace understood every word. She'd related some of her fears and dreams and plans, working through her own feelings about her new life in the process.

Somehow, talking to an empty room didn't seem quite the same.

And, oh my, but it certainly would have been good to have someone to talk to today of all days—someone who wouldn't comment or pass judgment but merely listen as she talked about the events of the day.

There was, of course, the advice she'd gotten from Cam about her baking venture. His opinion carried a lot of weight with her—he was intelligent, he knew the town and he knew her. Knowing she had his approval gave her the confidence she needed to carry through with her idea.

Yes, she should be planning her menus and shopping lists and identifying potential customers. Instead her traitorous thoughts kept circling back to that near-embrace that had resulted from her collision with the sheriff earlier. Yes it had taken her breath away and set her pulse to racing. But surely that was natural given how startled she'd been.

And it wasn't as if she had a lot of experience with that sort of thing. There'd been no time for courting back home in Ireland. After their mother's death she had become the lady of the house and had taken on many of the household duties that had formerly been her mother's.

If only her traitorous mind didn't keep returning to the sweet sensation of being held in his protective embrace....

So lost in her thoughts was she, that she nearly dropped her broom when someone knocked on the door.

"It's only me," Ben called from outside.

"Come in," she responded, glad for the moment to collect herself. Then, as soon as the door opened, "I've told you before there's no need for you to knock at your own door."

Ben shook his head as he wiped his boots on the rag rug she'd made to grace his threshold. "Wouldn't be right for me to barge in on a lady unannounced, even if that lady is sweeping my floor."

Nora had grown quite fond of Ben in the short time she'd been in Faith Glen. The impish quality he wore like a favorite suit made his age seem like a disguise. His dark eyes, hidden behind a pair of spectacles, seemed to look at the world with a youthful, mischievous air that made you both want to smile and to wonder what he had up his sleeve. Clouds of snow-white hair adorned the sides and back of his head, but only wisps clung to the top.

She leaned on the broom a moment. "If I'm in your way, I can work over at the jailhouse for a bit."

He waved her back as he crossed the room. "Nonsense. In fact, I came over here looking for a bit of company. Cameron and Gavin are out tromping through old Amos Lafferty's garden and it was getting lonely across the way by myself."

He pulled out a chair and sat at the small table, smiling up at her as he did so. "So, tell me more about your plan to start a business."

Glad to have a bit of company, Nora smiled and resumed her sweeping. "There's not a whole lot to tell, other than what you already know. The sheriff cautioned me to start slow, and I agree that's probably best—maybe two pies and one cake a day. Then, if it looks like folks really will buy my baked goods, I can do more."

"Oh, I have no doubt you'll do well." Ben tipped his chair back on two legs. "I just hope you don't get so much business you decide you don't need to work here anymore."

She smiled. "Don't worry, you three will always be my favorite customers. And let's not get ahead of ourselves. This may not work out."

He wagged a finger at her. "None of that false modesty. Folks are still talking about how good that cake you baked for the reception was."

Nora couldn't decide how to respond to that so she changed the subject. "Did you happen to check on the stew before you left the jailhouse?"

He nodded. "I gave it a good stir. The smells coming out of that pot are enough to tempt a stone. Those rabbits gave up their lives for a good cause."

Nora laughed. "Indeed. Rabbit stew was one of the first things my mother taught me how to cook, and it was my da's favorite dish."

Ben let the chair legs drop back to the floor. "Sounds like you had a fine family." Then he cocked his head to one side. "Speaking of which, I kind of miss having little Gracie around today. Of course, I know you made the right choice leaving her home in this weather."

"I miss her, too. But at least the sheriff is more comfortable not having her around." Nora wanted to take the words back as soon as they slipped past her lips. Yes, she was curious about his behavior, but she had no business fishing for information about her boss.

Ben gave her a searching look. "He's more fond of that little girl than you think, than even *he* thinks."

Nora tried not to let her skepticism show, but she found that very hard to believe. So she settled for saying nothing.

Ben studied her for a long moment, his expression unusually serious. Finally he nodded, as if he'd reached a decision. "There's something you probably ought to know about Cameron."

Chapter Seven

Nora felt a momentary touch of panic. Much as she'd like to learn the sheriff's secrets, this was wrong. She put a bit more force into her efforts with the broom, keeping her head down. "I didn't mean to bring this up, Ben, and I certainly don't want to pry into his past." Well, that wasn't entirely true, but wanting didn't give her the right to actually do it. "The man has a right to his privacy. If there's something he thinks I should know, then he'll tell me himself."

Ben shook his head. "You're wrong. I love that boy as if he were my own son, but he's got hold of some foolish notions that are ruining his life. And I think it's time someone else shared the burden of knowing about the nightmares that drive him. Someone who cares about him and wants what's best for him." He gave Nora a challenging look. "I was hoping you might be that person."

The sheriff had nightmares driving him? Hard to believe. He seemed so strong, so confident. Yet she'd sensed there was something troubling him.

But did she have the right to hear his story before he

was ready to tell her himself? Still, if Ben thought her knowing could help…

Almighty Father, I truly do want to help Cameron. He's a good man and he's been nothing but kind to me since I arrived in town. I'd like to return the favor and help him if I can. Maybe this is one way to do that.

Hoping she'd made the right choice, Nora slowly moved to the table and sat down across from Ben. "Tell me."

He smiled approvingly. "Good girl." Then he sobered. "I warn you, though, this won't be easy to hear. Cam didn't have a pleasant childhood."

Nora clasped her hands together in front of her and mentally braced herself. Suddenly she was very afraid of what she might hear. "Go on."

Ben patted her hands, then raked his fingers through his sparse hair. "Cam loved his mother deeply. From what he's told me of her, she was a God-fearing woman, hardworking and a loving mother." His face hardened. "Unfortunately, he wasn't so blessed when it came to his father. Douglas Long was a terrible man, a monster. He was a thief and a drunk who'd spend every penny of his money on liquor and gambling, then lash out at his wife for not putting food on the table. And worse, he was a mean drunk who beat both Cam and his mother regularly."

Nora couldn't repress her gasp. "No!" She could hardly take in the idea of someone treating another person that way, much less his own wife and child. How had Cam borne such cruelty?

Ben's gaze softened and he patted her hand. "I'm sorry to distress you so, but I'm afraid it's true. Cameron lived like that for the first twelve years of his life. He and his mother tried to protect each other as best they could, but they weren't a match for his brute of a father."

Her heart bled for the little boy Cam had been and for the mother he'd loved. "You said the first twelve years of his life—is that when his father died?" Her eyes burned with the effort not to cry.

"No, more's the pity. That's when his mother died."

How awful to lose the loving parent in such a situation. Why couldn't God have taken the brute instead? "Did his father cause—"

"No, thank the Lord. Both she and Cam worked at a factory and apparently there was some sort of accident there. After that, with nothing to hold him at home, Cam ran away. He lived on his own in the city for a while—this happened in Boston. Eventually, when he was about sixteen or so, he ended up here in Faith Glen."

She wiped her eyes with the corner of her apron. "And you took him in."

Ben shrugged. "It wasn't a hardship. Cam needed a job and a place to stay and I needed a deputy."

Nora knew it was much more than that—like Cam's hiring of Gavin. But she let it pass while she swallowed the lump that had formed in her throat.

"Anyway," Ben continued, "it took me a long time to get the story out of him. He wasn't big on trusting folks as you might imagine. But the important thing for you to understand is this." He leaned forward as if to emphasize what he was about to say. "Cam is absolutely convinced that if he was ever to have children of his own, he'd turn out to be just as bad a father as his own was."

Nora straightened, outraged. "That's ridiculous."

Ben spread his hands. "I know. But on this one subject, Cam is just not objective. And because he feels that way, he won't let himself get close enough to a woman to contemplate marriage. And he definitely wants nothing to do with being solely responsible for a child."

Nora couldn't believe what she was hearing. "But he's *nothing* like his father, and could never be. Even I can see that after knowing him for only a month. He cares too much about people, all kinds of people."

This time Ben raised his hands palm out. "You don't need to convince me. I'm on your side." He captured and held her gaze. "You do realize you can't let him know I told you, don't you?"

"But—"

Nora jumped as the front door opened.

"Ben, I need to talk to—" Cam halted on the threshold, obviously surprised to see Ben wasn't alone. "Well, don't the two of you look mighty serious. What have you been conspiring about in here?"

Cameron stared from Ben to Nora as he wiped his damp boots on the rag rug that was almost identical to the one Nora had placed by his own front door. Now just what had put that guilty look on both their faces?

Instead of answering him, Nora popped to her feet, grabbed the nearby broom and started sweeping. Was she pushing it with a bit more vigor than absolutely necessary? Something had gotten her all agitated.

When he turned back to Ben, his friend gave him an unrepentant grin. "I was just wheedling Miss Murphy here into taking a break from her work to keep a tired old man company."

Was that it—was she worried he wouldn't approve of her taking a break from her work? Cam snorted. "Tired old man, my foot. You have more energy than that puppy Gavin." He glanced Nora's way. "And Nora knows she can take a break anytime she wants."

Nora pushed the small pile of dirt she'd swept up toward the door. "I'll get out of your way so you two can talk business. I need to check on lunch anyway."

She turned to Ben and he felt some sort of understanding flash between them. "Thanks again for our chat. I appreciate your…encouragement for my baking business."

Ben nodded. "My pleasure. I have faith in you."

Cam watched Nora leave, frowning as something about her demeanor still seemed off.

But as soon as the door closed behind her, Ben spoke up. "That girl not only has a smart head on her shoulders but she has a good heart and isn't afraid of hard work. Some lucky man is going to snatch her up one day soon and we'll be stuck with each other's cooking again."

That prediction brought Cam up short. He didn't like that idea one bit. Only because it meant he'd lose a good housekeeper and cook, of course.

Ben hooked his elbow over the top of his chair. "Now what did you want to talk to me about?"

Cam shook off his momentary distraction and pulled up a seat. "About what I found out at Amos Lafferty's place."

"Are you telling me the garden intruder wasn't an animal?"

"I found some signs that it might be an animal of the two-legged variety."

"What kind of signs?"

"The rain washed most of the tracks away, but I found one footprint near his gate. And it was made by a foot much smaller than Lafferty's."

"You thinking the Grady boys might have been up to mischief again?"

"Maybe. Or maybe it was someone else."

Ben's gaze sharpened. "What are you thinking, Cameron?"

Time to let Ben in on his suspicions. "I'm just wondering if that little thief who tried to steal my horse is still here in Faith Glen."

"Now why would she be hanging around after almost getting caught? Makes more sense for her to move on to some place less…aware."

"I don't know." And that was what was worrying him. There was a part of this puzzle he hadn't figured out yet, and something told him it was a key piece.

"Did you mention this to Gavin?"

"Of course not. The fool boy is still half-besotted with her." He supposed a pretty face and an air of mystery and adventure would present a powerful attraction for a boy Gavin's age. But Gavin would have to learn to see below the surface if he was going to last as deputy.

"Besides," he said, focusing back on Ben, "I might be wrong, and you could be closer to the truth on the Grady boys. In fact, I think I'll have a word with them after lunch."

"Want company?"

"No need. Lem's a good man. If his sons are the guilty parties then I'll leave it to him to handle disciplining the pair. If they're not, then only one of us will have wasted a trip out there."

Ben didn't seem put out by Cam's answer. "Well, then, I think I'll wander on over to the Black house after lunch. Esther mentioned she might need some help with her garden while Will and Bridget are out of town."

Esther, was it? And when had Ben ever done any gardening? Had Nora been right after all about something developing between Ben and Will's mother? Come to think of it, Ben had become a regular at Sunday services lately and had inserted himself into the same pew as Cam, the Murphy sisters and the Black family. Cam had figured it was because he was in that pew, but the real draw might well have been something else altogether.

Cam was never one to beat around the bush, especially with Ben. "Nora seems to think you might be courting Miss Esther."

Ben smiled. "Now, didn't I tell you Nora had a smart head on her shoulders?" The older man got up and headed for the door, his step a bit jauntier than usual. "And speaking of Nora, you might want to keep an eye on her. If this bakery business does as well as I think it will, you might well be looking for a new housekeeper and cook soon even if she doesn't find herself a beau."

Cam refused to consider that possibility. "She seems to think she can handle both jobs."

Ben shrugged. "Let's hope she's right." He opened the door and his grin reappeared. "I'm off to Esther's. But tell Nora to save some of that lunch for me if I'm not back when she gets ready to serve it."

Cam followed more slowly, grinning at the idea of his old friend courting Will's mother. He supposed that proved it was never too late for a body to find love, or in Mrs. Black's case, find it again.

As for himself, well perhaps that didn't apply to everyone—

Tamping down the persistent image of Nora in his arms earlier and scampering away a few minutes ago,

Cam circled his thoughts back around to what he'd found out at Amos Lafferty's place.

And what it might mean.

Nora put away the last of the freshly washed lunch dishes and moved to wipe off the stovetop. What should she tackle next? She wasn't quite following her schedule today, which put her slightly out of sorts. Should she bake a loaf of bread to go with their evening meal? Should she work on the pile of mending the men had added to her basket? Or would it be all right if she just asked Cam for the rest of the afternoon off?

Nora chewed on her lip, fighting the urge to go with the latter choice. How were the Coulters faring with their nursemaid duties? Had they remembered to give Grace a bottle at midday? Were they keeping a close eye on her? Did they know to sing her a lullaby to help her sleep when nap time came around?

Did Grace miss having her near?

On the other hand, much as she missed Grace, Nora had to admit that she *had* moved through her chores much faster today. Without the precious distraction of tending to the baby's needs and pausing occasionally to just coo over her, she'd breezed through her tasks. Perhaps, instead of leaving now, if she continued to work for just another hour or so, she could complete all her normal chores and still get back to the cottage several hours earlier than normal. She'd make her sales pitch at the boardinghouse and general store tomorrow. And she could always take some of the lawmen's mending home with her to do there.

Pleased that she'd formed a plan that would allow her to fulfill all of her obligations, Nora gave the stove one last swipe with her rag, then turned.

But when she looked up, Cam was moving purposefully toward her. Remembering what happened the last time he'd been in the cozy galley with her, Nora felt her whole being tense in a not unpleasant anticipation.

But he halted just inside the doorway and leaned casually against the jamb.

She raised a hand to tuck a nonexistent stray hair behind her ear. "Hello there," she said, doing her best to sound casual. "Was there something you needed?"

He looked at her as if puzzled. Had he heard something in her tone? Could he sense the nervous energy thrumming through her?

"I didn't mean to interrupt your work," he said diffidently.

She shook her head, giving him a bright smile. "You aren't interrupting." She reached for the nearby broom, glad to have something to occupy her hands. "I've finished with the dishes and was about to sweep up in here. But if you have something else for me to do—"

He waved her words aside. "Actually, I had a different idea. Since the weather's cleared up, I was thinking we could head over to the livery so you can have a look at that horse and wagon I told you about. Oscar should have it all ready for you to inspect by now."

His tone indicated he considered it just a formality, that *of course* she would agree with his judgment. Didn't he understand by now that she had a mind of her own? "Of course. Best to get this inspection over with so we can move on to a more sensible solution if we need to."

He raised a brow, as if she'd just issued a challenge. Which, she supposed, she had.

"You have to promise me you're going to give this a fair consideration," he said pointedly.

"Naturally."

"Good." He straightened and nodded toward the door. "Then put the broom aside and let's go have a look."

The walk to the livery stable was pleasant. The rain had long since stopped but the sidewalks were still damp, and the road muddy. Still, the sunshine felt good and the air smelled fresh and rain-washed. They exchanged greetings with several folks as they passed by. Nora found even those casual exchanges worth a smile. She was still something of an outsider here but it was amazing how quickly that was changing, how the townsfolk were already beginning to accept her as one of them.

"When are Will and your sister due to return to town?" Cam asked.

"This evening. They didn't want to stay away from the twins for too long."

Cam nodded. "It's obvious those youngsters are already attached to your sister."

"I assure you that feeling is returned. Bridget will make a wonderful mother." The subject reminded her of her earlier conversation with Ben. "I've often thought being a parent must be one of the most blessed and fulfilling callings of all. Don't you agree?"

"It's a tremendous responsibility," he said evenly. "And not one that everyone is suited for."

He hadn't really answered her question. "Oh, I agree. One must be willing to see to their children's needs—and not just their physical needs. A parent should put their child's welfare above their own." She cut him a sideways glance. "Sort of the way you do for the citizens of this town."

He grinned. "Are you saying I treat the citizens of Faith Glen like a bunch of children?"

The man could be so frustrating when he got like this. He knew good and well that wasn't what she'd meant—he was just trying to bait her.

But before she could say more, they had arrived at the livery and the moment was lost. Oscar Platt stood just inside the large open carriage door and strode forward when he saw them.

"Good afternoon, Sheriff, Miss Nora. I assume you're here to look at the horse and wagon. They're already hitched out back and ready for your inspection."

They followed him to the back where several wagons were stored. The vehicle he led them to was similar to the one the sheriff used, with a single seat in front and a flat bed in the back. The bed of this one was much shorter than the sheriff's, but it was more than big enough for her needs.

It was the horse, however, that drew her attention. The mare had a reddish-brown coat with a darker mane and tail. She held her head up at an alert angle and had bright, intelligent eyes.

Nora approached the animal slowly. "My, my, aren't you a beautiful lady."

"Her name's Amber," Oscar said, giving the animal's side an affectionate pat. "She's a fine animal, fine indeed. And you'll see she's nearly as good a saddle horse as she is a carriage horse."

This was not at all the kind of animal she'd expected. She was no expert but even she could see that this mare was first rate, the kind to demand a premium from a prospective buyer. She would never be able to afford such a horse. "Mr. Platt, I'm afraid there's been some mistake. I'm looking for an animal that's not quite so... so *fine*."

The livery owner looked confused and turned to Cam.

"Tell her how much you're asking for the horse and wagon together," Cam said.

Oscar named a figure that brought a frown to Nora's face. Not because it was too high, but for the exact opposite reason. "May I ask why you're selling her for such a low price, if she's as grand as you say she is?"

"Well, I, that is..." Oscar rubbed the back of his neck and again cast a help-me look Cam's way.

Cam cleared his throat. "I told you, Nora, Oscar owes me a favor so he's giving me his bottom-line price on this." He spread his hands. "And I'm passing that good fortune on to you."

Nora stroked the horse's muzzle as she thought about that. She suspected there was more to this than Cam was letting on. But the offer *was* tempting.

"What do you think?" Cam asked. "Perfect for your needs isn't she? And the wagon, too?"

"They're everything you say. I just—"

He didn't let her finish her thought. "Why don't we take a little ride to test it out?"

"Well, I suppose." She glanced toward the livery owner. "I mean if Mr. Platt doesn't mind."

The man waved them on. He actually seemed relieved that they were leaving. "Not at all. You two go on with you. I'm sure you won't find anything wrong with the rig or the horse."

Cam offered a hand to help her onto the wagon, then took the seat beside her. "This seat has a nice solid feel to it, don't you think?"

She ignored that and settled herself more comfortably. "Shall we drive around the square then?"

"I have a better idea. Why don't we give this horse and wagon a more thorough workout? A short ride on Farm Road maybe."

Nora's lips curved up at that. The sky had cleared and the day had turned pleasant. A companionable ride would be very nice. And she hadn't had the opportunity to explore in that direction yet. What the locals called Farm Road headed west away from the ocean and, as the name implied, led to a number of small farms and homesteads clustered around the town.

She gave him a bright smile. "If you're sure you have the time, a short ride would be lovely."

"Actually, I have a bit of business over at Lem Grady's place. I thought I'd combine our ride and my work. It shouldn't take more than a few minutes."

"Of course." So much for thinking he wanted to take a casual ride with her. Not that it mattered. Besides, it would be interesting to see him at work on official business.

The Grady place was just past the edge of town, and they arrived within ten minutes. Once there, rather than going to the house, Cam stopped the wagon near an open field where Mr. Grady and his two boys were digging up an old stump in the rain-soaked ground.

He set the brake then turned to her. "There's no need for you to trouble yourself getting down. It's still muddy out here, and I don't plan to be long."

Nora sat back and folded her hands in her lap but she watched curiously as Cam crossed the field to meet the three Gradys.

As she watched Cam, Nora mulled over the earlier exchange in the livery, and a soft smile curved her lips.

Yes, Cam had been very presumptuous in the matter of selecting a horse and wagon. But it was also obvious that he'd gone to some trouble to convince Mr. Platt to give her such a good deal. It was all the more endearing because he'd never take any credit for it.

Nora sat up straighter. Not that she should read anything into his actions. Cam was always looking out for folks, that's all this was. She shouldn't forget her resolve to not open herself up to that kind of hurt, and instead to focus her affections on Grace.

Chapter Eight

Nora couldn't hear anything that was being said, but from their expressions and movements she thought she could make out some of the conversation.

Cam had approached the Gradys in his normal casual fashion and Mr. Grady seemed pleased to see him. The boys, on the other hand, looked guarded, and toe-digging-in-the-ground apprehensive. Had they done something they shouldn't have?

A moment later, Mr. Grady turned a stern eye toward his sons. The boys reacted with vehement head shakes and gesticulations.

Cam questioned them a few more minutes, then finally shook hands with Mr. Grady and headed back to the wagon. As he climbed up and released the brake, she noted he had a thoughtful, somewhat troubled expression on his face.

"Did everything go as you hoped?"

"I just ruled out a couple of suspects in a bit of ongoing mischief."

Was that a good thing or not? She couldn't tell from his expression. "If it's not out of place for me to ask, did this have something to do with the produce missing from Mr. Lafferty's garden?"

He nodded. "But Lem says he can vouch that his boys were both home all night because he heard Arnie snoring off and on and Evan hurt his foot yesterday and is moving pretty slow right now. Lem's not one to try to lie to keep his boys out of trouble, so I believe him."

"Are you sure the culprit wasn't a deer or fox like Ben first thought?"

Cam shook his head, his frustration evident. "Not entirely, but all the signs point to a thief of the two-legged variety."

"I know it's wrong to steal," she said, "but perhaps whoever is guilty of this had no other food. Surely we can be forgiving of such a trespass."

"That'll be up to Amos Lafferty. Assuming we ever find the culprit."

"Well, I'm certain you'll find him eventually."

"Your confidence is appreciated," he said dryly. Then he cocked his head, studying her thoughtfully. "And speaking of food, have you ever tried your hand at baking a blueberry pie?"

"What's a blueberry?"

He raised a brow. "You've *never* had blueberries? Well, then, we need to remedy that immediately. It's one of my favorite fruits. And you're in luck. I know where there's a fine patch of wild berry bushes and they're hitting their peak right now."

"But, shouldn't we get back to town so I can finish up my work?"

"Whatever you have to do will still be there tomorrow." He looked like a child about to partake of a rare treat. "This will be an opportunity for you to stock up on an ingredient you don't have to pay for." His expression seemed to be issuing her a dare. "Unless you're worried about getting a bit of mud on your shoes?"

She wouldn't let the challenge go unanswered. "My boots are up to a bit of mud. As am I." Besides which, she was curious as to what this fruit tasted like.

Cam stopped the wagon at the Grady farmhouse and borrowed a pail from Mrs. Grady. Fifteen minutes later he pulled the wagon to a stop beside an overgrown field.

They picked their way over the damp ground and past scraggly brush until Cam declared they had arrived. "Here we are," he announced with a flourish. "Prepare to taste one of nature's most delectable gifts." He plucked a berry from the bush and handed it to her.

She studied the dark blue, smooth-skinned berry for a moment, then popped it into her mouth. As soon as she bit into it she tasted the sweet, slightly tangy flavor. Immediately she could imagine how well this tiny fruit would lend itself to a pie, either on its own or paired with apple or other berries.

"I can see why you like these so much."

He grinned. "I knew you'd enjoy them. So what do you say? Want to gather some up?"

"Absolutely."

"All right then. The best way to make sure you harvest only the best is to hold the pail under the clusters and brush your hand across them. Those that are ripe will let go of the branch easy enough. Make sure you don't pick any that still have red coloring on them, and you don't want any that aren't firm." He picked another berry and popped it in his mouth, as if unable to resist. "If we work at it for an hour or so we ought to be able to fill most of this pail for you."

"Oh, but surely you plan to take half of whatever we pick for yourself?"

"Don't worry, I'll be eating as we go. And I expect to see a blueberry pie on our table one day this week."

"That sounds fair. After all, since I've never cooked with these before, I'll need to experiment a bit."

He straightened with a mock indignant look. "So that's how it's going to be, is it? You plan to save your best for your paying customers, and leave the castoffs to us?"

She lifted her chin and matched his tone. "Of course. I'm a businesswoman now."

He chuckled and they worked in companionable silence for a while. The time passed quickly and before Nora knew it the pail was nearly full and it was time to go.

Cam carried the pail as they strolled back to the wagon, swinging it slightly with one hand while he took her elbow with the other. After only a few steps, though, she stumbled over a piece of uneven ground and he quickly tightened his hold to steady her.

"Are you okay?"

Feeling foolish at her own clumsiness, she quickly nodded. "Yes, thank you."

"Good." Rather than simply loosening his hold, Cam linked her arm through his and drew it close to his side. "The ground's a bit rocky here—we'll take it slower."

He was merely being gentlemanly, of course. Still, Nora remained acutely conscious of his hold for the rest of the trek back to the road and waiting vehicle.

When they reached the wagon, Cam set the berries under the seat, then handed her up. But he didn't immediately go around to the other side. Instead he leaned against the wagon frame and looked up at her thoughtfully. "I didn't think to ask this earlier, but how much do you know about driving a horse and wagon like this one?"

Nora straightened and tried to appear confident. "I've never actually driven one myself, but I've observed others do it many a time. It doesn't look very difficult."

Cam rolled his eyes. "Slide over. I'm going to teach you how it's done and then you're going to drive this wagon back to the livery."

Not having much choice, Nora did as she was told. The idea of learning how to drive excited her, made her feel as if she were taking another step to gain control of her life.

Once Cam had settled in beside her, he instructed her to take the reins. "Hold them in your left hand, so you can guide with your right. You want to thread them through your fingers so that the left rein is between your thumb and middle finger and the right is two fingers below that."

As she attempted to follow his instructions, Cam leaned forward. "Here, let me show you." He adjusted her hold, threading the reins through her suddenly tingly fingers.

She was glad his focus was on her hands and not her face, because she wasn't certain her expression was as neutral as she'd like it to be.

When he seemed satisfied that she had the reins held properly, he glanced back up at her. "The trick is to get the tension just right. Hold the reins so that there's no slack, but don't pull them tight or tug on them unnecessarily. You want the horse to know you're here, but not to be made nervous by it."

To Nora, that sounded completely contradictory. Or was it just that her mind was unaccountably addled?

When she hesitated, he leaned forward again. "Here, let me show you."

His hand closed firmly over hers and it was all she could do not to jump.

As soon as Cam grasped her hand he felt his pulse jump. The warmth and fragility of her smaller hand under his made him feel both powerful and fiercely protective.

He pushed those thoughts away as best he could and focused his attention on teaching her to hold the reins properly. "Can you feel that?" he asked without looking up. "The horse is there, solid and ready for your direction."

All *he* could feel at the moment was her hand beneath his, small, warm, fragile. Was that racing pulse under his palm his or hers?

Clearing his throat, he again tried to focus only on giving her instruction. "Amber here is a good horse, gentle for the most part, so she shouldn't give you any trouble. But gentle doesn't mean meek. She's got some spirit in her, as well, so make sure she knows you're in control."

"You seem to know this horse pretty well."

He ought to. He'd spent quite a bit of time looking for just the right horse for her. But she didn't need to know that. "You wouldn't expect me to let Oscar sell you a horse I hadn't checked out first, would you?"

He didn't wait for her answer. "Now, there are a few simple procedures you need to learn. When you're ready to start, release the brake by pulling that lever back. Then give the reins a little flick and say 'get up.'

When you want to go left, tighten the left rein and when you want to go right, tighten the right. To stop, pull gently back on both and say 'whoa.'"

He leaned back. "Do you have any questions?"

"No slack, but don't pull too tight. She's gentle, but I should make sure she knows I'm in charge. Simple enough."

He smiled at her dry attempt at humor. "It'll probably take a little practice for you to get the feel of it, but you strike me as a fast learner."

"A lot depends on the teacher," she said with a half smile.

Was she doing that deliberately? "Well, then, start whenever you're ready."

She seemed nervous, but she gamely lifted her chin and reached down to release the brake. Sitting up ramrod straight, she took a deep breath, flicked the reins and gave the command to go. She seemed almost startled when Amber obediently moved forward. A moment later her lips curved in a triumphant grin.

Cam's chest swelled with an almost paternal pride, feeling her victory was a shared one.

They made the trip back to the livery without incident. Nora cautiously stopped the wagon well away from the building, but set the brake as if she'd been doing it for years.

Cam showed her how to tie off the reins then hopped down and helped her down.

Oscar was at the horse's head before she had her feet on the ground. "Well, what did you think?" His pleased-with-himself tone said he expected them to be won over. "The horse handles beautifully, doesn't she? And the wagon is sturdy and well sprung."

Cam decided to let Nora do most of the talking.

"It's just as you say." Nora crossed her arms. "And I've decided that if we can come to an agreement on the terms, we have a bargain."

Uh-oh. He recognized that stubborn tilt to her chin. Nora was going to try to wrestle control and do this her way. But at least she had decided to forget about the pony and cart idea.

"The terms?" Oscar looked confused again.

Cam almost felt sorry for the man. He hadn't intended for things to get so complicated when he'd involved Oscar in this negotiation. He just figured Nora would accept the deal better if it came from someone other than him.

"Yes." She drew herself to her full height and faced Oscar without blinking. But Cam noticed a blush of pink staining her cheeks, as well. "Unfortunately, I don't have the funds to make this purchase outright," she continued. "But, as you are aware, I am earning a regular wage. I'm hoping you will agree to let me pay you in installments. I would pay you an amount from my wages every week, with the understanding that the full amount will be paid within six months."

"But I thought—" Oscar rubbed the back of his neck and shot a quick look Cam's way.

Predictably, Nora would not allow herself to be ignored.

"While Sheriff Long did kindly offer to loan me the money," she said firmly, "I would prefer to take care of this myself. If my terms are unacceptable to you, then I will have to, regretfully, decline your generous offer."

Again Oscar turned to Cam.

Keeping to his plan to stay out of the discussion as much as possible, Cam shrugged. "You heard the lady. It's her you need to deal with."

"Well, I—" Oscar rubbed his chin, and once more cast a pleading look Cam's way.

Relenting, Cam gave a quick nod to the hapless livery owner, then turned to Nora. "Perhaps Oscar here would look more kindly on your offer if you gave him an added incentive."

Her brow furrowed. "Incentive?"

He grinned. "Say, throwing in one of your pies along with his weekly payment?" With that, he casually moved back to the horse, leaving the two of them to carry on without him. He'd done all he could to bring this negotiation to a happy conclusion. They were on their own now.

Happily, Nora jumped on his suggestion with alacrity. "That sounds fair to me. One fresh-baked pie with each weekly payment. Your choice of filling."

Oscar rubbed his chin. "I've always been partial to apple."

Cam hid a smile at the livery owner's befuddled tone.

"Does that mean we have a deal?"

"I suppose it does."

Cam turned in time to see Oscar wipe his hand on his pants and then offer it to Nora to shake, sealing their bargain.

Her expression was flush with victory as she walked toward him a moment later.

"It seems you now own a horse and wagon," he said dryly.

She gave him a diffident smile. "I hope you understand why I had to do it on my own."

Oh, he understood all right. The woman had too much pride for her own good. "Of course. You don't want to be beholden to me."

"Yes. No. I mean—" She took a deep breath. "I don't want to be beholden to *anyone*."

"You know, it's not shameful to accept help occasionally."

"But it's better to make your own way when you can." She brushed at her skirt. "Now, I'll go back to the jailhouse and finish up my work. It shouldn't take me more than another hour or so."

"How about you go home early today?"

He saw the flash of eagerness cross her face, followed immediately by a responsible frown. "But, I didn't finish—"

"As I said earlier, whatever it was you didn't finish will still be there waiting for you tomorrow. We should get this horse and buggy out to your place so James can get Amber settled in before dark. Besides, something tells me you're itching to see how Grace is faring with the Coulters."

Her expression turned sheepish. "Was it that obvious?"

He raised a brow. "In case it has escaped your notice, I'm a very perceptive person."

"Well, then, if you're sure you don't mind, I am a bit anxious to get back to her."

"I wouldn't have offered if I didn't want you to take me up on it."

She moved closer to the wagon. "I suppose you'll be relieved not to have to drive me home today."

Did she really think that was how this was going to happen? He hadn't worked this all out just to rob himself of the chance to drive her to and from her home. "Not so fast. You did well with that first lesson, but I don't think you're ready to go it alone just yet."

"But—"

"No arguing. As the sheriff, I'm responsible for making sure you don't put yourself or anyone else around here in danger. You can take the reins but I'm riding along with you."

"But how will you get back to town?"

"I've got two legs and your place is less than a mile away."

She tilted her head to one side, considering the matter. "I suppose I could have James drive you."

This was beginning to turn into a farce. "If it'll make you feel better, I'll saddle Fletch and tie him to the back of the wagon. Then I can ride him home."

She nodded. "Yes. That *will* make me feel better."

In a very short time his horse was saddled and tied to the back of her new wagon. He held his tongue but watched carefully as she took the reins once again. He was pleased to see she didn't falter. As he'd guessed, she had a natural aptitude for driving.

"One thing I didn't think about was the extra work this will mean for James," she said. "I hope it's not too big a burden for him."

"Don't worry about James. He used to be a groom, remember? He worked for the same prominent family in Boston as Agnes, that's how they met. Anyway, James managed an entire stable. He really likes working with horses. In fact I think he misses it quite a bit. So, in a way, you'll be doing him a favor by putting this horse and rig into his keeping."

The worry lines disappeared from her brow and she focused on her driving for the rest of the short trip to the cottage.

Cam relaxed, satisfied that Nora had finally accepted the situation. He'd never had so much trouble helping someone as he did this strong-willed woman at his side.

And if truth be told, he'd never gained such satisfaction from it before, either. Part of it had to do with the challenge she presented—he did love a good challenge.

The other part…well, he wasn't ready to dwell on that just yet.

Chapter Nine

As soon as Nora pulled the wagon to a stop, James was out the door and headed their way. "Well, well, what have we here?"

She set the brake, proud that she hadn't needed reminders or instruction. "It's my new horse and wagon. What do you think?"

James barely glanced at her and Cam—his attention was all for the horse. He ran his hands expertly over the animal, making noises in his throat that Nora couldn't quite decipher. Finally he looked up. "It appears you have yourself a fine animal here." He folded his arms. "I guess you'll be wanting me to care for her along with the other livestock."

Nora was relieved to see the eager anticipation behind his gruff question. "I'm sorry if this is going to cause you extra work. I promise to help as much as I can."

He waved a hand dismissively. "Ach, you have enough on your plate already, what with your job in town and the babe to look out for. You just leave the care of this fine animal and rig to me."

"I'll admit that would be very helpful. But only if you're certain…."

His chest puffed out slightly. "Certain as can be. Now get along in the house with you. I know you're itching to see Grace after being separated all day."

Cam moved to the back of the wagon and untethered his horse. "Need any help unhitching the wagon?"

James glowered at him. "Cameron boy, I was hitching and unhitching wagons when your pa was still a lad. Even with this bum leg of mine I can handle a simple rig like this one. You go back to your sheriffing and leave this to me."

Nora noticed Cam's smile wobble just the tiniest bit. Was it the reference to his father?

Cam led his horse over to where Nora stood and together they watched James lead the horse toward the barnyard.

"He really does seem to like working with horses," Nora mused. "I haven't seen such a spring in his step since I moved in here."

"Everyone likes to feel useful."

"And speaking of that, I suppose we should save you the trouble of coming out here every morning and evening. I'll just let James transport me and Grace to and from town." Though she *would* miss their morning and evening drives, and the accompanying talks.

Cam frowned. "I thought we already discussed this."

She tamped down her urge to agree with him. This was a matter of doing what was sensible, not what was more enjoyable. "*You* discussed it. And in your usual high-handed fashion, I might add. Surely you can admit that it's much more efficient for James to handle this now that transport is readily available."

"Nonsense. As I've already informed you, I have to make my rounds every day so this isn't the least bit out of the way."

In the end, they compromised. James would provide transportation in the mornings and Cam would take her home in the evening.

A few minutes later, Nora watched Cam ride off, reflecting on what a stubborn man he was. Still, she wasn't nearly as miffed that he hadn't given in to her as she ought to have been. Perhaps she was just tired.

The sound of a baby's cry caught her attention, and she bustled inside.

Tuesday morning dawned clear and warm. James had the carriage ready early and Nora smiled to see how proudly he sat there holding the reins. If for no other reason than that, she was pleased she'd agreed to this purchase. Conscious of the difficulty James had climbing, she insisted he not get down to help her up. Instead, Agnes held Grace while Nora climbed aboard, then handed up both the baby and Nora's basket of baked goods.

Nora said a silent prayer of thanksgiving as they made the short trip to town. Her life was good. She had Grace. She had a job that put food on the table for all of her household. And she now had the added measure of independence the horse and wagon afforded her.

Though part of her missed her morning chat with Cam, it felt quite satisfying to ride into town in her own wagon. She was one step closer to proving she could make it without having to depend on her sisters'—or anyone else's—charity.

Later, as she was finishing her after-breakfast cleanup

chores, the door to the sheriff's office opened and Bridget breezed in.

"Good morning, gentlemen," she greeted the lawmen.

All three men scrambled to their feet.

"Good morning, Mrs. Black." Cam was the first to speak. "Welcome back."

Nora stepped into the galley doorway, smiling at the emphasis Cam placed on Bridget's new title. "I'll second that."

"Hello." Bridget gave her sister a quick smile, then moved toward the basket at Ben's feet. "Ah, and there you are." She dropped into a graceful stoop to pick up Grace. "Oh my, you seem to have grown so much in just the few days I've been away."

"I can see which one of us you missed more," Nora said dryly.

Bridget laughed, lifting Grace to her shoulder and then crossing the room to give Nora a one-armed hug. "And you, dear sister, have not changed at all since I left."

"Glad to have you and Will back in town," Cam said as he raised a brow. "I trust you're not here on official business."

Bridget waved a hand dismissively. "Oh, no, nothing so serious. I was just hoping to catch Nora before she went out to do the marketing so I could accompany her."

"You're just in time." Nora untied her apron and grabbed her basket. "I'm on my way out now." She eyed her employer and his two deputies. "Any requests for your meals today?"

Cam waved her on. "Whatever you decide will be fine."

"One of those peach cobblers for dessert would be nice," Gavin added hopefully.

Bridget gave Nora an eager smile. "I brought Grace something from Boston."

"Oh?"

"It's for both of you really." Her grin broadened. "I can't wait to show you. It's right outside."

Her curiosity piqued by Bridget's obvious excitement, Nora let her sister lead her out onto the sidewalk.

And there sat a small, sturdy-looking wicker cart. It had four wheels and a handle, and had a leather shade on the side opposite the handle. The bottom was lined with a thick, soft blanket.

"It's a baby buggy," Bridget explained. "Do you like it? I thought it would make it easier for you to handle both Grace and your parcels when you had shopping or other errands to run."

"It's lovely." Nora ran a hand along the wicker edge, admiring the graceful curve.

"See." Bridget placed Grace inside and covered her with a lightweight blanket that had been tucked to one side. "She can lay here all comfy and cozy and leave your hands free for other things."

Nora gave her sister a hug. "Thank you. I love it."

"I'm glad. When I saw one of these on the sidewalks of Boston, I knew I had to get one for Grace."

Nora squeezed Bridget's hand before stepping back. "Well, it was very thoughtful of you." She eyed her sister teasingly. "You're looking so happy. Married life certainly agrees with you."

"Oh, Nora, I *am* happy and so at peace. I never thought I'd say this, but I'm actually grateful to Daniel McGarth for treating me as he did. If he hadn't left me at the altar last year I would never have come to this wonderful country and would never have met Will."

"The Almighty certainly has a way of working things out for us."

Bridget grasped the hands of the baby buggy and they headed toward the general store. "And I'm going to see even more of this wonderful country. Will has a business meeting in New York City next week. So we've decided to go as a family. And we're traveling by ship. Caleb has shown such an interest in sailing vessels that we thought this would be a treat for him and for Olivia, too."

"That sounds lovely. And I'm certain the children will see it as a grand adventure." She gave her sister a teasing smile. "And so will their stepmother if I'm not mistaken."

Bridget didn't deny it. "We're leaving on Friday and plan to return on Wednesday. Esther is staying behind—she says sailing doesn't agree with her. Oh, and Maeve and Flynn plan to come down on Monday to check on the progress their builders are making, so they will be available if you should need anything."

Nora tried not to take offense. "Really, Bridget, I don't need checking up on. I'll be perfectly fine. And if I do need help with anything, I've made a number of good friends in Faith Glen that I can turn to."

"I know. Still, I worry about you out there in that isolated cottage."

Nora straightened, happy to have a surprise of her own to share. "Not so isolated any longer," she said proudly. "I am now the happy owner of a fine horse and wagon which are already sitting in our barn."

Bridget paused midstep. "You are?" She started forward again. "That's marvelous, of course. But when… how?"

"I purchased them yesterday. Did you know that James was once a groom for a well-to-do family in Boston? You should see how much pride he takes in caring for them. He's been quite pleased with life in general since we brought the animal home."

"We?"

Now why would Bridget pick that word to pounce on? "Sheriff Long helped me with the selection and purchase. He also taught me how to drive the thing."

"You mean you actually drove the wagon?"

Nora laughed. "I drove it home from the livery myself. It's really not so difficult a thing. And I have a feeling James will be doing most of the driving in the future."

"But, and I don't mean to be indelicate, but how could you afford such a purchase?"

Nora brushed a bit of lint from her skirt. "I made an arrangement with Mr. Platt. I will pay him something out of my wages every week until the debt is cleared." She gave her sister a sideways look. "That and a pie a week as interest."

But Bridget didn't smile. "Nora, if you needed money, you should have come to us. Will would have been glad to—"

Nora didn't let her finish. "You weren't here when I struck the deal. And it's better this way. When the final payment is made I will truly feel as if I earned this purchase."

Bridget shook her head. "You have always been so stubbornly independent. But at least Cam helped you make the selection." She paused a moment. "Wait a minute. Does this mean he won't be driving you to and from town every day?"

Nora couldn't quite interpret the look Bridget was giving her and so decided to ignore it. "Yes and no. James will drive me and Grace into town in the mornings, and the sheriff will drive us back home in the evenings. He insisted."

"I see."

There was that look again. "It's only because I don't always finish at the same time every day. It saves James the trouble of waiting on me or me on him."

"Quite practical." Bridget gave her a knowing grin, then turned serious. "But, Nora, won't you let me help you with this? Remember, I know precisely how tight your budget is."

Nora gave her sister a teasing nudge. "It is less so now that we have one less mouth to feed." Then she sobered. "Actually, I've come up with a plan to help me supplement my wages and perhaps even build a little nest egg. I'm starting my own business."

"Oh my goodness, you're just full of surprises this morning. What kind of business?"

"A baking business."

"A baking business? Nora, you can't be serious."

Bridget's reaction stung just a tiny bit. "Don't you think my pies and cakes are good enough for folks to want to buy them?"

Bridget waved a hand, dismissing her question. "Don't be a goose. Of course they are. But baking is long, hot work. Where will you find the time or energy to do this?"

Bridget's words eased the sting somewhat. "The sheriff has agreed to let me do some baking during the day while I'm working, and I have Saturdays, as well."

"Of course he did. But still, that leaves you *no* free time to rest."

"I'll rest on Sundays." She didn't want to argue with her sister, especially not today. "Oh, Bridget, be happy for me. If this goes well, I'll have enough money to supplement what the purchase of the horse and wagon takes from my weekly wages and perhaps some extra to put toward the rest of the repairs at the cottage."

"How many pies and cakes do you plan to bake?"

"I'm not sure yet." At least Bridget had stopped trying to talk her out of this. "As many as I get orders for."

"So you haven't started yet?"

"Actually, I'm just about to." She lifted the cloth from her basket. "I have an apple pie to give to Rose Kenny over at the boardinghouse and a chocolate almond custard pie to give to Mrs. James at the general store."

"*Chocolate* almond custard?"

Nora smiled. She'd known that would divert Bridget's attention. "That husband of yours asked me to experiment with chocolate powder in my recipes and this is one of my better outcomes."

"It sounds delicious." Then her sister frowned. "Did you say *give?*"

Nora nodded, proud of her plan. "I thought I would show good faith by giving them their first pie for free. Then, if they are satisfied with how their customers react, they can place an order for more."

"Clever." Bridget's expression turned somber. "Are you doing this because you don't want to accept help from me or Maeve? Because there's no shame in accepting a helping hand from family."

"No, that's not it. At least not entirely," she added

honestly. "For the first time in my life I have a chance to determine how my life should be lived. I truly *want* to do this."

"Well, in that case, you can put me down for five pies every week. And I want one of those chocolate almond custard pies in my first order."

Nora gave her sister's arm a squeeze. "Don't be silly. If you want pies I'll give them to you."

"Oh, no. If you won't take charity from me then you can't expect me to take it from you."

"But it's not charity, you're family."

Bridget's raised brow and pointed look were quite eloquent. Nora laughed sheepishly. "Oh, very well. I'll have your first pie ready tomorrow." She gave her sister's arm a light squeeze. "That makes you my first customer."

By this time they'd reached the general store. Bridget lifted her chin. "Now, let's go inside and see if we can line up another for you."

Mrs. James seemed more interested in the baby buggy than in Nora's baked goods. In the end, however, she agreed to accept the pie Nora offered her, but was skeptical as to whether she would want to purchase any additional ones. But she promised to see if she could find a customer for it.

Rose, on the other hand, not only accepted the pie enthusiastically but immediately put in an order for two pies a day to serve her boarders, confessing that baking was her least favorite chore.

As they stepped out of the boardinghouse, Nora caught sight of a young girl scurrying quickly away. There was something vaguely familiar about her, but she couldn't quite place her.

"What is it?"

Bridget's words pulled her back to the present. "Nothing," she said, giving her head a mental shake.

"You looked miles away just now."

Nora waved a dismissive hand. "I just thought I saw someone I recognized, but she was gone before I could be sure."

"Should we try to catch up to her?"

"Oh, no, it wasn't important. Just one of those things that will nag at me until I remember."

Bridget tugged on her gloves. "Well, I should be getting back home. The twins will be ready for some outdoor play by now." She released the handle of the buggy and bent down to kiss Grace's cheek. "Tell James and Agnes hello for me and that I'll be out to the cottage for a visit soon."

Once her sister walked away, Nora headed back to the sheriff's office, pushing the buggy with a spring in her step. "Did you see what just happened, Grace? I already have orders for nearly twenty pies a week. I know that part of that order came from my sister, and is likely as much duty as desire, but I'm a businesswoman now and I must treat it as such."

Grace gurgled in response and Nora laughed. "You're right. I'm hardly a businesswoman yet. But, God willing, I will make this work."

Wednesday afternoon, Cam returned to the office from his midday rounds to find both of his deputies were out. He could hear Nora humming softly in the kitchen and could smell the enticing aroma of cinnamon and baked apples.

Almost without thinking, he crossed the room and leaned in the kitchen doorway, watching Nora at work. She was bent over the oven, removing a pie with a perfectly browned crust, so she didn't notice him right away. As soon as she set the pie on the counter, she slid a cake pan into its place. Then she stood and wiped the sweat from her brow with the back of her hand. He frowned as he realized how hot the small room was. Perhaps he should add another window in that north wall.

"A body could practically live on the smells coming from in here."

She jumped, then whirled around to face him.

"Sorry, didn't mean to startle you."

She relaxed. "Oh, that's okay. I didn't hear you come in is all."

Feeling the need to keep the conversation going, he asked the first thing that came to mind. "Do you know where my two deputies disappeared to?"

"Ben said he had to help Miss Esther with something—I'm afraid I don't remember just what. And Gavin went to help Andrew Dobbs get his cow out of a bog."

Cam grinned, glad he hadn't been in when the call came in for help with that particular problem. It would be a good learning experience for the boy.

He nodded toward the pie cooling on her worktable. "So, how many orders do you have so far?"

Her expression changed to one of pleasure. "Bridget wants one pie every weekday, Rose wants two, Mrs. James wants a pie and a cake every day and a few of the ladies around town who've heard about my undertaking have placed onetime orders."

He was pleased for her but Ben's warning that she might leave them niggled at the back of his mind. "I told you you wouldn't have trouble getting orders."

"And I'm very pleased that you were right." She started rolling out some pie dough on a floured surface.

He watched her for a moment, admiring her deft movements and air of confidence. "I've been wondering," he finally said, "is your baking skill something you come by naturally or did you have to work to learn it?"

"A little of both." She lifted the thin sheet of dough with practiced ease and set it into a waiting pie tin. "I learned from my mother, of course," she said as she began fluting the edges of the dough. "She was the best cook in our village."

Nora was such an intriguing mix of pride and modesty. "Yet your sisters aren't quite as talented as you are."

"Maeve and Bridget were younger than I when Mother passed on. Besides, they have other skills, other interests." She started spooning a mix of blueberries and sliced apples into the crust. "And cooking is something I've always enjoyed so I spent a lot of time in the kitchen with my mother."

He heard the wistful note in her voice. "How old were you when you lost her?"

"Fifteen."

He felt a pinch of sympathy. She'd almost been of an age to spread her wings, only to have them clipped by that loss.

Then she turned the table on him. "What about you? How old were you when you lost your mother?"

He shifted uncomfortably. His past was not something he was interested in talking about. But he'd started this conversation. "Twelve."

Her expression softened in sympathy. "That must have been a difficult time. Do you have any siblings?"

"No." He knew his voice was terse but she didn't seem to notice.

"Then it must have been doubly hard for you."

Given what his childhood had been like, it was probably a blessing that he *hadn't* had siblings to share his fate. "It taught me independence."

It looked as if Nora wanted to say more, but Grace started to fuss, effectively distracting her.

Relieved to have an end to that particular conversation, Cam turned to leave. But Nora wasn't quite done with him.

"Oh, dear, there are times when I wish there were two of me." She cut Cam a hopeful look. "Would you mind entertaining Grace for just a minute? I need to check on the cake I have in the oven."

Entertain Grace? How did one entertain an infant?

Chapter Ten

Cam glanced back over his shoulder, hoping against hope that Ben or Gavin had slipped in unnoticed. But no such luck.

Nora seemed oblivious to his discomfort. "Just talk to her and wiggle your fingers in front of her face. I'll only be a minute."

Okay, that didn't sound too difficult. And it wasn't as if she were leaving him alone with Grace. Cam moved toward the basket where Grace lay, her little face scrunched up as if she would be expressing her displeasure very soon and with great gusto. What did one say to an infant? He glanced toward Nora but she had her back to him.

"Okay, ladybug, if it's attention you're looking for, you've got it. I'm all yours."

She hushed and stared up at him as if she'd understood his words. He smiled at the fanciful notion. "That's better. Now, Nora says you need to be entertained but I think you just want to make certain we haven't forgotten you. As if we ever would. Nora thinks you are exceedingly special, and I must say, you do have a way of lighting up a room."

"I think she likes you."

Cam looked up to see Nora smiling at him with a softly approving expression on her face.

Cam straighten and cleared his throat, feeling as if he'd been caught doing something foolish. "Yes, well, I need to get back to work."

As he moved to his desk, Cam couldn't shake the image of the way she'd looked at him, as if he'd done something heroic rather than just distract an infant for a few seconds.

A man would do a lot to earn a look like that.

Nora's Friday morning routine got a welcome interruption when Bridget stopped by to tell her goodbye before leaving on the trip to New York. The two sisters had a nice long chat while Nora prepared the lunch ingredients to throw into the stewpot.

Bridget was understandably excited about her upcoming travel and chatted on about all of the family's preparations and plans, making Nora laugh out loud at some of her stories. Finally she halted in the middle of a story about Caleb's idea of what he should pack, and gave a self-conscious grin. "Listen to me. I haven't let you get a word in since I walked in here."

Nora smiled indulgently. "I enjoy listening to your stories."

Bridget snagged a blueberry from the bowl on Nora's worktable. "You always were a good listener. Now, your turn. Tell me what's going on with you. The bakery business seems to be going well. I'm hearing good things from your customers."

Nora felt a glow of pleasure that her baking was being so well received. "I feel truly blessed that the people here have been so willing to support my efforts. The whole thing has grown much faster than I expected. I had to do a bit of quick rearranging with my routine this week to fit everything in." Then she grinned. "And for the price of one pie a week of his very own, Gavin has agreed to do my deliveries."

Bridget laughed. "Was that his idea or yours?"

"I suggested it, based on a bargain I made with Mr. Platt, but Gavin jumped on it. He had been lamenting the fact that so few of my baked goods made it to their lunch table and the idea of having a pie all to himself perked him right up."

Bridget laughed again. "He's a growing boy." Then she sobered. "So is it all going as well as it appears?"

Nora grimaced. "Except for one thing. It seems I've reached my limit as far as what I can produce. I actually had to turn away a customer yesterday."

"But, surely that's a good thing?" Bridget placed her elbows on the worktable. "I mean, it's better than not having enough customers to buy your wares, isn't it?"

"Yes, of course. But it also means I'll never be able to earn more than I am today." Was she being greedy to want more?

"Oh." Bridget plucked another blueberry and chewed thoughtfully for a moment. "Is there some way you could find other items to bake, items that cook more quickly and can be parceled to more customers, things like cookies or tea cakes?"

Nora stopped what she was doing and looked at her sister with new appreciation. She'd never cooked those types of items before but she felt certain she could master them. "Bridget, that's a wonderful idea." Her mind started turning over possibilities. "I would have to do a little experimenting, of course, but I think I could get quite a few additional items baked each day if I worked it just right."

Bridget laughed. "Glad I could help." She wagged a finger Nora's way. "Just make sure you don't wear yourself out with all this extra work. There are people who count on you to be at your best." She reached down and adjusted Grace's blanket. "Like this precious babe given into your care."

"Don't worry, I won't take on more than I can manage." Nora went back to stirring the stew that was simmering on the stove. She appreciated her sister's concern but she was much sturdier than those close to her seemed to realize. In fact, to provide for her household and achieve her goals, she could be quite resourceful.

The outer door opened and Nora felt a little stab of disappointment to see it was Gavin rather than Cam. Silly of her, of course.

The young deputy sauntered across the room and sniffed the air. "It sure does smell good in here."

Bridget laughed. "The aromas from Nora's cooking are more alluring than any fancy perfume." Then she nodded toward the paper in Gavin's hand. "What do you have there?"

"It's a letter that just arrived from Mrs. Fitzwilliam. She said to tell you both hello."

"Everyone is doing well I trust," Nora said.

Gavin nodded. "Yes, but she's feeling frustrated that her investigator hasn't located her granddaughter yet."

Nora wiped her forehead with the back of her hand. "I've been praying for a happy reunion between them."

Bridget nodded. "As have I. I hope the girl is all right." Then she stood. "Well, I enjoyed the visit but I should be going now. I want to stop by and visit a moment with Agnes and James before we leave."

Nora nodded. "They'll be pleased to see you."

Bridget crossed the small room and Nora opened her arms for a hug.

"Take care of yourself," Bridget said.

"Of course." Nora squeezed her sister's shoulder then stepped back. "Enjoy your trip and make certain you pay special attention to all the wonderful sights. I want to hear all about them when you get back."

Bridget exchanged a few words with Gavin then gave a final wave as she headed out the door.

As Nora went back to her cooking, she reflected on the unexpected and interesting turn her sisters' lives had taken since they'd left Ireland. Still, she didn't envy them their big houses and ability to travel to exciting places.

But if she was honest with herself, she did envy, just the tiniest bit, the happiness and loving families they'd found. She offered a silent prayer asking for forgiveness for that envy, and then added another prayer for guidance.

She hadn't forgotten what Ben had revealed to her about Cam's childhood. In fact it had been on her mind quite a bit lately. She was certain the Almighty wanted to use her and Grace to help him somehow—she just hoped she recognized the opportunity when it came.

Which didn't mean she had changed her resolve to guard her heart. She wasn't sixteen any longer, she was a grown woman and she wouldn't repeat the mistake she'd made with Braydan Rourke. No, she was concerned for a friend, that was all.

Nora entered the cottage that evening with a smile on her face. She had dozens of ideas spinning in her head for how to implement Bridget's idea of smaller bakery items and, since tomorrow was Saturday, she planned to spend most of the day trying them out.

And Cam's announcement that he intended to come by tomorrow to "do a little work around the place" had only added to her happy mood. It would be good to see progress being made on the repairs to the cottage.

Why his upcoming visit would cheer her up beyond that she refused to consider.

She found Agnes in the kitchen, darning a sock.

"I understand your baking business is doing quite well," the woman said by way of greeting. "In fact I hear you've had to turn away a few customers."

So, apparently Bridget had discussed her concerns during her visit out here this morning. Nora felt a momentary twinge of annoyance which she pushed away as best she could. She placed Grace in the kitchen cradle and gave Agnes a smile. "A body can only do so much. And I'm working on a few ideas to help me produce more."

Agnes gave her a pointed look. "Wearing yourself out is not the answer. But what if you had some help?"

Nora paused. Surely Agnes knew she couldn't afford to hire anyone. "What do you mean?"

Agnes set her sewing in her lap and met Nora's gaze. "I mean *I* can help you with your baking."

Nora was deeply touched by the generosity of the older woman, but she had no intention of taking advantage of her that way. "Oh, that's very kind of you to offer but I couldn't—"

Agnes raised a hand to halt her protest. "Nonsense. I figure James and I are benefiting from this new endeavor of yours so we might as well do what we can to help. James is already taking care of your horse and driving you to town in the mornings. Helping with your baking will give me a chance to contribute, as well."

"But you already help me watch over Grace and do the housework. There's no need—"

Agnes sighed deeply. "Of course, if you don't think my cooking will be good enough, I'll understand."

Nora was horrified. She hadn't meant to hurt Agnes's feelings. "Oh, no, that's not it at all. I just don't want to impose—"

The grandmotherly woman beamed at her. "It's settled then. I know I'm not as good a cook as you are. But there are many things to be done that don't require a lot of skill. Like peeling and slicing apples, hulling nuts, measuring out ingredients, keeping an eye on the oven and such."

As Agnes picked up the sock and began plying her needle once more, Nora had the distinct impression that she had been rather expertly manipulated into accepting her friend's help.

Agnes was a lot more wily than her sweet appearance indicated.

The next morning, Nora rose before dawn and, as soon as she had Grace fed and freshened up, stoked the stove and went to work on her baking. Mrs. Ferguson, the wife of the foreman out at Will's chocolate mill, had placed a large order for a family gathering she was hosting Sunday afternoon. Happily, she had left the flavors up to Nora. Which gave Nora the perfect opportunity to do a bit of experimenting. She planned to try to mix Will's chocolate with both blueberries and maple syrup for what she hoped would be two very deliciously distinctive pies.

Nora sang softly as she worked, as much to entertain Grace as to keep herself company.

Before she could get the first pie in the oven, Agnes and James joined her in the kitchen.

Nora gave them a guilty grimace. "I hope my rattling around in here didn't wake you."

"Not at all." Agnes crossed to the cupboard to fetch two cups while James moved to the stove to get the coffeepot.

"No sense frittering the day away in bed," Agnes continued as she placed the cups on the table. "Getting an early start on your baking, are you?"

Nora nodded. "I promised Mrs. Ferguson I'd deliver her order this afternoon." She turned to James, who was filling the coffee cups. "I'm hoping you'll drive me to her place once I have everything ready."

"Of course." James lifted his cup and inhaled the steaming brew as if it were ambrosia. "I suppose you'll need something to pack your pies in so they're protected from the jostling. I think there are some bits and pieces of lumber out in the barn that I can use to fashion a few shallow crates from."

Nora started to protest that she didn't want to cause him extra work, then, remembering what Cam had said about folks needing to feel useful, thought better of it. "Oh, that would be wonderful, if you're sure it's not too much trouble."

"You just leave it to me." James's chest expanded noticeably. "I'll take care of it as soon as I tend to the animals."

When James headed outdoors a few minutes later, Agnes carried their cups to the counter. Then she turned back to Nora. "Have you had your breakfast yet?"

"The biscuits are almost ready to come out of the oven. I'll have one with a bit of jam in just a minute."

"Nonsense. That's not a proper breakfast. As soon as James brings in the fresh eggs I'll get a proper breakfast whipped up." She looked around. "In the meantime, what can I do to help?"

"If you would keep an eye on Grace for me while I roll out this pie crust that would be lovely."

"Of course." Agnes smiled fondly at the cradle. "But that's hardly work."

Nora smiled and waved toward a bowl on the counter. "Well, you did mention something about peeling and slicing apples."

Agnes nodded and moved toward the drawer where the knives were stored. Nora watched her, and offered up a quick prayer of thanksgiving. It was as if in her adult years she had been gifted with the grandparents she'd never known as a child.

Strange how it was that none of the three other people living in this house were related to her by blood, but she felt as close to them as if they were her true kin.

Thirty minutes later, as Nora and the Coulters were pushing back from the breakfast table, there was a quick knock at the back door and Cam stepped inside. "Mmm-mmm, it sure does smell good in here."

Nora waved him in. "If that's a hint that you're hungry, there are a couple of biscuits left from breakfast that you can have with some of Agnes's strawberry jam."

"Now there's an offer too good to refuse." He nodded toward the pie cooling on the counter. "Been hard at work already I see."

Agnes pulled a clean plate and coffee cup from the

cupboard. "Isn't it wonderful how well Nora is doing with this new business of hers?"

"That it is." Cam took a seat at the table. "The smells wafting from my office have made it a very popular place for folks to visit lately."

Cam reached for one of the biscuits from the platter, then paused. "Oh, I almost forgot." He dug into his pocket and pulled out a letter which he held out to Nora. "This came for you just before I headed here this morning."

Nora wiped her hands on her apron and accepted it. "It's from Maeve." Why would her sister send a letter when she was supposed to come for a visit in two days? Worried, Nora quickly ripped open the missive and scanned the enclosed page.

"I hope it's not bad news," Agnes asked, and Nora heard the anxious note in her voice.

A moment later her hand went to her throat. "Oh my goodness."

"What is it?" Cam pushed back from the table and stood. "Are your sister and Dr. Gallagher all right?"

Nora looked up quickly to find three pairs of eyes studying her in concern. "Maeve and Flynn are fine," she reassured them. "But there's been a terrible fire at a local hotel there in Boston." She closed her eyes momentarily before continuing. "Two people were killed and over thirty were injured, some of them quite severely. Flynn and Maeve are postponing their visit so they can provide medical assistance."

Agnes wrung her hands. "Oh, those poor people."

Nora sent up a silent prayer that the injured parties would find strength and healing. She would miss seeing Maeve and Flynn, but she knew they were doing what they needed to do.

She turned to Cam, who had returned to his chair. "Thank you for bringing this out to me."

"It was no problem. I just wish it could have been happier news."

James, who still sat at the table, leaned back in his chair. "You planning to do some work out here today?"

Cam nodded as he slathered a generous dollop of jam on his biscuit. "I thought I'd work on the roof."

"By yourself?" James asked.

"I know Will and Flynn have helped out before, but they're both busy men. I figure if I wait until they're able to lend a hand it might never get done."

"Anything I can do to help?" James asked.

Nora held her breath waiting for Cam's response, ready to intervene if he accepted James's offer. Allowing James his dignity was one thing, but there was no way she'd let the elderly man try to climb a ladder up onto the roof.

But she should have known Cam would handle it well.

"Thanks," Cam said easily, "but I can't let you do that. It wouldn't be right, being as Nora here is paying me for my labors."

Nora jumped in quickly. "That's right. Besides, James, you've already promised to fashion those crates for me."

Cam raised a brow. "Crates?"

That spurred a lengthy back and forth discussion between the two men on what James was trying to do and the best way to go about it.

Agnes and Nora exchanged knowing smiles and went back to their kitchen work.

By midmorning Nora was ready to escape the hot kitchen for a spell. Thinking that her handyman-for-the-day might be feeling something of the same, she grabbed a few items from the larder, placed them in a basket, then carried it and Grace outside. She set the basket down and shaded her eyes, looking up to find Cam pounding away at the roof with a hammer.

When he spotted her he paused and leaned back on his heels. "Well, hello there. Dare I hope you have something in that basket for me?"

She grinned. "If you're ready for a break, there's a jar of apple cider, some berries and a couple of slices of cheese I might be willing to share."

He stood, apparently quite at ease on the pitched roof. "Now, that sounds really good. Just give me a minute to climb down."

She watched him, admiring the animal-like grace with which he moved, and the play of muscles in his back and arms as he descended the ladder. Was it wrong of her to admire such agility and strength? After all, God had formed him this way.

Nora shifted her gaze to Grace. Not wrong perhaps, but dangerous to her peace of mind.

A moment later he had made it to the ground and she was able to give him a friendly smile. "I've been baking all morning which means the kitchen is nearly as hot as the inside of my oven. So I thought we might find a shady spot out here to have our snack."

He returned her smile, pulling a large handkerchief from his pocket to wipe his hands. "Good idea. How about under that tree over by the garden?" At her nod he scooped up the basket. "You *are* going to join me aren't you?"

She planted a kiss on the top of Grace's head. "We certainly are."

He gave a satisfied nod, then led the way, whistling.

Within minutes he had set the basket beneath the tree and spread the picnic cloth.

Nora carefully placed Grace on the blanket between herself and Cam, then pulled the simple fare from the basket.

"Colleen's Garden."

She looked up quickly to see Cam studying the weathered sign nailed to the nearby tree.

"Colleen was your mother's name, wasn't it? I remember it from the deed."

"Yes." Nora leaned back on her heels. "Apparently Laird O'Malley planted all of this for her." She looked around at the garden. She had done lots of weeding these past few weeks but it still needed a great deal of work to bring it back to life. "It must have been quite lovely at one time."

Knowing Cam was bound to be thirsty, she shook off the wistful musings and poured him up a large glass of the cider.

He drained it quickly then held his glass out for more. As she poured, he glanced toward an old rickety bench that sat a little ways from the tree. "Looks like that was part of the original setup, as well. It doesn't appear to be very safe, though. Probably best no one tries to sit on it until I can get it fixed."

"Don't worry. None of us here plan to risk our necks that way. Though it would be lovely to have a comfortable place to sit out here." She sat back again as he retrieved the glass from her, then she watched as he absently swatted at a fly that flew a little too close to Grace's face. How could this man ever believe he would harm a child placed in his care?

Please, Heavenly Father, give me the words and the

opportunity to help Cam see how wrong his thinking is on that score.

He set his glass down, bringing her focus back to the present. She smiled at him. "Now, if you'd say grace for us please…"

Cam did as she'd asked and then they both helped themselves to the simple fare.

As she munched on a handful of berries, she studied the roof. "You're making good progress, but I don't want to take advantage of you. Please don't feel obligated to get it all done today."

He reached for a piece of cheese. "It's my day off and I don't have anything else to take up my time at the moment. Besides, another few hours and I should have this roof all squared away."

That was good news. She wouldn't have to worry quite so much about the next rainstorm to come through. "I certainly appreciate all of your efforts. I know how hot it must be up there."

He gave her a dry smile. "Don't forget you're paying me. It's not like I'm doing this just to be nice."

He wasn't fooling her. To be nice was exactly why he was doing this.

Before she could comment, though, he nodded toward the house. "I think the next project we should tackle is to work on the windows. I noticed the pane in one of them is broken and that several of them have cracks around the sills."

She agreed. "Let me know what materials are needed and I'll talk to Hattie over at the general store about ordering them."

"I can take care of that for you."

She eyed him suspiciously. "Just make certain it goes on my tab."

"You're the boss." Then he grinned. "Out here at least."

If only she was certain he believed that.

"I take it the baking you're doing this morning is for one of your customers. How many items are in the order?"

"Mrs. Ferguson ordered four pies and two cakes for a special dinner party she plans to hold tomorrow. I tried a couple of new flavors for her, and incorporated some of the chocolate from the mill. I hope she likes them." Then she felt her cheeks warm as she realized that he wouldn't be interested in her experiments.

But he didn't seem particularly annoyed. "I'll be glad to deliver those baked goods for you when I head back to town this afternoon," he offered.

"That's very kind of you. But I wouldn't want to cheat James of the opportunity." She smiled in response to his raised brow, then expanded on her statement. "I do believe James is looking forward to having an excuse to hitch up the wagon today since he didn't need to take me to town this morning."

Cam nodded. "I see. In that case, I shall withdraw my offer."

She leaned back, supported by her palms. "He and Amber have become best of friends, you know. In fact, I'm almost certain I'm missing an apple from my baking supplies this morning and there was a suspicious bulge in his shirt pocket when he went out to milk Daisy. I wouldn't be at all surprised to learn that apple somehow made its way into Amber's feed bag this morning."

She saw him brush away another fly that had gotten too close to Grace's face and decided to try a little experiment of a different sort.

Chapter Eleven

Nora popped up, and brushed the dust from her skirt. "I just remembered, I meant to bring some of my new cookies out here for you to try." She gave him a bright smile. "If you'll keep an eye on Grace for a minute I'll be right back."

She saw the sharp flicker of emotion in his eye. But he didn't refuse outright. "That's not necessary. There's more than enough here to—"

"Nonsense. It's a new recipe and I'd like to see what you think." She moved toward the house, not giving him time for further protest. "I'll be quick as a sneeze."

She kept moving forward, resisting the urge to look back. He might not be comfortable watching over Grace, but she wanted him to see that she didn't have even the tiniest concern that Grace would come to any harm under his care.

Cam's even-tempered disposition, however, was another matter altogether.

Cam rubbed the back of his neck, watching Nora abandon him with little Grace. Then he looked helplessly at the baby. "Well, ladybug, it looks like you're stuck with me for the moment. How about we make a bargain to make the best of it?"

Grace looked up at him with wide eyes, her arms and legs pumping jerkily in a movement that nevertheless communicated pleasure.

"Good girl. I'll take that as a yes." He lowered a finger to tap her chin and before he knew what she was about she'd latched on to it. He froze and then felt a strange pressure in his chest.

He stared at her hand, wondering at how tiny and fragile it was, yet how perfectly formed. The child was so utterly helpless, yet blissfully unaware of her fragility, blindly trusting that all her needs would be met. And deep inside him, an aching desire to protect her took hold of him. This child deserved a father, someone to cherish her and keep her safe.

It caused an almost physical hurt to know that someone could never be him. She deserved better. "Yes indeed," he whispered softly, "I do believe you're going to be a heartbreaker when you grow up."

"She's easy to talk to, isn't she?"

Cam started, surprised he hadn't heard Nora's approach. He slid his finger out of Grace's grasp, surprised to find himself doing it reluctantly.

"Probably because she isn't much of a talker herself." He stood and brushed off his pants. "Thanks for the refreshments and the company, but I really should get back to work now."

She smiled softly, as if seeing through his words to what he was feeling inside. Which was a ridiculous thought since there *was no* deeper meaning to his words.

"Aren't you going to taste these cookies?" she asked.

"Of course." He took one from the dish she held out and bit into it. And smiled. "*Very* good. If you're planning to add these to your wares I predict they'll sell well."

He reached for another and lifted it in salute. "I think I'll take this one with me."

He headed toward the ladder, hoping that putting some distance between himself and the two females behind him would clear his head. Those thoughts he'd been having about Grace were an impossible dream, and a dangerous one at that. He'd forgotten for a moment that he was the last person alive who should be responsible for a child's welfare.

He couldn't let himself forget that again.

Nora watched Cam climb the ladder back onto the roof, then she slowly bent down to collect the items from their picnic. What had just happened? She was certain Cam had been enjoying his time with Grace, had noted the soft smile he gave the babe and the easy way he spoke to her.

So what had sent him scurrying away just now without a backward glance?

She worried at her bottom lip. At some point she would have to tell him she knew about how his father had treated him. Would he feel betrayed?

She stroked Grace's cheek with a knuckle. "If anyone can convince him that he can be trusted around children, I do believe it has to be you, young lady. After all, you're his ladybug." She smiled again, pleased that Cam had a nickname for Grace. It gave her hope that he wasn't completely opposed to interacting with little ones.

Perhaps this *had* been progress of a sort.

And perhaps it was another test of her patience.

* * *

By midafternoon, Nora had finished her baking. She carefully packed her baked goods in the shallow crates James had devised—praising him for their clever construction—and helped him load them into the bed of the wagon. In addition to the goods for Mrs. Ferguson, Nora also packed up two dozen of her cookies to be split between Rose and Mrs. James as an enticement for them to order some in the future.

As James headed the wagon toward town, Nora noticed Cam was no longer working on the roof. She glanced around and found him working on that rickety old bench in the garden and her heart did a strange little flip-flop.

It was one thing for Cam to see to the soundness of her home—one could almost argue that he did it out of a sense of responsibility since he'd been looking after the Coulters for the past few years. But to fix something like the bench, something almost frivolous—its only function was to give her enjoyment—that could only come from the goodness of his spirit, and it touched her deeply.

How could he *not* know his own worth, his innate goodness? Humming, she went back inside and poured a glass of apple cider, then carried it out to him. "Hello there. You look like you could use a bit of refreshment."

Cam glanced up and wiped his forehead with the back of his hand, the one that still held his hammer. "Thanks. I could at that." He looked around. "Where's lady—Grace?"

"In the house. Agnes is keeping an eye on her." She nodded toward the bench. "It was so kind of you to work on this after all your hard work on the roof."

"It turns out it only needed a little shoring up." He

patted one of the arms. "I just finished up. What do you think?"

"It's lovely." The broken boards on the back of the bench had been replaced with sturdy new ones and the arms were now attached securely. The seat was freshly braced and no longer seemed in imminent danger of collapsing. And all of the wood looked smooth and clean—freshly sanded perhaps? "May I try it out?" she asked.

He stood and waved an arm with an exaggerated flourish. "Of course."

Nora sat on the restored bench and spread her skirts primly as if seated on a throne. "Very nice. And very comfortable."

"So you approve?"

"Absolutely." She smiled up at him. "In fact, I can easily see Grace and me spending many an hour out here, enjoying the beauty of the garden."

He gave a satisfied nod. "Then I guess I'm finished for today." He bent down to pick up a small saw and handful of nails from the ground. "I'll see you at church service tomorrow."

She felt a stab of disappointment that he was leaving. "You could stay for dinner if you like."

He smiled. "Thanks. But dinner is still a couple of hours away and I have a few things to take care of before dark."

Cam saw Nora's cheeks pinken and realized she probably felt rebuffed by his refusal of her invitation. That hadn't been his intention, he really did have something to take care of. He planned to do a little more scouting around to see if he could find where the horse thief he was convinced was still in the area might be hiding.

But he didn't want to go into all that right now, so instead he gave her a reassuring smile. "By the way, I think with three to four more Saturdays like this one, we'll have the whole place weathertight and ready for the winter."

He saw her expression change to one of relieved delight. "Do you really think so? Oh, that would be wonderful. I can't thank you enough." Then the practical side of Nora stepped back to the fore. "But don't forget to figure out what I owe you for today's work."

He nodded. "I won't forget. I plan to keep track of everything you owe me and then we'll settle it all up when the job's done."

She gave him one of those suspicious looks that let him know he hadn't entirely fooled her, so he decided to take his leave before she had a chance to say anything else.

Saluting her with his hammer, he turned and made his way to his horse, and his thoughts turned back to his mission.

Why was the horse thief of a few weeks ago performing minor acts of mischief around town? And what was keeping her here? Did she have ties to the community? Or had she found herself somehow stranded here? Or was he completely wrong and were the horse thief and the mischief maker two completely different people?

Whatever the case, he aimed to get some answers, and get them soon. Because the idea of leaving Nora and Grace vulnerable to whatever plans a possible criminal might have in mind was totally unthinkable.

* * *

Nora added a little more salt to the pot of squash on the stove and tasted it again. Perfect!

James was out in the barn taking care of the evening milking and Agnes was in the parlor doing some mending, so she moved the pot away from the hottest part of the stove. She set it down on a spot where it would stay warm and at the ready until they were gathered for dinner.

Glancing out the window, she smiled at the sight of the garden bench. All in all it had been a lovely day and Nora felt a sense of deep satisfaction and renewed optimism that she really could make everything work out as she'd hoped.

She moved toward the cradle, checking on Grace. She exhaled a sigh of relief to see the little girl was now blissfully sleeping. Grace had been more than normally fussy this afternoon and, much as Nora loved her, it was nice to finally have a moment of peace and quiet. As if she'd heard Nora's thoughts, Grace stirred restlessly. Nora hummed softly for a few minutes until the baby quieted again.

Nora eased the muscles in her neck. It was stuffy here in the kitchen—maybe she should carry Grace to the parlor. Then again—Nora chewed on her lip, considering her options. She really didn't want to risk waking Grace up again after it had taken so long to get her settled. Perhaps she'd just open the outer door for a bit.

Putting thought to action, Nora crossed the room and propped open the back door. A slight breeze had stirred up and she stood on the threshold for a moment, savoring the cooler air and the peaceful evening. The sun hadn't gone down yet, though it was already reaching for the horizon.

Today's baking had exhausted her supplies—and her. But with the money she'd earned this week she should be able to replace everything and have enough left over to pay Mr. Platt what she owed him this week.

Thank You, Father Almighty, for all the many blessings You showered on me today, and every day. Help me to remember that, even in the dark times, You are there watching over me.

She moved back into the room and checked on Grace again. The child stirred in her sleep and Nora lightly brushed her cheek with a knuckle. What a joy and a blessing to have this precious child in her life.

Unbidden, she thought of Cam. He deserved to know this kind of joy, as well. And if she had it within her to help him, she would. Even if it was a joy he'd share with someone else.

She sighed and restlessly pushed her thoughts in a different direction. Perhaps now would be a good time to make her shopping list. She checked once more that Grace was sleeping well, then moved to the roomy larder, leaving the door open so she would hear if Grace started crying.

She studied the shelves. Another sack of flour was definitely needed. There was still enough sugar on hand, but she was short on salt. She was running low on chocolate but should have enough to last her until Will and Bridget returned.

Nora paused as she heard Grace fuss. But the baby quieted almost immediately and Nora relaxed. Taking a nap this late probably meant the baby wouldn't sleep through the night, but Nora didn't really mind. Tomorrow was Sunday, a day of rest. They could both nap in the afternoon if they needed to catch up on missed sleep.

A minute or two later she stepped out of the larder, satisfied she had a complete list. Perhaps she would also look at the seeds when she went to the general store. It wouldn't hurt to expand on their small kitchen garden. It had probably been all Agnes could manage on her own, but Nora was here to help her now. The more fresh herbs and vegetables they had, the better. And before spring arrived, Grace would be ready for some soft foods. Best to put up a good supply now.

Speaking of Grace, she was sleeping well. Nora moved toward the cradle, wanting to take another peek at her.

Then she froze and felt the blood drain from her face.

The cradle was empty.

Chapter Twelve

Where was Grace? Nora felt a momentary touch of panic jangle through her, then the only reasonable explanation occurred to her. Agnes must have picked her up when she started fussing earlier. Nora headed to the parlor, exasperated that the older woman would take the baby without telling her, but relieved that it was nothing worse.

But when she reached the parlor, Agnes was bent over her sewing, with no infant in sight. A cold finger clawed its way down Nora's spine. "Agnes, where is Grace?"

Agnes looked up, a puzzled frown on her face. "Isn't she in her cradle?"

Nora didn't answer. Instead she spun on her heel and raced back to the kitchen. Perhaps James had taken her outside. *Please God...*

She shot out the back door, wildly scanning the area behind the cottage for James, trying to reassure herself that there was no need to worry. A heartbeat later she spotted a figure running toward the tree line. And from the description she'd heard, she recognized that long yellow braid.

It was her—the horse thief who'd nearly run right over Gavin a few weeks ago. And the bundle in her arms was wrapped in Grace's blanket.

No! Dear Jesus, don't let her get away with my baby!

Nora took off at a run, yelling at the fleeing girl to stop. She had to catch up with her, had to make her give Grace back. What could she possibly want with Grace? *Don't let her hurt my baby, please...*

But the kidnapper disappeared into the woods while Nora was still several yards away. A moment later Nora plunged into the thicket behind her, ignoring the thorns and whip-like branches while calling frantically for Grace. She tried to pray, but all that came out was *God please, please, please* over and over.

The third time she stumbled, she stayed down, struggling to catch her breath. Panic threatened to suffocate her when she realized she had no idea which direction she should go in. She needed to be still, to just listen. Surely she would hear the girl running, Grace crying—something to tell her where they were. But the only sounds that she heard were the wind, the birds and insects.

A noise like the crack of a branch came from somewhere to her right, and Nora was up and running again.

Sometime later—minutes or hours, she wasn't really sure—a pair of arms grabbed her from behind. Nora screeched and began struggling for all she was worth. Did the little thief have an accomplice? Well, they would have a harder time taking her than they had with Grace...

"Nora, hold still, it's me."

She finally quieted and focused on her captor. "Cam." She said his name dully. Then she started struggling again. "We have to stop her. She's got Grace. That horrid horse thief has my baby."

He pulled her close against his chest. "I know. James rode into town and told me what happened."

The fight drained out of her. "Why did she do this? Oh, Cam, what if she's hurt?"

Cam had never seen his proud, no-nonsense house-keeper so distraught. There was a brittleness about her, as if she would shatter at the slightest touch. Her normally tidy hair had escaped its pins and was framing her face in wild disarray. There were scratches on her arms and face that she didn't seem to know were there. Her dress had two rips that he could see, and likely more. And worst of all, she was trembling.

Cam smothered an oath, directed against the kidnapper and against his own inability to fix this right this moment. The thought of any little one, much less Grace, at the mercy of a conscienceless criminal was tearing him up inside. He had to get his ladybug back safe.

"I know, Nora honey. And we'll find her. But you need to let me take you back to the cottage in case the person who took her decides to bring her back."

He saw a desperate kind of hope flare in her eyes. "Do you think that's possible?"

He tried to balance between reassurance and not promising the impossible. "Anything is possible. Now come on. Gavin is right over here. He'll see that you get home okay and stay with you."

"But—"

He had to get her home before she hurt herself or made herself ill. "Agnes and James are very worried. You need to be strong for them."

She stiffened stubbornly. "I want to keep looking."

He brushed the hair from her face, wishing there was something he could do to comfort her. "It'll be dark soon. And time spent standing here arguing with me is time I could be out looking for Grace."

He saw the struggle play out on her face. Finally her shoulders drooped in acceptance and she nodded. Then she placed a hand against his chest. "Please, find her."

"I will." He desperately hoped he could keep that promise. *God, I know I haven't been much for praying, not in a long time, but please help me find Grace. Not for me, but for Nora and Grace herself—they need each other.*

An hour later the sun had gone down, blanketing the countryside in darkness, and Cam was forced to call a halt for the night. Even with lanterns it was too dangerous for the searchers to be stumbling around out in the woods. Still, he himself kept looking in the more open areas for another hour until he finally accepted that it was useless. In the dark he could walk within a few feet of the kidnapper and never know it.

He trudged up to the cottage, dreading having to tell Nora that Grace had not yet been found.

Before he got very close, the door flew open and Nora raced outside. The light from the half moon revealed in aching clarity just how much of a toll the wait and worry had taken on her. From the corner of his eye he saw Agnes and James standing in the doorway, holding each other. Gavin stood in the shadows behind them.

But his focus was all on Nora.

She halted a few paces from him and he saw the

hope drain from her expression, quickly followed by anger.

All he could say was "I'm sorry."

She launched herself at him, beating against his chest with balled fists. "How could you come back without her? You promised. You never liked her, did you? If you won't keep looking then I will."

Her words stung more than her blows, but he pulled her close, trapping her fists between them. "Neither one of us is going back out there tonight. We won't do Grace any good by tripping all over ourselves in the dark. The kidnapper has obviously gone to ground somewhere—we could pass right by her any number of times and not find her."

Her eyes blazed up at him, angry and defiant. "That's not true. You should at least be able to hear her. You promised to bring her back to me. Grace wouldn't be totally quiet while so much was going on, especially if she hasn't had her dinner. Not unless—"

He put a hand to her lips. "Shh. Don't think that way. Grace is fine. Why would the girl take her if she didn't want her for herself?"

Her angry determination finally gave way to resignation. "Oh, Cam, why did she take Grace? It makes no sense."

He almost preferred her anger to this air of numb defeat. "As soon as we find her, we'll ask her," he said as bracingly as he could. "And we *will* find her." He gently squeezed her arms then released her. "Now, let's go inside where we can sit."

She nodded and allowed him to lead the way back to the cottage.

Agnes straightened as they approached. "You must

be tired and hungry," she said to Cam. "There's still some food left from dinner."

He cut a quick glance Nora's way. Would she want him at her table or was she still angry? "I wouldn't turn down a bite to eat."

With a nod, Agnes moved down the hall, tugging James along with her.

Gavin remained just inside the doorway. "Any sign of her at all?"

"Nothing concrete." Cam turned back to Nora. "Why don't you go on with Agnes and I'll follow in a minute."

She eyed him suspiciously. "Is there something you're not telling me?"

He tapped her chin then traced an X over his chest. "Cross my heart, there's nothing new to report. I just need a word with my deputy."

She didn't appear convinced, but finally nodded and then trudged down the hall toward the kitchen.

He turned back to Gavin. "I think the kidnapper has a home base of some sort where she's been hiding these past few weeks. We'll need to thoroughly search all of the inlets and woodlands. For now, go on back to town and get some sleep. Pass the word that we're starting again at first light and that the sheriff's office will be the gathering point. And we need everyone to report on any abandoned outbuildings, thickets and caves they can think of where someone wanting to hide might take refuge."

Gavin nodded, his expression sober. "Do you really think we'll find her?"

"We have to." He couldn't let himself believe otherwise. If for no other reason than Nora needed him to be strong. "You can take my horse. No point in you doing any more walking than you have to."

"But what about you? No offense, but you must be worn out. It wouldn't be right for me to ride and you to walk. Unless you're planning to take Miss Nora's horse."

"I'm not planning to take Miss Nora's horse and I don't intend to do any more walking tonight." At Gavin's confused expression, he elaborated. "I'm staying right here."

Gavin's brow rose to near his hairline. "You mean all night?"

"That's exactly what I mean." Though he had a feeling he'd have to argue the point with Nora. "Someone should be here in case the kidnapper tries to come back. Just make certain you have Fletch back here at first light."

For a minute it looked as if Gavin would say more, but apparently the boy thought better of it. With a nod he stuffed his hands in his pockets and moved toward the paddock.

James met him in the hallway as soon as he stepped inside the house. "Don't mind what Nora said," the older man told him. "We all know you're doing your best."

Not Nora. "Apparently my best isn't good enough."

"Don't say that." James patted his shoulder. "You're going to find our Grace and bring her back. Just have faith."

Cam desperately hoped James was right. When he entered the kitchen Agnes was just setting a glass of what looked like apple cider on the table. Nora stood next to the counter with her arms wrapped around herself as if she were afraid she would fly apart otherwise. A heaping plate of food sat on the table, ready for him.

Agnes tsked when she saw him. "Your arm is bleeding. You should have said something."

Cam, who'd barely felt any of the scrapes and scratches he'd received, looked down to see a particularly deep scratch above his wrist, covered with dried blood and dirt. He grimaced as he studied it. "Sorry, but I don't think I tracked any blood into your house."

Agnes waved that comment away. "As if that was what I was worried about. Nora, see if it needs bandaging while I finish getting his meal served."

Nora nodded and motioned him over, but didn't speak and didn't meet his gaze.

Cam washed his hands and face, then let her take a look at his cut.

"It's started bleeding again," she said dully, "but it looks clean and not too deep." Her gaze remained fixed on his arm. "I don't think it'll need much doctoring beyond wrapping it."

She put words to action, winding a long strip of gauzy cloth around his wrist.

Though she seemed to have her emotions under control, she still wouldn't look up to meet his gaze. Was it deliberate? Was she still angry that he'd failed to find Grace?

He couldn't blame her—he was angry at himself, as well. This was partly his fault. If he'd tried harder to find the girl after she took his horse or if he'd warned Nora to take extra precautions because the criminal might still be skulking around here, then maybe Grace would never have been taken in the first place.

As Cam took his place at the table, Agnes stood. "If you will excuse us, James and I are going to retire for the night." She eyed Nora. "Don't you worry about cleaning the kitchen tonight—I'll take care of that in the morning."

Nora nodded, but didn't respond otherwise.

Cam ate in silence, watching her peripherally as he did so. She stood as if carved from stone, stiff, silent and cold.

Finally he couldn't take the silence any longer. "Do you want me to send word to your sisters?"

"No, thank you." Her tone was flat, unemotional. "I'm not certain we could get word to Bridget before she's due to head back. And Maeve and Flynn have those burn patients to tend to."

She had obviously already given this some thought.

Nora took a deep, ragged breath. "Besides, we'll have Grace back before either of them can get here." Her fierce expression dared him to disagree.

Cam made a noncommittal sound, not trusting himself to say the right thing at this point.

She rubbed both her arms. "I saw you send Gavin off on Fletch. I want you to take Amber when you go, and please don't argue with me. You need to be at your best tomorrow when you start the search again."

So she wasn't totally oblivious to what was going on around her. "There's no need. I'm not going anywhere."

He was surprised when she didn't immediately protest.

"That sofa in your parlor is bed enough for me for the time being." He braced himself for her to argue with him now that she'd had a moment. It said something about her state of mind that she merely nodded.

The dark smudges under her eyes worried him, as did the fragility of her appearance. If only he had the right to hold her and offer her a bit of comfort. "I know you probably think sleeping is an impossibility right now," he said as he stood, "but it's best if you at least try to rest." He carried his plate to the counter and she drew herself in as he passed, as if wanting to avoid the least bit of contact.

He wasn't certain how much more of this he could take. "Tomorrow is going to be a long day," he said gruffly. "So upstairs with you."

For a moment he thought she'd argue. The Nora of this morning certainly would have. But this Nora didn't say a word.

After a moment she pushed away from the counter. "I'll lay a sheet on the sofa for you. Good night." The words were uttered in a hoarse whisper, then she crossed the room and headed for the stairs. Cam had to force himself not to go after her.

But even if he did, what then?

He sat back down at the table, folded his hands and bent his head. *God, I know I messed things up in a big way again, but please don't let that sweet little girl suffer for my mistakes. Do what You will to me, but bring Grace back home to Nora.*

And to me.

Chapter Thirteen

Cam was a young boy again and a woman was crying, hunched over so he couldn't see her face. But he knew the sound of that sobbing and knew it was his mother. He wanted to help her but his feet remained rooted to the floor. Then the figure shimmered and changed and now it was Vera McCauley holding the broken body of her three-year-old son. She looked up at him and her tearstained face twisted into a mask of hatred. Still, he couldn't move and couldn't look away.

Cam struggled to wake up, aware that he was having that old nightmare, but unable to escape from it. Then the image changed again. Now it was Nora, sobbing over a too-still Grace.

No! This wasn't real.

Finally he woke, flailing at the tangled sheet, damp from his sweat, breathless from the effort to push through. He ran a shaky hand through his hair. It had been years since he'd had that nightmare. He'd thought—hoped—it was gone for good. Now it was back, with an additional ugly twist.

He sat there for a moment, waiting for his racing

pulse to slow, for his ragged breathing to return to normal.

Then his head came up. What was that noise? Cam forced himself to go very still, straining to hear. A moment later he heard the sound of muffled movements coming from the kitchen. Had the kidnapper returned? Between one heartbeat and the next he was on his feet and moving stealthily into the hallway. The sounds were more evident now and there was soft lamplight spilling out from the kitchen doorway. Whoever was in there was being mighty bold. Or mighty careless.

He reached the end of the hall, his senses on full alert, his body ready to pounce on whoever had dared break into Nora's home.

The rattle of dishes brought his brow up. Had the intruder decided to steal a meal? "Stop right there," he ordered as he stepped into the room.

With a tiny squeak of fright, the shadowy figure spun around to face him, a hand to her chest.

It was Nora. He was disappointed not to be facing the kidnapper, but it wouldn't do to let her see that. "Sorry, I didn't mean to startle you."

She took a deep breath. "That's okay. I hope all my fumbling around in here didn't wake you."

"No, I woke on my own." No need to mention his nightmare.

"I couldn't sleep either. I thought I'd come down and fix a cup of cocoa. Would you like some?"

"That sounds good." What sounded even better was that there was no hardness, no hint of accusation in her tone.

She added some extra milk to the pan on the stove, then stirred in some cocoa powder and sugar.

A few minutes later she had poured them each a cup and carried them to the table. But she didn't take a seat right away. She took a deep breath and then met his gaze. "I want to apologize for the way I acted earlier."

The tightness in his chest loosened the tiniest bit. "There's no need for that."

"Yes there is. I know with complete certainty that you did absolutely everything you could. And I know that you'll keep looking. You've been nothing but kind to me ever since I arrived here and there's no excuse for me to say such awful things to you."

Cam wished he deserved such accolades. "I know this is hard on you. If beating on my chest and yelling at me helps you feel better, then you just go right ahead."

She gave him a watery version of her normally dry smile. "You may live to regret you said that."

"It's all part of being the sheriff," he said, trying to match her tone. Then he sobered. "We're going to start back up at first light. Nearly every able-bodied man in town will be out looking."

She nodded and swallowed. Her eyes cut toward the baby bottle that still sat on the counter, waiting. Her clasped hands tightened, whitening with the effort.

He moved closer, touching her arm, trying to comfort her with his presence. "Grace will be all right." *Please God, let that be true.*

"That awful girl should have taken the bottle, too. How will she feed her? *What* will she feed her? Does she even have access to fresh milk?" Nora met his gaze, her eyes filled with unshed tears. "Oh, Cam, my baby is out there, probably frightened and hungry."

"Ah, Nora honey." He opened his arms and she stepped into them. He hugged her in a protective embrace, aching to do more, knowing it wouldn't be fair to her, and wouldn't be enough for him. Her tall, slender form felt so soft, so fragile. She was trembling and he longed to protect her from all hurts, all ugliness, to slay any dragon that would dare approach her. But he knew with aching certainty that there was nothing he could do that would ease this particular pain. She probably wasn't even fully aware that his arms were around her.

So instead he just stood there, silently holding her, trying to wrap her in whatever comfort he could provide by his presence. He swayed, almost as if they were dancing, until finally her trembling stopped.

"She'll be all right," he whispered. "We *will* get Grace back safely." *Dear God, please don't let me fail another child, another mother.*

Don't let me fail Nora.

He couldn't resist planting one soft kiss to the top of her head. Nora turned her face up at that and suddenly his lips were on hers. She didn't push him away; in fact, her arms went around his neck. She tasted sweet and innocent and totally wonderful. He wanted to communicate all he was feeling into that kiss—all of his protective urges, his desire to comfort her and absorb her hurts, his love—

That thought drew him up short and he used every bit of willpower he had to pull away.

Nora looked up at him, her eyes wide, her expression confused. She tucked a strand of hair behind her ear with hands that visibly shook. "I'm sorry. I—"

"Don't you dare apologize." Didn't she realize it was him who'd taken advantage of her? He took a deep breath. "We're both tired and worried, that's all."

Something in her expression flickered, there and gone before he could identify it. She nodded and swallowed hard, then gave him a shaky smile. "I'm afraid our cocoa has gotten cold."

Relieved that she'd let it drop, he returned her smile. "It's summer. It'll probably be better cold."

Her eyes were overly bright orbs in a too-white face. "I don't want to be alone right now," she whispered.

"Then you won't be." He led her to a chair and seated her. His hand itched to stroke her hair but he picked up his cup of cocoa instead. "Why don't you tell me what life was like for you in Ireland."

He watched her as she talked and tried very hard not to think about that kiss.

And that one very unsettling thought.

Thirty minutes later, Nora yawned widely, then gave Cam a sheepish grin.

His answering smile had a teasing quality to it that warmed her to her toes. "Looks like someone might finally be ready for a bit of sleep."

"I've been sitting here talking your ear off and keeping you up half the night." She pushed her chair back from the table.

He stood, as well. "You didn't make me do anything I didn't want to." Then he gave her a probing look. "Are you going to be okay?"

She nodded and made an effort to smile. "I might actually be able to get a little sleep before the sun comes up." Though she doubted it. But it wasn't fair of her to keep him awake longer than she already had. She lightly touched his shoulder. "I appreciate you keeping me company."

As she moved toward the stairs, Nora realized how inadequate that thank-you had been, but she had been too much of a coward to say more. The way he'd held her tonight, keeping her together when she'd felt that she would shatter into a million pieces, had touched her on a level she didn't even fully understand right now. As for that kiss, that had touched her in an entirely different way. For one blissful moment she had felt cherished and loved and had been filled with certainty that this man holding her would slay all her dragons for her. Then he'd apparently come to his senses and disengaged.

She knew he'd merely been trying to comfort her. But somehow, it had felt like more. Or maybe, she thought as she trudged up the stairs, that was just wishful thinking.

Perhaps she'd turned into what she feared most. Someone doomed to experience an unrequited love.

Nora was downstairs before dawn the next morning. She'd gotten very little sleep, and when she awakened from her third doze she'd decided it was useless to keep trying. When her mind wasn't dwelling on the way that sweet kiss had made her feel, it was going over all the terrifying possibilities of what might be happening to Grace. Even if the kidnapper meant Grace no harm, would she know how to feed a baby or even have access to milk? Did she have clean nappies? Would she be gentle and sing her lullabies?

As early as she had risen, Cam was up before her. She found him pulling on his boots as she entered the kitchen.

He gave her a probing look. "Good morning."

She nodded, willing the heat to stay out of her cheeks. "James must still be in bed—the stove is cold. As soon as I get the fire going I'll fix you some coffee."

"No need. I'm headed out right away."

She wanted to protest—no doubt he needed some nourishment. But her desire to have him find Grace stopped her. "At least take some of this bread left over from supper."

He stood and accepted the bread, eyeing her as if trying to read her mood. Good luck to him on that— she wasn't sure of it herself.

"I feel so useless," she said as she paced the room. "I should be out looking for her myself."

Cam shook his head. "Like I said before, you need to be here in case the kidnapper brings Grace back. And there *is* something you can do to help."

"What?" Anything to keep her hands busy, to feel she was doing her part.

"We'll use this as a check-in point for the search teams. If you can keep a full pot of coffee and something to eat for when they report in, that'll be a big help. It doesn't have to be anything fancy—just filling."

She'd hoped it would be something more directly related to the search, but she nodded. "Of course." Cooking was something she could do, something to keep her occupied.

Cam placed a hand on each shoulder, stopping her from pacing. "You have to keep strong, not give up. We *will* find her."

Unable to say anything, Nora merely nodded.

"You have to keep strong," he said again, "for all of us." Then he gave her shoulders a light squeeze. "For me," he whispered.

The way he was looking at her stirred something inside Nora, caught the breath in her throat, pushed the rest of the world away. For one long moment she thought he might kiss her again.

Then the sound of activity outside broke the spell

and turned both their heads. Without a word, Nora all but ran to the front door, only vaguely aware that Cam followed. Could it be—

In the shadowy morning light, she spotted Gavin riding in on Fletch. Trying not to let her disappointment show, she waved to the young deputy. "Come on back to the kitchen when you get the horse tethered. I'll have some breakfast ready in just a bit."

"Thanks. That sounds real good." Gavin dismounted and wrapped the reins around a fencepost, then moved toward the cottage. "That is, if there's time before we set out."

"You won't be part of the search party," Cam said firmly. "I need you to stay here with Nora and the Coulters."

Gavin stopped in front of Cam, a mutinous expression on his face. "But, I want to help look for Grace."

"I know you do, and I appreciate that, but you're needed here."

"Needed for what?" There was something suspiciously like a pout coloring Gavin's tone and expression.

"There's always the chance that the kidnapper will return, either to bring Grace back or do further mischief. We need someone here who can keep watch for anything that looks suspicious."

Cam's jaw tightened. "I need to know that you are here so I can fully concentrate on the search."

Nora felt her heart flutter slightly at that. Did Cam really believe what he'd said or was he just trying to placate Gavin?

Whatever the case, Gavin seemed somewhat mollified, "I suppose I can do that."

"Good, because I'll be counting on you."

* * *

Nora had all but forgotten it was Sunday. Wanting to stay close to home in case something turned up, she, Gavin and the Coulters decided to hold a small prayer service of their own, led by James. He selected Romans 8 to read from, a chapter that brought her great comfort, and then he spoke with simple but surprising eloquence on what the passage meant to him.

Afterward they sang several hymns and Nora was surprised by the purity of Gavin's voice. One of the hymns, "The Solid Rock," spoke to her in a way it never had before.

Dear Jesus, she prayed silently, *I know I tend to try to control everything myself rather than leaning on You for help. Please help me to remember, especially when I go through trials, that You indeed are my hope and my rock. That whatever shall come to pass, You are always in control and that You will never put me through any trials that I cannot bear.*

Later, as Nora was preparing lunch, Gavin pulled up a chair at the table to keep her company. He plucked an apple from a bowl on the table and polished it against his sleeve. "I can't believe I ever wanted to get to know that girl better," he said. "I wish now she'd never come to Faith Glen."

Nora had no trouble agreeing with that sentiment. But that kind of thinking wouldn't help anything. "Well, she did and there's nothing we can do to change that."

"Even so, I sure hope when we catch her that the sheriff throws her in jail and never lets her out."

At least he said "when" and not "if." But she couldn't

let his comment go unchallenged. "That's not a very charitable thing to say."

"Surely you can't tell me you're feeling kindly toward that sneaky little thief after what she did."

"Kindly" wasn't what she was feeling at all. But Nora chose her words carefully. "I will admit that I would find it hard to give her a hug. But I've been keeping her in my prayers. Not because I'm particularly charitable. But because she has Grace and I cling to the hope that she is a good person at heart and that she is being kind and loving toward my baby." *Please, God, let that be the case.*

Gavin didn't say anything for a few minutes and she saw him think things over as he bit into the apple. Finally he nodded. "I suppose that makes sense. Maybe I ought to say a few prayers for her myself."

She gave him an approving smile. "That would be very nice."

The rest of the day seemed to drag on forever. Ben and a few other men came by at noon to report on their progress and to grab a quick bite to eat before heading back out. Gavin tried, with little success, to pretend he didn't mind being left behind again.

Throughout the afternoon, ladies from the town came by with offerings of food and kind words. Esther Black was among the first to arrive and she stayed until just before dusk. She'd brought her knitting with her and calmly sat in the kitchen keeping Nora and Agnes company, chatting over inconsequential matters, and letting the conversation ebb and flow comfortably.

Nora was both grateful and surprised by the woman's gentle strength. And when Ben came by to take her home, Nora had no doubt Esther and Ben would do quite well together.

And through it all, she kept an eye out, hoping to see Cam return with her baby in his arms at any minute.

Cam's shoulders sagged with defeat as he trudged up to Nora's front door. He tried to steel himself for the disappointment he would see in her eyes as he returned empty-handed yet again, but still, when he saw it, it hit him like a physical blow. He would actually prefer to have her pound angrily against his chest as she had yesterday.

She gave him a tremulous smile, then waved toward the back of the house. "Come into the kitchen and I'll fix you something to eat." She led the way. "Esther brought a ham and Mrs. Donnelly brought by some shepherd's pie. You can have your pick. Or both if you like."

Cam heard the strain in her voice. She was very close to breaking down. "I think perhaps we should go ahead and send word to your sisters in the morning."

She turned and her gaze flew to his.

He recognized the question and the fear she was trying to hold at bay and he touched her arm reassuringly. "No, I'm not giving up, not by a long shot." He'd keep searching for that little girl until she was found, no matter how long it took. "But I think you need to have your sisters here with you. And I think they deserve to know what's going on."

"But—"

He didn't let her finish her protest. "Nora, honey, I know you're a strong, proud, independent woman. But if this was happening to one of your sisters, if it was one of their children who was taken, wouldn't you want to know about it, to be there for them?"

"Yes, of course I would."

"Then don't you think they deserve the same consideration from you?"

"I… Yes, I suppose you're right."

He gave her shoulder a squeeze. "Good. I'll have Gavin send someone to Boston with a message at first light. Who knows, Flynn may even have a way to get word to Will and Bridget."

She nodded, looking at him with such trust and heartache that it was all he could do to not take her in his arms right then and there.

To comfort her of course. But he'd already strayed too far across that line.

He took a deep breath. "Now, I'll join you in the kitchen in a minute. I just need to have a word with Gavin before he heads back to town."

A few minutes later Gavin was dispatched with instructions to get word to her sisters and Cam took a seat at the kitchen table.

Nora set a plate in front of him then stepped back and clasped her hands together. "I want to apologize again for the way I attacked you last night."

"I told you, there's no need for that." Especially since he was still burdened by his own guilt.

"Yes there is." She took a deep breath. "Knowing what I do about your upbringing, I realize it must have brought back painful memories for you."

His gaze sharpened and he went very still.

Chapter Fourteen

Cam couldn't believe that now, in the middle of this nightmare, his past was rearing its ugly head. "My upbringing?" he said softly.

"Ben told me about your father."

Cam swallowed an oath. "Ben should mind his own business."

"Please don't be angry with him." She took a chair across from him. "He cares about you."

He could do with a little less of that kind of caring.

She leaned forward, putting her still-clasped hands on top of the table. "I won't even try to say I understand what you went through."

The last thing he wanted from her was pity for the poor mistreated boy he'd been. He wasn't that boy anymore, hadn't been for quite some time.

"What I do understand, and thank the Almighty for, is that you are a much more honorable man than your father was."

He jabbed his fork into his shepherd's pie with a bit more force than necessary, wishing she would drop this whole line of talk. "You don't know me nearly as well as you think you do."

"I know with every fiber of my being that you would *never, ever* strike a child or a woman. Or anyone else for that matter, unless it was in defense of someone."

Her championing of him would be flattering if it wasn't so misguided. "There are other ways of hurting folks besides hitting them."

Her brow furrowed. "What do you mean?"

He had to shut this off—now. Time to be blunt. "Let's just talk about something else."

She leaned back, her posture stiffening and her lips pinching together. "Very well," she said primly. "What would you like to talk about?"

This was ridiculous. His tired mind couldn't think of anything but the kidnapping. Then he figured if Ben could discuss his personal life, then he could talk about Ben's. "How about your suspicion that something might be brewing between Ben and Esther?"

That brought a gleam back to her eyes. "Oh? Has Ben said something?"

"Not specifically. But ever since you mentioned the possibility, I've noticed my deputy has been spending a lot of time in her company. And he's been keeping an eye on things over at the Blacks' house while Will and the rest of the family are out of town."

"Oh, it would be such a wonderful match. They're both such good people. They deserve to have a bit of romance at this point in their lives." She sighed. "Everyone does."

She started then, as if embarrassed by what she'd said. Pushing her chair away from the table, she stood. "Let me get you some dessert. I made buttermilk pie today."

Cam watched her cross the room, wondering if she included him in that "everyone."

And why did that matter to him so much?

Nora lay on her bed trying to wait for the darkness to fade into the gray of near-dawn. The cradle lay next to her bed, haunting her with its emptiness. She missed Grace so much it was like a physical ache. She could almost hear the echo of Grace's cries. Would she ever hear that sound for real again?

Father, You are the Great Comforter, the Almighty One. You have Your eye on even the tiniest sparrow, and it's not possible for anyone to hide from You. So I know You're watching over Grace, wherever she is. You know how much I want to have her back with me, but if that's not in Your will, please, please keep her safe and happy.

Nora uttered her amen aloud, then glanced at the window again. Had the sky lightened just the slightest bit? She had no doubt Maeve would come as soon as she got word, and it *would* be good to have one of her sisters here with her. They'd always looked out for each other and drew strength from each other.

Cam was putting on a strong front when he was with her, but she could tell he was taking this every bit as hard as she was. Whether he would admit it or not, he cared a great deal for her little girl.

That faint mewling sound wafted in through the window again, and this time she sat bolt upright in her bed. That hadn't been her imagination—it had been a real cry. It might just be a stray cat but she had to be sure.

Trying not to get her hopes up too high, Nora climbed out of bed and slipped on a robe as she headed down the stairs. The house itself was eerily quiet, as if holding its breath. The parlor and Coulters' bedroom were both at the front of the house and the sound had come from the back, so perhaps no one else had heard it.

She didn't attempt to light a lamp—her eyes were accustomed to the dark. And she knew she had to be very quiet so as not to frighten away whatever, or whoever, it was.

God, if You'll give my baby back to me I won't even try to catch the kidnapper. I won't look for vengeance, just joy. I'll leave it to You to deal with her in Your own way, Your own time.

When Nora reached the foot of the stairs, she started toward the kitchen.

But the nape of her neck prickled as she sensed a presence behind her. Whirling around, her heart in her throat, she put a hand to her lips to stifle a scream a heartbeat before she recognized the shadowy figure as Cam. A question formed on his lips and she quickly transferred her fingers to his mouth, indicating he should be quiet.

He nodded, then, when she moved her fingers, "Why are you up?" His words were a mere whisper of sound.

"I heard something outside. I wanted to investigate."

She could sense his whole being come to full alert. He nodded, then quickly stepped in front of her, indicating she should wait.

Nora didn't argue, but there was no way she planned to obey that command.

He moved with surprising speed and stealth to the back door.

There was another fussing sound and this time she could tell Cam heard it, too.

He was out the door in a flash, and Nora was right behind him. Luckily the sky was clear and the first fingers of dawn were lightening the horizon so she could make out shapes. The girl, bent over a basket lying at the edge of the garden, was taken by surprise at their sudden appearance. She spun around and took off at a run.

Cam, still barefoot, gave chase but Nora ignored both of them. Heart pounding like fists against her chest, breath catching in her throat, she raced toward the basket. *Please, God, please, God, please—*

And there, her face scrunched up in a peevish grimace, lay Grace.

Nora dropped to her knees and started laughing and crying at the same time. Her whole body was trembling so hard she barely trusted herself to pick Grace up, but she couldn't hold back for long. With a cry, she lifted the squirming infant, hugging her against her chest, rocking back and forth. "Oh, my sweet, sweet girl, I was so worried, so scared I'd never see you again." Then she held her away, anxiously studying her. "Are you truly okay, my sweet little one?"

To her relief there were no signs of injuries. "Thank you, Heavenly Father. Oh, Grace, I promise I'm going to take such good care of you. You won't—"

Gavin appeared around the corner of the house just then, carrying a package wrapped in butcher paper. "Miss Nora, what are you—" Then he spotted Grace and his steps quickened. "Well, glory be! You found her. Is she okay?"

Nora was still studying every inch of Grace in the increasing morning light. "She sounds hungry, but otherwise I think she's fine." Her nose twitched as Gavin neared and her mind registered that his package undoubtedly contained fish. Apparently the townsfolk were still sending food as tokens of support.

Before she could inquire, though, angry squeals coming from the distance snagged her attention. In her joy at finding Grace she'd almost forgotten that Cam had given chase to the kidnapper. She turned to see him holding on to the arms of a twisting, kicking blonde whirlwind.

"I'm coming!" As if suddenly realizing what was happening, Gavin dropped his package and sprinted toward the pair.

Nora pulled Grace back against her chest. No one would take her little girl away from her again.

"Praise God Almighty, is that really Grace?"

Nora turned back toward the house to see James and Agnes standing on the back stoop. She stood, and started back toward the house. "Yes it is."

"But how…"

"I'm not certain, but I think the kidnapper brought her back." Nora tilted her head toward the three who were slowly moving toward them. "The sheriff and Gavin have her in custody."

"Oh my goodness."

Then Grace started crying in earnest. "I think she must be hungry."

"Well, of course she is." James stepped down from the stoop and touched Grace's cheek briefly with one work-roughened finger. "I'll go right now and get a pail of fresh milk so you can feed her proper."

Nora saw the moisture in his eyes and smiled her thanks.

"Let's get her inside," Agnes said. "I'll get the stove warmed up and we'll fix coffee for the menfolk."

Nora carried Grace into the kitchen, rocking her in

her arms and crooning a lullaby. It was so good to feel that sweet weight in her arms again, to have that tiny heart beating against her own. She felt as if she would never let her go again.

A moment later, Cam and Gavin escorted the disheveled and cowed-looking kidnapper as far as the kitchen stoop.

"Do you mind if we come inside for a minute?" Cam asked through the open door.

Why would he feel the need to ask? "Of course not. Come on inside."

"All three of us?"

Oh, that was it. He was worried about her reaction to the girl. "Yes, of course. Agnes is working on getting breakfast ready."

Cam all but dragged the reluctant girl inside, while Gavin carefully guarded the rear, as if he expected the girl to somehow break away and make a run for it.

But from the way she stood there, it appeared to Nora that there was no fight left in the girl.

"Have a seat." Cam led the girl to the table and pulled a chair out with his free hand. "I'm going to let go of you, but if you so much as make a move to get up, I'm going to get a rope and tie you down. Understand?"

The girl nodded, her eyes downcast.

"Now, let's start with your name."

"Mollie Kerrigan."

Nora started at the sound of her voice. The girl was Irish—a recent immigrant from the sounds of her.

"Well, Mollie," Cam continued, "you've been causing quite a bit of trouble here the past few weeks. I've got a lot of questions for you. But we're going to start with why you kidnapped Grace."

The girl didn't say anything.

Nora, feeling slightly more charitable now that Grace had been returned and had apparently suffered no ill effects, tried a softer tone. "Please, tell me why you took my baby."

The girl looked up finally and stared at Nora defiantly. "She's *not* your baby."

Nora recoiled, clutching Grace tighter. "Of course she is. Or as close as makes no never mind."

"No, she's not." The girl's chin lifted. "I know, because I'm her *real* mother."

Chapter Fifteen

Nora felt the blood drain from her face and had to sit down before her legs buckled. Mollie was lying. What she said was impossible.

Cam moved to stand behind her and she looked up, searching for his gaze. She wanted to protest, to restate her own claim on the baby, but her mouth refused to form any words.

He gave her shoulder a light squeeze, then turned back to the girl. But his hand stayed where it was, lightly resting on her shoulder.

"You have any proof of that?" he asked.

"Only my word." Mollie must have realized how empty that sounded to the rest of them, because she tried again. "I had the baby aboard the *Annie McGee* just one day out from port. I wrapped her in a scrap of gray wool and left her between sacks of oatmeal in the kitchen's storage room because it was warm and dry there, and because I knew there was a woman who'd come by soon to find her. I didn't want a man to find her."

Nora finally found her voice. "Anyone who was on

board the ship could know all that. It doesn't prove you're the mother."

Mollie faced Nora defiantly. "She has a small birthmark on her back just below her left shoulder. Other than that, she's absolutely perfect."

Cam turned to meet her gaze, a question in his eyes. Nora nodded, reluctantly acknowledging the truth of what Mollie had said. Then she turned back to the girl, still not ready to believe her claim. "You've had her for the past few days, so of course you know about the birthmark."

The girl's lips pinched together. "When I placed her in the storeroom, I made her a pallet out of an empty flour sack and an old apron that I found hanging on a peg by the door. The apron was folded in quarters."

Nora's doubts were starting to fade and she was grateful for the warmth of Cam's hand on her shoulder. "If you're truly her mother, why did you abandon her?"

The air of defiance sloughed away, replaced by drooping shoulders and downcast eyes. "Because I was alone, and scared, and didn't know what else to do."

Cam cleared his throat. "Where is Grace's father?"

Mollie's face turned scarlet and she didn't say anything for a long moment. "We were planning to run away to America together as soon as we could earn enough money for our passage." Her voice wavered. "But when Elden—that's his name—found out I was going to have a baby, he ran off without me."

Nora felt her heart stir in spite of herself. To be abandoned like that, just when Mollie would need her husband the most, must have been a terrible blow.

"So you got on that ship to follow your husband to America?" Cam asked.

If anything, her face grew redder. "Elden's not exactly my husband. He never married me like he promised he would when we ran away together."

Nora heard a gasp but wasn't quite certain who it came from.

"I loved him," Mollie said defiantly. "My parents are dead and my grandmother hates me. But Elden was really nice to me, kind and caring. At least at first. And he promised if I came with him we would have wonderful adventures together." She rubbed her arms. "I thought he loved me."

She looked so forlorn, so lost, Nora had to hold herself back from offering a hug.

"And yes, I stowed away on the *Annie McGee* because I wanted to follow him here." Mollie seemed unable to stop talking now that she'd started. "And I gave my little girl away because I thought if the baby wasn't around, maybe Elden would want me again. Besides, I knew I couldn't take care of her myself and she'd have a better life with someone who could."

Mollie cast a longing glance Grace's way before lowering her gaze again.

"But I couldn't seem to put her out of my mind like I thought I could. It wasn't long before I realized what a fool I'd been to give up my precious baby for a faithless man."

Nora tried not to let the girl's story touch her. "You could have come forward and claimed her at any time before we docked."

The girl's shoulders drooped further. "I had nothing to offer her. I was stealing whatever scraps of food I could find just to survive, which meant I went to bed hungry most nights. And I was a stowaway. If I'd come forward there's no telling what the captain would have done to me."

Nora had a feeling Captain Conley would have been more understanding than Mollie feared but there was no point saying that now.

"I truly planned to leave her in your care. I could tell that you and your sisters were fond of her and you had more to offer her than I did."

Nora was still trying to find some hole in the girl's story. "So why did you follow us to Faith Glen?"

"I just wanted to make certain my little girl would truly be okay. That was all I planned to do, honest, and then I intended to go away and never bother you again."

She met Nora's gaze with eyes that begged her to understand. "But I couldn't make myself leave. The more I saw of my baby, the more I wanted to be with her. And besides, I didn't really have anywhere else to go."

Nora wanted to yell that Grace was *not* her baby, but the tense, uneasy feeling in the pit of her stomach mocked that assertion. Instead she pushed harder on the other points. "So rather than coming to me, you just snuck in and took her out of my home, leaving me to worry about Grace until I was nearly sick with it."

"I didn't mean to. I knew the sheriff was looking for me and that it was only a matter of time until he found me. So I planned to leave."

Cam had been looking for her? Nora swung her gaze around to his and saw the truth of that in his face. Why hadn't he said something?

From the corner of her eye she saw James slip inside with a pail of milk and basket of eggs. She started to get up, then saw Agnes reach for the bottle. Grateful, she settled back in her chair and returned her focus to the conversation around the table.

"I couldn't leave, though," Mollie was saying, "without getting one last look at her. Then I saw you," she nodded toward Nora, "leave the baby all alone in the kitchen and I realized I could get a closer look, maybe even touch her cheek, kiss her forehead, say goodbye proper-like."

Cam must have realized the guilt she felt at Mollie's words because he gave her shoulder another gentle squeeze.

"But you didn't just look." Nora couldn't control the accusatory tone that colored her words.

"I didn't plan to take her, truly. She started fussing and I picked her up just to quiet her. It was the first time I'd held her since the day she was born. She was so small and perfect, and when I held her she stopped crying and smiled at me. Just like that, something came over me, all of a sudden like. The next thing I knew I was running out of the house with my baby in my arms."

Nora tried again to tamp down any softer feelings toward this girl who had claim to her baby. "Her name is Grace."

"That's a very nice name." Mollie looked up again. "I know it was an awful thing to do, especially since you've been so good to her and all. I know you must have been worried something awful, and I'm really, truly sorry for that. But she's my baby and I wanted her with me."

You can't have her. "But you brought her back."

"After I stopped running, I realized I'd made a terrible mistake. Much as I wanted her with me, I knew I couldn't take care of her. I tried, but truth is I can hardly fend for myself. I want better for her than that. I want her to have the kind of life someone like you can give her."

The girl turned to Cam. "What do you plan to do to me?"

Cam dropped his hand from Nora's shoulder and she wanted to protest. Instead she hugged Grace closer.

"By your own admission, you're a stowaway, a thief and a kidnapper." Cam's voice held an authoritative, no-nonsense edge. "I'll have to arrest you."

Mollie nodded, seeming resigned to her fate. "I thought so."

Cam turned to Gavin. "Head back to town and let the other searchers know we've found Grace and there's no need to keep looking. Let Ben know exactly what's happened and to get the cell ready for a prisoner." He glanced Nora's way. "I'll borrow your wagon, if that's okay, to transport her into town."

Gavin nodded and headed for the door.

Agnes, who'd been working at the stove while the discussion with Mollie was going on, handed Nora the baby bottle and turned to Cam. "Before you leave I insist you eat breakfast. No point in all this food I've cooked going to waste."

While the others ate the eggs and ham Agnes had prepared, Nora gave Grace her bottle. The little girl sucked at it greedily, obviously more than ready for her feeding. Had Mollie fed her much at all?

Mollie dug into her plate of food with nearly as much enthusiasm. It was likely the first decent meal she'd had in quite some time. Nora also noticed her slipping glances Grace's way throughout the meal.

"Just out of curiosity," Cam asked, "where did you hide out?"

Mollie stopped eating long enough to answer his question. "There's an abandoned shack out in the woods about a half mile south of town. It's not much but it had a roof and four walls to keep the weather and the wild-life out."

Cam nodded. "I know the place—Lem Grady and his boys were supposed to check it out first thing yesterday morning."

"They did. I hid and watched them go over every corner of it. Then as soon as they left, I figured it would be safe to hide out there for a while."

Mollie seemed proud of her cleverness and Nora had to admit she seemed to have a good head on her shoulders, in a cunning, not-quite-trustworthy sort of way.

Once the meal was over, James volunteered to hitch the wagon. Agnes offered to hold Grace while Nora ate, but Nora turned her down. As foolish as she knew it was, she couldn't bring herself to physically let go of Grace until Mollie was out of the house.

Once breakfast was over, she followed Cam and Mollie as they headed outside. The three of them walked in silence until they reached the wagon and then Cam turned to her. She hadn't had a chance to say anything to him since he'd captured Mollie, and suddenly words failed her. A simple thank-you seemed inadequate for all he'd done, yet right now they were the only words she could muster. "Thank you. For everything."

"Just doing my job." But his eyes told her a different story. Then he touched her arm. "You've been through a lot these past few days. I don't expect you to come in for work anytime soon. Take as much time as you need."

"I appreciate the offer, but I'll be there tomorrow." She jiggled Grace. "We both will."

He appeared ready to say more, but then seemed to think better of it. Instead he nodded and turned to hand

Mollie up onto the wagon seat. When he turned back to Nora he smiled. "Thanks again for the use of your wagon. I'll bring it back later today after I get our prisoner settled in."

Nora nodded, trying to sort through the emotions swirling inside her. She'd sort through her feelings for Cam later.

As for Mollie…

Part of her wanted to dislike this girl who had caused her so much anguish, and who had the potential to cause so much more. But the other part of her felt a stirring of unwanted sympathy for everything she had endured.

A moment later she watched Cam head the wagon toward town, and let out a deep, shuddering breath, releasing her ambivalent emotions with it. For now, at least, she would ignore everything but her joy at the miracle of having Grace back, safe and sound.

The rest could be sorted out later.

Chapter Sixteen

Nora spent most of the morning fussing over Grace. She bathed her and put a fresh gown on her. She cooed over her, crooned to her and examined her multiple times for any signs of injury she might have missed. Even when Grace took her nap, Nora hovered over her cradle, watching her sleep.

Near noon, Cam returned with the wagon. He helped James unhitch the horse, then joined Nora and Agnes in the house.

"Lunch will be ready in another thirty minutes or so," Nora said by way of greeting. "Would you care to join us?" She felt unaccountably shy, as if something in their relationship had shifted these past few days. Would it return to normal soon? Did she want it to?

He grinned, apparently feeling none of her ambivalence. "My timing was in no way accidental. I was hoping for an invitation." He glanced toward the cradle. "How's Grace?"

Nora beamed. "She's fine. In fact she doesn't seem to have suffered any ill effects at all." Then she asked a question of her own. "Is your prisoner settled in?"

"As much as can be expected."

He didn't sound particularly pleased. "Is something wrong?"

He waved a hand. "I've been dealing with gawkers most of the morning. Ever since I brought Mollie in, no fewer than two dozen townsfolk have made excuses to stop by. It seems everyone wants to get a look at the female kidnapper who caused all the fuss the past few days."

"That's natural I suppose," Nora said. "The search did disrupt a lot of lives for a short time." Though it hadn't seemed such a short time while it was happening.

Before Cam could respond, the sound of a carriage intruded.

"Now who—" Then realization hit her. "Oh my goodness, I forgot we told Gavin to send word to Boston."

Nora popped up and ran to the door. Sure enough the carriage had stopped and Maeve was already halfway out of it. Nora wasted no time running to meet her.

"Nora, oh, Nora, I'm so sorry. We came as soon as we heard."

The sisters nearly collided in their desire to embrace.

"It's all right now," Nora reassured her sister. "We have her back." She squeezed her harder. "We have her back," she repeated. Oh, how she'd missed having her sisters nearby. She hadn't realized how much until just this moment.

When they finally separated Nora noticed that Flynn had stepped out of the carriage behind Maeve and was talking to Cam in low tones. He had his doctor's bag with him at the ready. Apparently he'd come prepared for the worst.

"We would have been here sooner," Maeve said,

"but the young man who carried your message got lost trying to find us." She looked around. "Where is Grace? I have to see her for myself."

"She's inside with Agnes and James." Nora linked her arm through Maeve's as they moved toward the open door. "I'm so sorry I didn't send word when we recovered her. My mind has been a bit scattered."

Maeve gave her arm a squeeze. "Of course it has. I'm just glad it all turned out so well." She searched Nora's face, as if looking for reassurance. "Grace *is* okay, isn't she?"

"She seems none the worse for the experience. Of course if you and Flynn would examine her just to be sure I'd be most grateful."

Flynn spoke up from behind them. "I don't mind at all. In fact, I insist."

As soon as they entered the kitchen, Maeve gave James and Agnes a quick greeting and then reached for Grace. "Oh, dear, sweet Grace, let me have a good look at you. How you've grown since I saw you last."

Flynn performed a thorough examination and pronounced Grace healthy, then they all gathered around the table.

"So, tell me what happened." Maeve looked from Nora to Cam. "All I know is that Grace was taken. How long ago did this happen? Who did this terrible thing and how did you get our baby back?"

Nora spoke first. "It happened on Saturday." Was that really just two days ago? "Do you remember the day Bridget, Grace and I moved into this cottage? How this strange girl came out of nowhere and stole Cam's horse? Well, she's the same person who kidnapped Grace."

Maeve leaned forward. "But who is she and why would she do such a thing?"

"Her name is Mollie Kerrigan." Nora paused a moment, then took a deep breath. "And she claims to be Grace's mother."

"Grace's... But how... I don't..." Maeve looked as shocked as Nora had felt when she got the news.

Nora gave her a sympathetic smile. "I know, it's difficult to believe. But Mollie stowed away on the *Annie McGee* and didn't have anyone or any resources to take care of her baby, so she left her where she'd be easily found. Then she followed us here because she wanted to be close to Grace. Of course, I didn't learn any of this until she brought Grace back this morning."

"She *brought Grace back?*"

Nora stood and moved to the stove. "Yes. Because she realized she couldn't be the mother Grace needs, and she believed that I could." She stirred the contents of the pot, then moved it to a cooler area of the stove. "Now, the fish soup is ready and the bread is already cooling on the sill. There's more than enough for everyone so let me get the dishes on the table and we can continue this discussion over lunch."

Maeve rose and went to the cupboard. "It smells wonderful. Flynn's cook is really good at what she does, but I've missed your cooking."

They talked throughout the meal, Maeve and Flynn asking additional questions about what had happened the past few days, and Cam and Nora providing what answers they could. Then Nora asked them to share a little of what they had experienced working with victims of the fire in Boston. Once again Nora admired the dedication of the newlywed pair for the healing work they did.

When they were done with the meal, Agnes shooed them from the kitchen, insisting that she and James would take care of the dishes while the "young folk" had a nice visit. Cam and Flynn drifted out to the barn where Nora suspected they would have a more frank discussion about the kidnapping.

Nora and Maeve carried Grace out to the garden to enjoy the bit of afternoon breeze.

Maeve smiled in delight when she spotted the bench. "Oh, you've had it repaired! It looks nice."

Nora nodded. "Cam took care of that. He's been making repairs around the place for me."

Maeve gave her an arch look. "Has he now?"

Nora felt her cheeks warm. "I intend to pay him for his labors, of course," she added quickly.

"Of course."

Maeve's dry tone warmed Nora's cheeks further. She hadn't had much time to reflect on how her and Cam's relationship had changed over the past couple of days. All that she knew right now was that it *had* changed in some subtle, mysterious way.

As they settled themselves on the bench, Maeve reclaimed her attention. "That reminds me. Bridget stopped for a quick visit before they headed to New York and she mentioned you were starting a bakery business."

Nora nodded. "I'm just beginning but I think it's going well."

"Everyone always said you were the best pie maker in all of County Galway. Some even said you were better than Mother herself."

Nora waved off the compliment and gave her sister's hand a squeeze. Then she changed the subject. "I'm sorry if I pulled you and Flynn away from those poor hurting people who need medical help. But I'm selfish enough to be glad to have you here for a bit."

Maeve returned her smile. "There are other doctors to see to the patients, but I only have two sisters." Then her lower lip trembled. "Oh, Nora, when I think of all you must have gone through! That must have been such an awful, wrenching experience. Are you truly sure you're okay?"

Nora took a deep breath. "I won't deny it was a nightmare while it was happening. But it's over now and it turned out fine."

Maeve's expression took on a slightly accusing cast. "You should have sent word sooner. We would have come right away to support you through it."

"I knew you had other responsibilities taking care of your patients. And I kept praying they would find her any minute."

Maeve gave her hand another squeeze. "But you're my sister. Besides, I love Grace, too, you know."

Nora laid a hand on hers. "Oh, Maeve, I didn't mean to imply you didn't. To be honest, I don't think I was quite rational at the time it was happening. Forgive me?"

Maeve's face cleared and she leaned over and gave her a hug. "Of course I do." When she settled back she grimaced. "Is that wicked girl truly Grace's mother?"

Nora felt her thinking shift and certainty settled into her heart. "She is." Saying that out loud cut worse than she'd thought it would.

Maeve didn't appear convinced. "But, just because she claims she is doesn't make it so. She's done so many awful things—how can you be so sure she's not lying about this?"

"She knows too many details about Grace. And

there's a similarity in their features that can't be denied. She's Grace's mother all right."

"Where is she?"

"Cam has her locked up over at the jailhouse."

"Grace's mother, a criminal. So hard to believe."

Nora winced at that stark description. Her ambivalent feelings of this morning began to surface again, stronger than ever.

"What's she like?" Maeve asked.

Nora thought it best to let Maeve form her own opinion. "You should meet her and see for yourself."

Maeve shook her head. "Not right now. I don't think I could be very nice to her at the moment."

Nora couldn't imagine her little sister being deliberately mean to anyone. "There'll be time enough later I suppose. She's not going anywhere." She touched Maeve's arm. "But please, meet her before you return to Boston."

Maeve was silent for a long moment, then reluctantly nodded. "If I remember correctly," she said, "Gavin seemed smitten with the girl during his last encounter. How is he reacting to her now?"

"His infatuation with her ended as soon as she took Grace," Nora said dryly. "I think he's been harder on Mollie than anyone else. Except maybe Cam."

"I must admit, I have trouble feeling very charitably toward her myself."

"I don't think she would ever have deliberately hurt Grace. Even when she abandoned her on the *Annie McGee,* I think she was only trying, in her own way, to do what was best for her daughter."

"What's going to happen to her now?"

"I suppose she'll end up going to prison for a time." That idea didn't sit so well with her.

Maeve apparently sensed some of her ambivalence. "And how do you feel about that?"

Nora tried to gather her scattered thoughts. She wanted to say that justice was being done, that Mollie was getting what she deserved. But it wasn't that simple.

When she looked at Mollie she saw the girl-woman who had lied and cheated and stolen to get herself where she was today. The person who'd taken Grace from her and put her through two days and nights of gut-wrenching, heartbreaking worry. The person who could still lay claim—

No! She wouldn't even think of that possibility right now.

Yet this was also a girl who was hurting and needed a friend. A girl who'd felt alone, abandoned and scared. A frightened girl who had given birth alone while hiding in the dank bowels of a ship. A girl who'd eventually decided to do the right thing for her baby and risked capture to do so. A girl who, for all her faults, was still a child of God.

Finally she met Maeve's gaze. "I want to help her."

Chapter Seventeen

Cam and Flynn stood out by the barn, leaning against the newly patched fence. Cam had already filled Flynn in on the grittier details Nora had left out of her recounting, and reassured him about Nora's and Grace's ongoing safety. He'd even admitted, with some trepidation, his spending the past two nights in the house and was relieved when Flynn merely thanked him for the protection he'd offered his sister-in-law.

Now they stood in companionable silence, staring at Amber prancing about the enclosed barnyard.

When they heard steps approaching, Cam knew before turning around that it was Nora. Strange how attuned he was to her presence.

"That's a fine horse you've acquired," Flynn said.

"Thank you, but Cam here had more to do with the selection than I did."

Cam smiled. Nice to hear both her easy use of his name, and her acknowledgment of the part he'd played.

"Still," Flynn continued, "I know it'll be a relief to your sisters to know you have a means of transportation now." He straightened. "And speaking of your sisters,

I did send word to Will and Bridget about this matter before we left Boston. I imagine they'll be here tomorrow at the latest."

Cam sensed something different about Nora, something unsettled. "Is something the matter?"

She met his gaze and straightened. "Actually, I've made a decision, and I'd like to have a family meeting to discuss it."

Family meeting. Surprising how deeply that exclusion cut. "I suppose I should be getting back to town anyway. Ben is probably ready for—"

Her look stopped him. "Actually," she said with a diffident smile, "if you have time, I'd like for you to join us, too. This is going to affect you as much as anyone. And I'd really like your thoughts on the matter."

That last comment made the invitation feel much less like an afterthought. He nodded. "Of course."

Cam and Flynn followed her back to the kitchen and the whole group took seats around the table, including Agnes and James. Grace lay sleeping in a cradle situated between Nora and Maeve. Cam was seated on Nora's other side. He wasn't sure if that had happened naturally or not, but he was glad to be there.

For a while no one said anything as Nora seemed to take a moment to gather her thoughts. The sober, determined look about her made her appear isolated. Cam wanted to give her hand a squeeze but held himself in check.

Finally she looked around the table. "I've been doing a lot of thinking this morning about what's happened, and about Mollie herself. I know she's done some terrible things, but she's suffered through a lot of hardship and pain, as well. Is it really necessary to have her spend time in jail? I mean, does it serve any useful purpose?"

Had she let the girl's story soften her heart? "She broke the law, Nora," he said, refusing to apologize for locking up a confessed kidnapper. "I had no choice but to arrest her."

Nora gave him a reassuring smile. "I know you were doing your job, Cam, but if Grace is truly her baby, can we really call it kidnapping?"

He refused to be swayed by such slippery logic.

But Flynn spoke up before he could. "That's not the only law she broke."

Nora shifted her gaze back to the others at the table. "I know. She also tried to steal Cam's horse, but she didn't keep it long."

"She didn't *try,* Nora," Cam protested. "She actually succeeded in stealing Fletch. How long she kept him is beside the point."

"But if you don't press charges on the horse stealing…"

"Why wouldn't I? Nora, she's a *criminal.* She's done lots of very bad, unlawful things."

"She abandoned her baby," Maeve said. "Twice."

Cam could see Nora trying to hold her frustration in check.

"But look at how young she is," she argued. "And her life hasn't been easy. It appears she hasn't had much in the way of family or friends to help her along the way."

"We had a difficult time too," Maeve insisted. "But we didn't resort to stealing."

"But we had each other," Nora reminded her. "And then you found Flynn."

Maeve glanced quickly at her husband and squeezed

his hand, then turned back to Nora, a softer look on her face.

Cam frowned. Nora might be winning her sister over, but not him. "I'll admit, if what she told us is true she's had lots of trials and troubles to deal with. But how do we know she's telling the truth?" He raised a hand to stop whatever counterargument she was about to make. "And even if she is, that's no excuse for breaking the law. As your sister pointed out, other folk have had it as bad or worse and they got by without turning to crime."

Her expression immediately softened and the sympathy in her expression told him she was thinking of his past. He quickly spoke up again. "No matter what her situation, she could have just asked for help, rather than stealing and lying."

"Yes, she could have. But, for whatever reason, she didn't and we can't go back and change that. I want to help her now."

Nora's willingness to forgive was admirable, especially after all that had happened, but he didn't understand this misguided determination from a woman who was usually so practical and levelheaded. "Why? Why would you want to help someone who wronged you so deeply?"

"Because she's Grace's mother."

That simple statement silenced them all for a moment.

Finally Flynn spoke up. "What do you suggest we do? Surely you don't think she shouldn't have to suffer *some* sort of consequences for what she's done?"

"Of course not. Just because someone is sorry doesn't mean they don't have to make reparations for what they've done. But putting her in prison doesn't do her or any of the people she wronged any good. Especially since I don't think she's a danger to anyone or likely to repeat her crimes."

Cam wasn't so sure about the last part but decided to hold his peace on that score—for now. "So, as Flynn asked, what do you think we ought to do?" He knew she'd have a plan—she always did. And he also knew he wasn't going to like it.

"Wouldn't it be better," she replied, "not just for Mollie but for everyone involved, if she did what she could to make it up to the people she wronged? We could make a record of everything she's stolen and everywhere she's trespassed, and determine the lost value. Then we give her a way to earn money so she can pay it all back."

She'd obviously already put a lot of thought into this scheme of hers. "You do realize that letting her out of jail might not be doing her a favor, don't you? She might not be interested in working off her debts."

"If she doesn't want to work in exchange for her freedom, then I'll drop this whole plan without another word. But I really don't think that'll be the case. I sense that, deep down, there is something good in Mollie. We just have to help her find and nurture it."

"Everyone in town knows her story by now." Cam was still trying to get her to see reason. "Who do you think will be willing to take a chance and hire her?"

"You will." She lifted her chin. "Mollie can help me do the cleaning at the jailhouse and at your and Ben's places. That way you can keep an eye on her, the townsfolk can see you trust her, and she can pay you for the use of your horse and earn a little toward paying the shipping company for her passage."

He raised a brow. "But that's taking away money you need."

"Actually, I can use the time I save to spend more hours on my bakery business. It will let me fill those orders I've had to turn away."

Cam found his own frustration level growing. "And suppose she tries to run away again the first chance she gets?"

"Then you'll find her and bring her back, and this time she'll have much harsher consequences to deal with. But fear that she might not accept our help is no excuse not to offer it."

She looked around the table, and he saw the way she braced herself. "And there's another thing. Mollie will need a place to stay. Renting a room would take most everything she earns so that's not a good solution."

Cam sat up straighter. He had a good idea what was coming next and if he was correct he didn't like it one bit.

She took a deep breath. "So I plan to invite her to stay right here at the cottage."

He'd been right. Of all the fool, pigheaded, poorly thought-out notions. Apparently Maeve and Flynn felt the same way. Their protests were swift and overlapping.

"Oh, Nora, you can't let that girl near Grace—"

"Absolutely not. You're my wife's sister and I have a responsibility to—"

Cam was in complete agreement. Just because Nora was feeling softhearted didn't mean he would allow that girl to live under the same roof as her and Grace. Not to mention the Coulters.

When she turned to him, he gave her his answer in one terse sentence. "Not on my watch."

He refused to be moved by her obvious disappointment.

"It's the right thing to do," she insisted. "Mollie needs

good people around her to teach her to trust again." She stared Cam down. "The way Ben did with you."

That approach wasn't going to work with him. "Ben didn't have to arrest me to get my attention."

She brushed aside his comment. "Besides, if she lives with me, she'll be able to spend some time with Grace under my and the Coulters' watchful eyes. I can also teach her how to care for a baby and observe to see if she really can take on such a responsibility."

He saw her hand slide down to touch the edge of the cradle.

"You can't seriously be thinking about handing Grace over to her?" Maeve asked.

"No, of course not. But as Grace's mother, Mollie has a right to be part of her life."

Cam tried again to make her see reason. "I know she seems sympathetic enough now that she's been caught, but she has yet to prove herself trustworthy. She could even be dangerous."

"I don't think so. Remember, she *did* bring Grace back of her own accord."

Was she so determined to look for the good that she could ignore the bad? "Nora, she didn't once offer to make amends for any of her wrongdoings. She left Grace out in the yard, *hoping* you would find her quickly, and then up and ran off again. She's here now *only* because we caught her. If we hadn't, she'd still be out there doing goodness knows what."

"You need to listen to what he's saying," Flynn added. "I can't agree to leave that criminal here with you unless I'm absolutely convinced she's harmless. And maybe not even then."

"But—"

"No buts." Flynn could sound very authoritative

when he tried. "If Cam wants to allow Mollie to work off her debts rather than go to prison, that's his business. But allowing her to stay here with the four of you is completely out of the question."

Nora leaned forward earnestly. "But I truly believe, for Grace's sake as well as her own, that Mollie needs to spend time with Grace. And the only way for that to happen is for her to stay here with us. Please, trust me to know what I'm doing."

"I have to ask this." Cam locked gazes with her. "Do you really think you can trust that girl not to try to abduct Grace again?"

He saw a vein in her throat jump, but she nodded. "Yes, I do."

Cam let out a frustrated breath. "That's very trusting and even charitable of you, Nora, but you need to let common sense prevail over your softer instincts."

Nora grimaced. "I'm no paragon." She expanded her gaze to include them all. "I still have trouble forgetting that Mollie abandoned her newborn baby. And that just a few days ago she stole that beautiful little girl away from me without so much as an explanation, leaving me to worry my heart and soul raw over Grace's fate." She took a deep breath then let it out slowly. "But in her own way, I think Mollie really does love Grace, so I have to believe she has good in her. And when it comes down to it, I have no right to judge her." She glanced around the table again. "None of us do."

She looked to the Coulters. "But I'm not the only one this affects. Agnes, James, can you be comfortable having her in the house with us?"

Agnes looked at her husband and took his hand in hers. There seemed to be a moment of silent communion between them, then she turned back to Nora. "Everyone deserves to have someone who believes in them, to have a chance to make things right with their life if they're willing to take it. We're willing to stand behind your decision to help the girl."

Nora gave them an approving smile. "Bless you for your generous spirit."

"Well, my spirit is not so generous." Flynn's tone was firm. "I cannot allow you to endanger yourself this way. And I know Will will feel the same way when he hears of it."

"It is kind of you to be concerned about my welfare, Flynn, but I'm capable of deciding this for myself. I'm only discussing this with you all because I want you to understand why it means so much to me."

Cam hid a smile at this appearance of her stubborn, independent streak. There was a lot to admire in her spirit if not in the plan itself.

"Nora, be reasonable," Maeve pleaded. "Your heart is in the right place, but if you won't think of yourself, think of Grace and Agnes and James."

"Mollie wouldn't hurt us," Nora insisted. "She's not violent. And if she steals from us or runs away, then we will survive just fine."

Flynn softened his tone. "You want to believe everyone is as well-intentioned as you and your sisters are, but the truth is that there are bad people in this world. And until I'm convinced that she is as harmless as you believe, I can't allow you to put yourself or Grace in danger." He gave Maeve's hand a squeeze, as if to reassure himself that she was safe, as well.

Cam's jaw tightened. Flynn had a brother's right to look out for Nora, and while he didn't out and out mention his partial ownership of the cottage, Cam knew

Nora was aware of her brother-in-law's ability to enforce his will in this matter.

He couldn't bear the hurt, defeated look in her expression, especially not after all she'd gone through the past few days. "What if she had protection here?" he asked impulsively.

Flynn frowned. "Are you talking about giving Nora a weapon? I don't think—"

"No, not a weapon." How could Flynn think he would do something so reckless? "A person."

Flynn studied him suspiciously. Cam couldn't blame him. "What did you have in mind?" the doctor asked.

"As lawmen, Ben, Gavin and I all have a responsibility to provide protection to the citizens of Faith Glen, including this group here. In that role, we could take turns staying here at night, acting as prison guards." Not that he intended to let Gavin and Ben take very many "turns." "Sleeping in the parlor, of course," he added quickly.

Flynn frowned thoughtfully. "That seems to be a possible compromise. But I'm still not certain this is the right thing to do."

Nora crossed her arms. "I am."

Maeve placed a hand on Flynn's arm and a look passed between them. Finally Flynn turned back to Nora. "Let us agree to this much at least. We'll make no decision until Will and Bridget return and we can get their input."

Nora jumped on the suggestion, obviously relieved that the door hadn't been shut completely. "Agreed."

"Bridget offered us rooms in her home." Maeve was obviously ready for a change of topic. "We plan to stay there at least until they return. Longer if you need us to."

Cam still had one more issue he wanted to nail down. "In the meantime, supposing you got your way in this, where exactly would you have Mollie sleep?"

"She could take Bridget's old room," Nora answered, "the one upstairs across from mine."

Cam stood and turned to Flynn. "I think the two of us should have a look and see what would be required to make it secure."

"All right. At the minimum we'll want to be able to lock it from the outside."

Cam noticed Nora open her mouth to protest, but then she clamped it shut again. At least she was learning to pick her battles.

Nora watched Cam and Flynn leave the room together and felt some of the tension ease from her body. Cam's last-minute change of heart toward her plan had been both welcome and unexpected. Did he finally believe in what she was trying to do? In her?

She knew Flynn was only looking out for her, but she hated that he had such control over what she did. The sooner she could buy her sisters' shares of the cottage, the happier she would be.

"Don't blame Flynn." Maeve placed a hand over hers on the table. "He only wants what's best for you and Grace. We both do."

"I know. But you understand why I want to do this, don't you?"

"I understand that you have a good heart and that you always try to take care of those who have no one else."

Nora smiled at her sister's exaggerated praise, and her avoidance of a direct answer. "I keep thinking about what might have happened to us if we hadn't had this place to come to. Mollie didn't have that chance."

"I know. And I agree that she had a rough time of it." Maeve's expression grew solemn. "But you need to see the other side of this, as well. She wasn't in our situation, not really. It sounds like she had a good home and a grandmother to watch over her at one time. Even if the woman didn't treat her well she provided for her. And Mollie threw that away to run off with a not-so-nice boy who made shiny promises she couldn't resist."

Nora was surprised by Maeve's rather straightforward assessment. When had her baby sister developed such a mature outlook? "I'm not blind to her weaknesses," she explained. "Mollie looks for the easy way out of her troubles, she doesn't take responsibility for her choices and she doesn't realize what havoc her actions cause. But she wants what's best for Grace and she has now seen how difficult life can be. I think she's ready to learn a better way and she deserves a chance to do so. So yes, I know she's not without her faults, but neither is she a villain."

Maeve gave her a hug. "Then that's good enough for me. I'll support you in any way I can." She released Nora. "Now, let's talk about how we're going to convince the others."

Chapter Eighteen

The next morning, Nora walked into the sheriff's office, pushing the baby buggy before her.

Cam frowned. "I told you not to worry about coming in today."

She glanced toward the cell, nodding a greeting Mollie's way, then turned back to Cam. "I know. But I'm ready to get back into my regular routine."

He studied her closely. "Are you sure?"

She nodded. "I wouldn't be here if I wasn't."

He smiled. "To the point as always. In that case, welcome back. We'll all be glad to have something besides our own cooking to eat."

Cam walked over to the stroller and had a look at Grace. "How's ladybug doing this morning?"

Nora smiled. "She's doing fine. And if you'll keep an eye on her for me I'll get breakfast started."

He grinned down at the infant. "I think you and I have the better part of that deal," he told Grace.

Nora's heart swelled with happiness as she went into the jailhouse kitchen. Cam had come a long way from not wanting anything to do with Grace. Was he finally beginning to understand that he was not his father?

Humming, she grabbed a bowl from the shelf and pulled eggs from her basket. Behind her she heard Gavin come in.

"Miss Nora's here!"

She smiled at the obvious pleasure in his voice. "Good morning, Gavin," she called over her shoulder. "Is this a two- or three-egg morning?"

"Three please." He stepped into the doorway. "It sure is good to have you and Grace back."

"Thank you. I'm happy to be back." And she most definitely was.

"Did you bring any of those big fluffy biscuits with you?"

She laughed. The hopeful question made it quite clear just what Gavin was most happy about. "I certainly did. And I brought along some plum jelly to go with them."

The sound of Ben entering and talking to Grace completed her feeling of things returning to the way they should be. These three very different men were part of her family now.

A few minutes later, Cam took Gavin's place in the doorway. "Smells good."

She smiled over her shoulder. "I'll be ready to serve in just a minute." Did he feel that same little tug of anticipation when they were together, that extra little tingle of awareness?

"Anything I can do to help?" he asked.

She shook her head. "Thanks, but there's no need. I'm almost finished."

He didn't move away but rather crossed his arms and stared at her with his smoky blue eyes. "I saw Flynn over at his building site when I made my rounds yesterday evening. The house looks like it'll be finished soon."

"It'll be good to have him and Maeve here permanently." Why did the room always feel so much smaller, more intimate, when Cam was in here with her? She wouldn't let herself wonder if he felt the same way. No, he'd made his lack of interest in her beyond friendship perfectly clear.

She lowered her voice. "Did you say anything to Mollie about my plan to help her?"

"Not yet. I thought we'd wait until Will and Bridget returned home and a definite decision was made."

Nora nodded. "That's probably best." She arranged five plates of food on a large wooden tray, then selected five cups from a nearby shelf. "Do you know if she prefers tea or coffee?"

"Tea."

Pleased that he'd taken the time to find that out, Nora prepared enough tea for two cups while she poured up three cups of coffee for the men.

She met his gaze, trying not to be distracted by the way he was looking at her. "I think it would be safe to let Mollie eat with us, don't you agree? I mean, it's not like she can escape with all three of you here keeping an eye on her."

Cam rolled his eyes, then nodded. "But only while she's eating. Then it's back inside the cell she goes."

"Of course. You're in charge."

And she wouldn't have it any other way.

Cam wandered out of the kitchen and moved to his desk. He had found himself on edge around Nora ever since Grace had been taken. At first he'd put it down to the tension that had permeated that whole situation.

It was only natural, after all, that the heartbreak she'd been going through would touch him—it would have touched any man with half a heart. And the fact that she'd turned to him for comfort had only made it that much more intense.

But he was no longer sure that was the whole story.

Because he was ready to concede that she'd gotten under his skin way before that terrible incident, he just hadn't wanted to admit it before now.

The thing was, what did he plan to do about it?

She knew the whole ugly business about his father and it hadn't seemed to change her opinion of him. That was a testament to her own goodness. After all, if she was willing to forgive Mollie who'd wronged her so terribly, why wouldn't she have sympathy for someone who'd gone through what he had?

What she didn't know about, though, was his darkest secret. The one that triggered his nightmares. The one that kept him from ever pursuing the future he longed for. The one that no one, not even Ben, could ever know about.

So he had his answer. What did he intend to do about it?

Not a single thing.

Nora got word midafternoon that Bridget and her family were back home. It was Cam who gave her the news and he insisted Nora immediately take Grace and go reassure her sister that everything was okay.

And Nora, in turn, insisted that he accompany her.

By the time they arrived at Bridget and Will's home, Nora could tell that Maeve and Flynn had updated them on most of what had happened.

Bridget ran to greet Nora, hugging both her and

Grace as if afraid they would suddenly disappear if she let go.

When they all finally took their seats in Bridget's parlor, Nora looked around and suddenly felt as if she was on trial.

"Maeve and Flynn told us what you're wanting to do," Bridget said. "And we've all been discussing it at great length."

Nora couldn't discern from Bridget's expression how she felt about it.

"We think your motives are admirable," her sister continued, "especially given what you've been through."

Nora sensed a "but" coming.

"But we're concerned that your trust may be misplaced," Maeve said, right on cue. "However, we also know how much this means to you and how determined you can be to follow through on your plans to help someone."

Did this mean she would have their blessing?

"Cam's offer to volunteer his and his deputies' protection for your household seems like a good compromise," Flynn conceded. "But we have a few stipulations."

Stipulations? Nora braced herself. "And those are?"

"I had an idea yesterday while I was inspecting the construction on our home," Flynn explained. "We could add a structure to your cottage, a simple, single room on the back that was connected to the cottage but that had a separate entrance. It would allow Cam or one of his deputies to stay there as a guard in relative comfort and close proximity, without giving anyone cause for censure."

Nora wrinkled her nose. "Add a room? But doesn't that seem a bit extreme?"

"Not at all." Flynn tugged on one of his cuffs. "In fact, the men I have working on our home can take care of something simple like that in one, maybe two days."

Will leaned forward. "And since Flynn plans to take care of having the room built, I will see that it's furnished properly."

Nora tried to sound grateful. "That's very generous of you gentlemen, but it's really not necessary. I'm sure after just a few days' time, you will all see that Mollie is no danger to anyone and it will no longer be necessary for anyone to stay at the house to act as her jailer."

"We're going to build an extra room onto the cottage," Maeve said firmly. "And Will and Flynn are going to take care of the costs and the details."

Wasn't Maeve supposed to be on her side? "But—"

"And while we're at it we're going to make certain that the existing structure is weathertight," Bridget added.

Nora tried to protest again.

"It won't do you any good to argue," Maeve said firmly. "As you well know, Bridget and I each own a share of the cottage, and we want to do this, so you're outvoted."

When had her sisters gotten so bossy? They had never ganged up on her so forcefully before. She swallowed her pride and nodded. "I see I don't have much choice in the matter. And if this is what it takes for you all to feel comfortable going forward with my plans, then so be it."

"Good." Flynn looked genuinely pleased. "You can expect the work crew first thing in the morning."

Nora stood and reached for Grace. "I'll take my leave of you now. I still have work to finish up at the jailhouse before I head home this evening."

Cam stood. "There's no need—"

She shot him a determined look. "I plan to put in a full day's work for a full day's pay." She hefted Grace to her shoulder. "Besides, we may have settled this matter amongst ourselves, but I have yet to speak to Mollie about it."

As they made their way to the door, Bridget moved beside her. "Don't be angry, Nora. We are only trying to do what's best for everyone."

She gave her sister a tired smile. "I'm not angry. I just wish it could have been handled differently."

Later, as Cam drove her back to his office, she let out some of her frustration. "One day I will own that cottage outright. But now, with the addition of this room, it will cost me more to do so."

"Why is it so hard for you to accept help?" he asked mildly.

"It's not that. It's just—" She stopped. What *was* it? "It's just that I don't want to be a burden on my sisters," she finished lamely.

"You're not a burden. Both Will and Flynn can afford to help you without any hardship whatsoever."

"But they shouldn't have to," she insisted.

Cam shook his head, his disagreement with her attitude obvious, and they made the rest of the short trip in silence.

When they arrived back at the sheriff's office, Cam was still trying to decide what he thought of the way this plan had been worked out among Nora and her family. But right now he needed to give Nora a bit of privacy to speak to Mollie. First he sent Gavin out to return his horse and wagon to the livery. Then a quick, meaningful look Ben's way was enough to have Ben remember an errand he needed to run.

Once they were alone, Cam unlocked Mollie's cell door and Nora went inside and sat next to Mollie on the cot.

He moved his desk chair to just outside the cell. He intended to keep a close eye on this little interaction. He figured he'd learn quite a bit about Mollie's character in the next few minutes.

"I want to talk to you about something," Nora began.

Mollie cast a quick glance his way, then focused all of her attention on Nora. "Yes ma'am. What about?"

"What do you think will happen to you now?"

Mollie picked at some threads on her raggedy skirt. "I suppose there'll be a trial and I'll go to prison for a long time." Her voice trembled slightly.

"What if I said there was another way for this to turn out?"

Hope flared in the girl's eyes. "What kind of other way?"

"Well, Sheriff Long and I, along with my family, have been talking things over, and we don't think you'll be helping any of those folks you wronged by spending your time in prison. In fact, we're wondering if you might better serve them and yourself by paying them all back instead."

The hope in her eyes died immediately. "That sounds good, but I don't have any money."

"You could earn it."

Mollie perked up. "How would I do that?"

"You could help out different people around town. And you could start by working here at the sheriff's office."

Mollie gave her a confused look. "But, don't *you* work here?"

"That's right. And I would still do the cooking and mending. But I'm trying to start a new business which is going to require more and more of my time. I thought perhaps you could take over the cleaning and we would split the wages."

Cam mentally shook his head. She had managed to make this sound as if Mollie would be doing her a favor.

"Then if you do a good job here," Nora continued, "and prove yourself to be trustworthy, we could find other work in other places for you to do."

"I'd work very hard for a chance like that." Mollie lifted her head. "When Elden and I first ran off, I scrubbed floors at an inn to earn money and the inn-keeper said I was a good worker."

Nora folded her hands in her lap. "Of course you'd have to turn over most of your wages to the sheriff to pay off your debts."

Cam raised a brow at that. So he was going to play banker in this little scheme of hers, was he?

Mollie glanced his way again and nodded emphatically. "I understand that, Miss Murphy. And I won't use any more of that money for myself than I need to. Why, I'll pitch a tent beside the road to live in if I have to. It'll just be good not to have to always be running and hiding anymore."

This time it was Nora who cast a quick glance his way. He gave a small nod of encouragement, more to show support for her than for her plan.

With a small smile, she turned back to Mollie. "That's the other thing I wanted to talk to you about. I would like for you to come stay at my home."

Mollie was obviously surprised. "Why would you do that?"

At least the girl recognized how extraordinary the offer was.

"Well, for one thing," Nora said, "I'm one of the people you need to pay back. If you lived at my place you could do some odd chores in the evenings to take care of your debt."

Interesting. No mention of Mollie needing to spend time with Grace.

"I'm afraid there'd be lots of rules for you to follow," Nora continued, "and some restrictions on your freedoms, especially at first."

"I understand. I just appreciate that you'd trust me enough to give me this chance."

Nora sat back. "Then I guess the question is, are you willing to follow the rules and work hard to repay your debts? And to live under my roof?"

"I am." Mollie glanced toward the buggy where Grace slept. "In fact, I'd like that a lot." Then she turned back to Nora. "Mind if I ask you something?"

Nora sat up straighter. "Of course not."

"Why are you being so nice to me?"

Nora tucked a stray hair behind her ear. "I think everyone deserves a second chance." She stood. "Please don't prove me wrong."

Cam stood and opened the cell door for Nora to exit.

Then he leaned against the open doorway and stared down at Mollie. "There are a few things I need to say before we go through with this plan Nora just described to you."

"Sir?"

"First, you're going to be watched closely. Me or one of my deputies are going to be nearby at all times.

If any of us gets even a hint that you're thinking about running off or breaking the law in any fashion again, then the deal is off and it's back to jail you go."

"Yes, sir. And I promise you won't have any trouble like that out of me."

"Next, we're going to sit down and you're going to tell me every single thing you stole or person you wronged from the time you slipped aboard that ship headed for America. And I do mean everything. I warn you, I know some of it already so I'll more than likely know if you leave anything off."

"Yes, sir, every single thing."

"We're going to make a list and then, where possible, we're going to let the victims set a value on how much you need to pay back for them to feel compensated, including your passage to America. And until you've paid it all back you won't be completely free to do as you please."

"Yes, sir."

"Promptly at eight o'clock each night you're going to go into the bedchamber Nora here assigns you at her home and someone is going to lock you in for the night. You are not to attempt to leave that room until it is unlocked the next morning."

Nora made a disapproving sound behind him. "I don't think—"

He didn't turn around. "I'll have no arguments, from either of you, on that point."

"It's okay, Miss Nora," Mollie said, "I understand. I haven't given any of you much reason to trust me yet. But that's going to change, I promise you."

Cam nodded. She was saying all the right things, but did she mean them? "All right then. Me and Nora's family have some work to do out at her place to get things ready for your stay. Once that's done, we'll give this plan of hers a try and see how it all works out."

For Nora's sake, he hoped the girl was as eager to make amends as she seemed. He couldn't bear to see Nora disappointed again.

He waved Mollie out of the cell and over to a chair by his desk. He lifted his own chair and followed her. "In the meantime, let's get started on that list."

Just as Flynn had promised, bright and early the next morning, four workmen showed up at the cottage, accompanied by three large wagonloads of lumber and other equipment. Right behind them were Flynn and Maeve, Will and Bridget, and Cam.

Did her sisters' husbands and the sheriff plan to roll up their sleeves and get to work, as well? Within minutes it was obvious they did, as they helped unload the wagons. Once that was done, everyone went to work. James took care of the horses and wagons while the rest of the men started on the construction. Maeve and Bridget joined Nora and Agnes in the kitchen, each carrying a large basket.

"What's this?" Nora asked suspiciously.

Maeve started unpacking her basket on the kitchen table. "A pair of already plucked chickens and some fresh vegetables. Bridget has two jars of lemonade and some blueberries. We figure there's going to be quite a few mouths to feed for lunch today."

It wasn't enough that they were building her an addition to her home—they thought they had to put food on her table, as well. "I had planned to take care of that," she said stiffly.

"Don't worry," Bridget said with an unrepentant

grin. "We intend to let you do all the cooking while we visit with Agnes and Grace."

Nora felt some of her annoyance ease and she returned her sister's grin. "I'm going to hold you to that."

Throughout the morning the hammering continued. It made Grace fussy so the sisters carried her out into the garden and then took walks along the beach with her. Nora joined them when she could get away from the stove and enjoyed the time spent with them. They did a lot of catching up with each other's news and slipped into the easy camaraderie she was afraid might have been lost to them when they went their separate ways.

When the men stopped to take a break, the ladies stepped outside to admire their work.

Nora tried to imagine what it would look like when it was completed. "It's so much bigger than I expected. You could almost fit both upstairs bedchambers in there."

Cam shrugged. "It's nearly as easy to build a large room as a small one."

Will nodded. "And we figured that when this is all over, you might want to move into it yourself."

The room was situated on the back side of the house and opened into the small room next to the kitchen that Laird had apparently used as an office when he lived here. It also had an outer door that faced the kitchen stoop. Then Nora looked again at the roofline that was taking shape. It extended well beyond the walls of the new room. "Are you planning to build a porch back here?"

"That we are," Flynn answered.

"But that wasn't part of the deal." Though if she was honest with herself, she was quite taken with the idea.

"We're not doing it for you," Cam said with a completely straight face. "It's for James. We're building it so he has a place to take off his boots before tracking into your kitchen when he comes in from the barn every morning."

"That's right," James answered. "I can't stand to have Agnes go on about my dirty boots every morning. That wife of mine is quite determined to drive me to distraction on the subject."

Nora couldn't resist a smile as she gave in. "Well, I wouldn't want to have that happen. And I'm sure we'll all enjoy having a back porch and will make good use of it."

By noon the four walls were up and the workers were constructing the roof and the floor of the porch. Because of their numbers, they ate in shifts and Nora found herself grateful that her sisters had brought along the extra foodstuffs. Those carpenters had worked up quite an appetite.

Cam was among the last of them to sit down at the table and she joined him. For a few minutes they had the kitchen to themselves. "So, do you think you'll manage to survive having to accept this generous gift from your sisters and their husbands?" he asked.

He knew her so well. "It will be difficult, but yes, I think I will survive."

He reached over and squeezed her hand. "That's my girl."

His words and tone as much as his touch set her pulse racing unexpectedly. He felt it, too—she could tell by the way his eyes darkened and then focused more sharply on her, as if she were the only thing he could see, the only thing he wanted to see.

For a moment neither of them moved, barely breathed. The tightness in her chest had become almost unbearable.

"Nora—"

Whatever he was planning to say was lost when Maeve bustled into the room. They simultaneously yanked their hands back and focused on eating their lunch.

"Bridget thinks Grace is ready for another bottle," Maeve said with a laugh. "I declare, that child is growing so fast, she—" Nora's sister paused, looking from Nora to Cam as if sensing something was wrong. "Sorry, did I interrupt something?"

"Not at all," Nora answered quickly. "We're just getting a bite to eat."

"I see." A secretive smile curved Maeve's lips. "Well, don't let me stop you. I'll just fix this bottle and be on my way again." Maeve reached for the pail of milk, humming cheerfully as she did so.

Nora and Cam continued to silently focus on their plates, even after Maeve had departed. Finally, Cam stood. "Thank you. That was delicious, as usual."

Was he going to leave it at that? "Cam, what—"

"I think we should be able to finish things up today." Cam didn't turn around as he placed his dish in the sink. "That means we can begin your project with Mollie tomorrow if you think you'll be ready."

Okay, so he didn't want to talk about it. "Of course."

He rubbed the back of his neck. "Which reminds me, I need to make certain that bedchamber door can lock securely from the outside. I'll grab the materials I need and take care of that right now." And with that he headed out the back door.

Nora slowly moved to the sink with her dishes, feeling totally dissatisfied.

What was going on with Cam?

Just as Cam had predicted, the workmen finished the construction, right down to the installation of two glass-paned windows, well before dark. Then they tackled the other critical repairs to the house, tightening loose boards, repairing or replacing sills, patching over chinks in the walls. When they were done, Nora was certain she no longer had to worry about drafts and leaks. They'd be able to face the coming winter with a snug, dry home.

Finally, Flynn walked up and gave her a short bow. "We're ready for your inspection."

Surprised by their desire to have her review their work, Nora nodded. Accompanied by her sisters, she walked through the large new room, inhaling the scent of sawdust and paint, admiring the craftsmanship of the well-sealed windows and square corners, enjoying the solid feel of the floors and the warmth of the sunlight streaming in through the windows. She pictured the curtains she would hang there, something light and cheery but not too feminine. And maybe some colorful rag rugs to warm up the floor.

Smiling, she opened the side door and stepped out onto her new back porch. The workmen were all standing there, including the sheriff and her brothers-in-law, waiting for her reaction. Agnes and James stood there, as well.

"I love it," she said with absolute sincerity. "It's perfect."

The men all smiled back at her.

"I have a chocolate blueberry pie and a buttermilk

pie fresh from the oven waiting in the kitchen. I insist you all have a large slice and a cup of coffee before you go."

Before anyone could move, the sound of horses and wagons intruded.

Bridget clapped her hands. "That must be the furniture Will and I are giving you."

Sure enough, several wagons paraded into her front yard. In addition to the bed, which she had expected, she saw a chest, a padded chair, a small table, two rocking chairs and something she couldn't quite make out.

"Oh, Bridget, this is too much. I can't take all of this."

Bridget didn't even turn around. "Of course you can," she said brightly. "All you have to do is stand back and let the workmen do their jobs." Then she went back to directing the men unloading the wagons.

Within short order, the bed, complete with bed linens, along with the padded chair, chest and small table had been installed in the new room. The remaining items, the two rockers and what turned out to be a porch swing, were installed on the back porch.

She looked around at the circle of her family and friends who had done this for her and realized once again just how blessed she was. She might not want to lean on them so heavily as they seemed to wish, but they loved her and that was what mattered.

"Thank you all for this," she said, her voice catching for a minute. "And not just for the construction and the furnishings, but for caring so very much."

Her sisters squeezed her in a hug. "Goose!" Bridget said. "Of course we care. We love you."

"You're our big sister," Maeve added. "We need you at your best to look out for us."

How could she have doubted her sisters' motives, their undiminished love for her? Just because they were starting new lives didn't mean they were going off and leaving her behind.

It was she who, out of her fear and loneliness, had erected unnecessary barriers.

But no more. The Murphy sisters were family, come what may. Whatever they did for each other, they did out of love. She knew that now.

She saw Cam out of the corner of her eye. Somehow she had to reach him, help him understand how, like her, his thinking was painfully flawed in one small but important area of his life.

But how could she get through to him?

Chapter Nineteen

The next morning when Nora arrived at the sheriff's office, Cam opened the cell door and set Mollie free.

"You don't ever have to go back inside there," he told her, "if you stay on the straight and narrow. But if you do anything to hurt Nora or Grace, or slip back into any of your old ways, then our deal is off and it's back in here to face the music. Understand?"

"Yes, sir."

Nora immediately put the girl to work scrubbing floors while she herself started in on cooking their breakfast. She kept a close eye on Mollie, though she tried not to be obvious about it. Gavin, however, had no such compunction. He was still angry at the girl for the kidnapping and no amount of reasoning could change his mind.

After breakfast, Nora led Mollie across the way to Cam's and Ben's living quarters, with Gavin trailing closely behind. As they climbed the stairs to Cam's place, Mollie looked back over her shoulder at Gavin.

"You're the one I nearly ran over with the horse that day at Miss Murphy's place, aren't you?"

Gavin's scowl deepened. "I am." His tone was curt.

Nora opened the door and led the way inside. She didn't comment, deciding to let the two work this out on their own.

"Well, I'm very sorry for that and I'm glad you weren't badly hurt. I know that probably doesn't mean much, but I truly am. When those children saw me I got scared the sheriff would catch me. I knew if he found out I'd come here as a stowaway he'd throw me in jail."

"As he should." Gavin wasn't showing any signs of softening.

She nodded. "You're right. And if I'd known he was such a good man I wouldn't have feared it quite as much." She gave a sketchy grin. "But even so, being put in jail is never a pleasant thing to consider."

"Then you shouldn't do anything illegal."

Nora figured that was enough discussion on that topic. "Okay, Mollie, let me show you where the mop, broom and cleaning rags are, and go over what needs to be done. Ben's rooms are downstairs and you'll do the same down there as up here."

Once Nora was certain Mollie understood what needed to be done, and had observed her work for a few minutes, she left the girl under Gavin's watchful and very suspicious eye. Crossing back to the jailhouse, she placed Grace back in her buggy and headed for the general store.

Mrs. James greeted her with a smile. "Good morning, Nora. Glad to see everything is well with you and little Grace."

"Thank you. I'm starting back into my baking today. Would you like to place an order?"

"Two of your cinnamon pound cakes and an apple pie if you can manage that."

"Of course. I'll have them ready for you this afternoon."

Nora made quick work of her shopping, then eyed the dry goods section, intending to get the seeds for the kitchen garden. But then she spied the bolts of fabric. She'd noticed this morning how soiled and tattered Mollie's dress was. The girl very likely only had the one.

Making up her mind, Nora pushed the stroller toward the fabrics, then studied the bolts, selecting a simple green color that she knew would complement Mollie's complexion and eyes.

Mrs. James cut it to the proper length for her, then folded and handed it over. "That will make a lovely dress for you," she said. "Are you making it for a special occasion?"

Nora smiled. "No, nothing special." Not feeling the need to volunteer anything else, she quickly paid for her purchases and returned to the sheriff's office.

She got lunch started and placed a pie in the oven, then relaxed and gave Grace her bottle. Once the infant was sated she lapsed into a morning nap.

Nora returned to the kitchen, ready to do more baking. She hummed as she worked. There was her standing order to complete, of course. But she also did a little experimenting, trying a new combination of flavors in one pie and playing with size and thickness in a batch of cookies. It was fun to try new things, new ways of making her desserts.

"Sounds like someone is having a good time."

Nora glanced over her shoulder, surprised she hadn't heard Cam return. "I'm playing with flavors in here and they're turning out well, if I do say so myself."

"Dare I hope me and my deputies will get the benefit of some of your experiments?"

She smiled piously. "One should always have hope."

He shook his head at her rejoinder, then looked around. "So where is Mollie?"

Nora put the pie she'd been assembling into the oven, then turned back to him. "She's cleaning across the way. Gavin is keeping an eye on her."

"How is she doing so far?"

Nora didn't hesitate but chose her words carefully. "She doesn't do things exactly the way I would, but then everyone has their own ways, and she's getting the job done. I truly have no complaints about what I've seen of her work or her attitude so far."

She moved forward, stepping past him. "In fact, while I've got a few minutes, I probably should go check on how she's doing."

She bent over the buggy and saw Grace was sleeping. "Oh, she's napping. Would you mind keeping an eye on her for a few minutes? I won't be long and I hate to wake her."

She saw that familiar distressed look in his eyes.

"I don't think that's such a good idea. I mean, I might be called away on official business."

"You can always just step out the back door and call if you need me to come tend to her."

"Still, I think it best—"

Ben walked in just then, interrupting Cam's protest. As if he'd just been rescued from a burning building, Cam greeted his deputy with a broad smile. "Ah, Ben's here. He'll be glad to help you, I'm sure."

"Of course I will," Ben said agreeably. "I'm at your disposal, Nora girl. What do you need?"

Recognizing defeat when she saw it, Nora smiled

Ben's way. "Just keep an eye on Grace for a few minutes while I step out back. She's napping and I don't want to wake her." She shot Cam a frustrated look. "Seems the sheriff here is afraid his official business might get in the way."

Cam cleared his throat. "That's right. You never know when an emergency situation might arise."

Ben made a shooing motion with his hands. "You just go on about your business now, we'll watch over little Gracie for you."

As Nora crossed the narrow alley to the lawmen's quarters she shook her head in disappointment. She'd thought Cam was beginning to get over his apprehensions about being around children, but apparently she'd been wrong.

This misguided fear of his was robbing him of the potential for so much happiness. She had to find a way to help him see the kind of man he truly was.

The kind of father he could be.

That thought set a fluttering in her stomach.

Father Almighty, I want to help Cam see the truth of this matter, but I'm not sure how anymore. Please help me to find a way. Present me with the right opportunity, the ability to recognize it and the courage to act on it.

Later that afternoon, when Cam drove them home, Nora found herself seated between Mollie and Cam. The addition of an extra adult forced her right up next to Cam. During that short ride, which felt unusually long today, she was all too aware of his presence beside her. Every bump and sway of the wagon caused them to brush against each other, and each brush sent tingles through her. Did he feel even the tiniest bit of that unsettling reaction? Or was he truly as unaffected as he seemed?

* * *

"This will be your room."

Mollie looked around at what had briefly been Bridget's room. "It's nice. In fact, it's been a very long time since I've slept in a place so clean and comfortable looking. Thank you for letting me use it."

Nora studied Mollie thoughtfully. "Don't you have any possessions to store here at all?"

"No. I had a few things I hadn't already sold off when I boarded the ship—some extra clothes, a hairbrush and mirror, a couple of hair ribbons—but I lost it all when my carpetbag was stolen on the docks in Boston."

Nora led her from the room and back down the stairs. "Well, then, you'll have to borrow one of my dresses and a nightdress until we can get you some additional clothing of your own. Do you sew?"

"I've done a bit of embroidery work and some mending, but I've never actually made an article of clothing before."

Nora nodded to herself. She thought she'd detected undertones of a genteel upbringing in the girl's voice. This reference to embroidery work and lack of practical sewing skills confirmed it. What had driven Mollie to leave that life behind for this one? "No need to worry," she said. "Agnes and I will teach you. You never know, that's a skill you might be able to use at some point to help you earn some money."

"I'm willing to try to learn anything you want to teach me."

The girl was certainly making an effort to have this arrangement work out. Nora moved toward the kitchen. "Now, I think a nice long bath may be in order before we do anything else."

Mollie stopped in her tracks. "Do you mean it, Miss Murphy? It's been so long since I've had more than a dip in a pond or a quick wipe with a wet rag."

"Yes, a *real* bath. Now, the washtub is in the back room, right through there." She pointed to what had formerly been Laird's office. "I'll put the large kettle on the stove to heat up some water. There's a bucket over by the back door you can use to start hauling water to fill the tub."

Once Mollie was happily settled in the tub, Nora went to her room and looked over her dresses. It didn't take much time. Besides the one she had on, she had three others, and one of those was the special blue dress she'd worn to Bridget's wedding.

She picked up the brown one—serviceable but not too worn—grabbed her sewing bag and went downstairs. She paused long enough to scoop up the basket that held Grace and went out on the back porch.

She set Grace's basket on the floor of the porch near the swing, then sat down and threaded her needle. It was so nice to sit out here and enjoy the evening breeze. And the swing was quite comfortable.

She smiled as Grace gurgled, swinging her arms with such abandon. Apparently Grace liked it out here, as well.

When she looked up again she saw Cam headed back from the barn. He stepped on the porch and sat in one of the rockers. "Getting some mending done?" he asked.

"I'm shortening this so it will fit Mollie."

"Giving her the clothes off your back now?"

"Just until we can get her some of her own."

"And where *is* Mollie?"

"She hasn't run off if that's what you're worried

about. She's taking a bath." Nora grimaced. "And I told her to wash the dress she was wearing while she was at it, so I need to get this finished quickly." She looked up momentarily from her sewing. "By the way, I meant to ask, how did the list of her transgressions turn out?"

"She was surprisingly forthcoming. Perhaps it was because she wasn't certain how much I already knew. But the list is long. Mostly small stuff, though. Like the produce from Amos Lafferty's garden."

"Have you talked to any of the people affected yet?" she asked. "Do you think they'll be satisfied with having her pay them back rather than serve time in prison?"

"Oh, I think getting reparation is going to be accepted by the victims quite well. It's the rest of the townsfolk you'll have worry about."

Nora's hands stilled for a moment. "What do you mean?"

"They're not getting anything out of this and to their way of thinking I'm letting a thief, and maybe worse, walk free among them." He raised a brow. "Don't forget, it was just a few short days ago that they were scouring this area because she'd kidnapped an infant."

How foolish of her not to have realized that. "Do you think that'll mean problems for Mollie?"

Cam shrugged. "If she works hard, does as she ought and doesn't get into any more trouble, I think folks will eventually accept her." He paused but she could tell he wasn't finished. "*Your* attitude will go a long ways toward smoothing the way for her," he finally added. "If folks see that you've forgiven her they are more likely to look for the good in her themselves."

Nora nodded and resumed her sewing. What Cam had said made sense, but the responsibility that added to her shoulders seemed daunting. She offered up a silent prayer for help not to stumble in her efforts.

Cam watched Nora ply her needle, the quick efficient movements counterbalanced by the soft frivolity of her humming. It was so reflective of the contradictions that made her so uniquely Nora that it made him smile. He watched the light breeze tease a wayward tendril into escaping her bun and he itched to twine it around his finger to see if it felt as soft and playful as it looked.

This is how God meant for family life to be, he thought. Not the dark, ugly thing he'd grown up with that was filled with fear and hate and guilt. But this— this sense of warmth and peace and fulfillment, along with just a touch of mystery and the push-pull of attraction.

A gusty breeze scurried across the porch just then and Nora lifted her face into it, eyes closed and lips slightly parted, as if welcoming a lover's kiss.

It was a spontaneous, artless gesture, but the sweet arch and smoothness of her neck, the innocent pleasure in her expression, took his breath away. What would she do if he closed the distance between them, took her in his arms and gave her the kind of kiss he longed to, the kind of kiss a suitor gave to his lady to communicate the depth of his feelings?

Cam stood abruptly, caught off guard by the turn his thoughts had taken. When had he started feeling this way?

It didn't matter. He wasn't her suitor. And he wouldn't ever be.

And he'd better find somewhere else to be before he forgot that.

Chapter Twenty

After dinner that evening, Mollie helped clear the table and clean the dishes. Once that was done, it was time to feed Grace. Nora quickly filled the bottle with milk fresh from the evening milking, then picked Grace up.

Glancing across the room, she caught Mollie watching them. The girl looked away and busied herself with wiping the counter, but not before Nora had seen the sad longing in her eyes.

"I'm feeling the need for a bit of fresh air," she said impulsively. "Mollie, would you like to give Grace her bottle tonight?"

She could feel Cam staring at her but refused to look his way.

"Me?" Mollie's expression was both hopeful and fearful at the same time. "I don't…I mean, I might not do it right."

"Of course you can. Grace does most of the work anyway. Come, sit here at the table and I'll show you."

Mollie slowly walked to the table. "I don't think she likes me. I mean she mostly cried when I had her last."

When you took her from me you mean. Nora quickly pushed that ugly thought aside. For this arrangement to work, she had to let go of all those feelings.

"One of the things you need to understand," she explained to Mollie, "is that Grace can sense your mood. If you're nervous, or irritable or frightened, she'll feel it and it will make her fussy, as well. So when you're holding her, focus on *her,* not on your own feelings. Think about how beautiful and precious she is, and how blessed you are to have her with you. Because if what she feels is your love, she'll feel safe and secure, and it will soothe her like nothing else can."

"She *is* precious."

Nora wanted to hold on to Grace, to make it clear that Grace belonged with her and no one else. Instead she nodded. "That she is. Now, hold out your arms."

Mollie did as she was told and Nora gently eased the infant into her waiting embrace. "Very good. Just make sure you support her head properly. Like that, yes."

Mollie stared down at her sweet burden.

"Here," Nora urged, "take the bottle and touch it to her lips. She'll latch on quickly enough." Grace started sucking at the nipple, right on cue. "There now, looks like you have the hang of it already."

Mollie couldn't seem to tear her gaze away from Grace. "She's so beautiful. She has my mother's eyes."

"Just about the most beautiful baby there ever was."

"Does she have a middle name?"

Mollie's question caught Nora unawares. "No. I mean, when we found her we had to give her a name so we could call her something other than 'baby,' so we decided to call her Grace. We never moved beyond that."

Mollie continued to stare down at the feeding infant.

"I always thought that if I had a little girl I would name her after my mother, Abigail. Do you think we might give her that as a middle name?"

"I think Grace Abigail is a very lovely name."

Mollie smiled softly and stroked Grace's cheek. "Hello, little Grace Abigail."

Nora felt a lump form in her throat and tamped it down as best she could. "Well, now, time for that fresh air."

Mollie looked up, her eyes wide and staring as if her lifeline was being taken away.

Nora managed to smile. "Don't worry. Agnes is here to help you if you have questions. She actually has much more experience with babies than I do." Then with a wave, Nora headed quickly out the door.

She'd barely stepped off the porch before she heard someone step out of the house behind her. It was Cam, of course—she didn't even have to turn around to be certain of that. She didn't stop but in a moment he was beside her, matching his steps to hers.

"You're not worried Mollie will run away?" she asked. Better to keep the conversation on neutral ground.

"Agnes and James will keep an eye on her for me."

She stumbled over a bit of uneven ground, and he grabbed her elbow to steady her. Then, instead of letting go, he tucked her hand on his arm. She thought about pulling away but decided it felt good there.

"That was a very kind thing to do," he said quietly.

She shrugged. "It's just a feeding."

"We both know it was more than that."

Sometimes she wished he didn't know her quite so well. "It's why I brought her here." But she hadn't planned to start so soon.

"I know."

Neither said anything else for a while, and soon they were strolling along the beach. Nora tried to lose herself in the muted slap-lapping sound of the waves and the crunching sand beneath their feet, in the brisk scent of salt water and sea spray, in the awe-inspiring sight of an ocean that seemed to go on forever.

Finally the panic within her subsided.

She slowed her pace and found a grassy dune above the beach to sit on. She wrapped her arms around her knees and stared out at the water. "I'm not giving Grace up, you know. Not yet."

"I know."

"Mollie has to prove herself worthy and able first."

"I know."

"And maybe not even then. I mean, Mollie and I could both raise her, together." She laid her head on her knees and turned her neck to finally look at him. "Couldn't we?"

His smile was achingly gentle. "You could. Absolutely."

It wasn't until he touched a finger to her cheek and pulled it away damp that she realized she was crying.

Cam pulled Nora to him and placed her head on his chest. He'd give his right arm to be able to take the hurt from her, but he was helpless to do so.

"This is silly," she said with a slight catch in her voice. "It's only one feeding."

Cam made a noncommittal sound, not wanting to lie. Because he could see the writing on the wall. It was happening just as he feared it would. Nora was too honorable a woman to separate a mother from her child, even if she had to shred her own heart in the process.

How she would be able to bear this he couldn't fathom. Because she loved that little girl as deeply and sacrificially as if she were her own flesh.

Nora finally lifted her head away from him, but remained in the circle of his left arm. His chest mourned the loss of her warmth, but his arm rejoiced in the sweet weight it supported.

He looked down and saw that her tears had stopped. But he knew the hurt hadn't.

She met his gaze and smiled softly. "You love Grace, too, don't you?"

"She is lovable," he answered lightly.

Her nose wrinkled in irritation. "Be serious, Cam. I saw the way her kidnapping ate at you and I see the way you look at her sometimes, like you can't help yourself. You love that little girl. Admit it."

Why was this so important to her? "All right, yes, I care a lot about her."

"Yet you won't let yourself get any closer to her."

"I have my reasons. Personal, *private* reasons."

"But this is so wrong, in so many ways. You'd make such a wonderful father, Cam. Don't you *want* children of your own someday?"

He pulled his arm back, grabbed a rock from the ground beside him and flung it as far as he could. "Yes! Is that what you want to hear? Yes I want to have children of my own, to have a family of my own. There are times when I see other fathers with their families and know I would give just about anything to be them for just a day." He stopped just short of saying *I want to have a family with you.* "But I know better than to pine after something I can't have."

She touched his arm, sending shock waves clear through to his gut.

"If this is about your father," she said, "then you have to see how blind you're being. You are not like him. You will never be like him. You are an honorable man."

She was pushing again, making him think about things he'd rather forget. "It's not about my father. At least not entirely."

"Then what is it?"

Cam stood and brushed off his pants. "Let this be, Nora. You can't fix everyone and everything. Some wrongs can never be righted."

He held out his hand to help her up and she took it. But to his surprise, when they were face to face, her eyes were filled with sorrow. "I'm disappointed in you, Cam. I thought you were a man who was fair and honest."

"I am."

"No, you aren't. You encouraged me to share my stories with you, how my mother and my da died, how we were run out of the only home we knew with no place else to go—or so we thought—and of the difficult decisions we faced. And in talking to you, I learned to see God's hand in everything that came to pass. You winnowed out of me my dreams of independence and you are helping me find a way to realize them. And you helped me see that it's naught but sinful pride to refuse help when it comes from a loving, generous spirit."

He rubbed the back of his neck, a little embarrassed by her recitation of the many things he'd done for her. "I was just trying to—"

Her eyes blazed back at him. "I *know* what you were trying to do. You were trying to help me without making me feel beholden to you. Because you're a good man, a good friend."

Did she think of him as *only* a friend?

"But if you are truly such a good man," she continued, "then you need to learn to take help and godly counsel as well as give it. If you don't trust me enough to share your worries, then talk to Ben or the preacher or Will." She spun on her heels and headed back toward the cottage.

As he followed in the gathering dusk, Cam let her words roll around in his mind, testing them for soundness. Could she be right?

Then the image of Vera McCauley's grief-twisted face screaming up at him blotted out everything else and Cam shuddered. Never again. The only way to prevent a repeat of the tragedy was to go on as he had before.

He stared at Nora walking away from him and ached for what might have been.

Then his lips twisted in a self-mocking smile. Whatever else had happened out here this evening, he'd succeeded in making her forget her own pain, if just for the moment.

Chapter Twenty-One

For Nora, the next three weeks passed both quickly and slowly at the same time. It felt almost as if her whole world were changing yet again and there wasn't anything she could do to stop it. She wasn't even sure if she *should* stop it.

The closeness that had developed between herself and Cameron was gone, replaced by the kind of casual friendship one had for a likable acquaintance. They talked every day, ate most of their meals together and he continued to drive her home every evening. And as for those evenings, there was no "taking turns" to stand guard over Mollie. Cam seemed to be a permanent resident of the new room at the cottage.

But there was no casual chatting in the doorway of the kitchen, no accidental brushing of hands and no repeat of that walk on the beach together. And the more time that passed, the less likely it seemed that they would be able to go back to what they'd had before.

Nora felt bereft, as if she'd lost something very special. Had this been her fault? Should she not have pushed him so hard? How could she help him if he wouldn't let her get close anymore?

But romance was definitely in the air for one of the lawmen. Ben finally proposed to Esther and the two declared their intention to get married in a few short weeks. Ben turned in his resignation at the same time, announcing that he and Esther planned to do some traveling after they got married.

Nora was tickled pink for them. She could see the joy in both of their faces and was happy that two such giving, generous people had found each other in this autumn of their lives. God's timing was truly perfect.

Gavin, too, was pleased by the announcement, but Nora knew it was for entirely different reasons. He was pleased, of course, that his friend had found happiness. But with Ben's retirement, Gavin was no longer just a deputy in training but was now Cam's right-hand man. And it also meant he would be able to move into Ben's place once Ben and Esther tied the knot. He seemed understandably thrilled that he'd soon be able to give up sleeping in a jail cell.

On the other hand, Nora's bakery business continued to grow beyond anything she had imagined. Now that Mollie was handling most of the cleaning Cam had hired her for, Nora had more time for baking, and the townsfolk were buying everything she could produce. She had learned to make miniature pies, and those, as well as her cookies, were big hits with the workers over at the chocolate mill. Her current goal was to save enough money to buy a second stove.

Things with Mollie were going very well, also. The girl was proving herself to be as good as her word. She tackled every job assigned to her and did it conscientiously. She took instruction from Nora and Agnes on how to sew and glowed with pride when she completed the work on her first dress. She even used the leftover scraps to make a little bonnet for Grace, utilizing her embroidery skills to add pretty touches to the finished project. On Sundays Mollie accompanied Nora and the Coulters to church services and was appropriately demure and teachable. She was beginning to win over many of the townsfolk.

Even Gavin, who remained intractable when she was under his watch, looked on her with something approaching approval when he thought no one was watching.

But the biggest change in Mollie, from Nora's perspective at any rate, was how comfortable she was becoming with Grace. Nora continued to care for Grace during the day, but in the evening, when they were back at the cottage, she turned over more and more of the responsibility for Grace's care to Mollie.

Nora tried to stay optimistic. She had grown fond of Mollie. Perhaps, if the girl wanted to settle down permanently here in Faith Glen after her debts were paid, and live at the cottage with Nora, then they really could both have a hand in raising the little girl.

When Maeve and Flynn's house was finally completed, the extended family members were all invited to take the grand tour of the place. The couple was planning a larger gathering the next day, an open house for the whole town to get to know their new doctor, but first Maeve had declared she wanted a "family only" gathering.

Nora looked around when she arrived, surprised at what a crowd her "extended family" now included. Bridget and Will were there of course, along with their two children and Esther. And now that Esther was an engaged woman, it also included Ben. Nora herself had brought Grace, of course. Agnes and James had come, as well, as had Mollie, who was now like a niece to her. And because Mollie came, Gavin felt the need to be there, as well, to "keep an eye on her."

The last person to show up, to her surprise, was Cam. Why was he here? Did he consider himself part of the family?

But Maeve stepped forward and welcomed him literally with open arms. "Sheriff, I'm so glad you accepted my invitation. The party wouldn't be complete without you."

So perhaps she had misunderstood what Maeve meant by "family only."

"Now that everyone is here," Maeve announced, "I'd like to show you through our new home."

The home was indeed beautiful. Spacious and elegantly furnished, there were six bedchambers, a large dining room, a study, a library, a visitors parlor, a private parlor and a music room. There was even a bathing room furnished with the latest and most luxurious of fixtures.

When the inside tour was complete, Flynn and Maeve led them through wide glass doors out of the music room and onto an elegant stone terrace. They all took positions along the low stone wall that edged it, admiring the view that encompassed a gracefully sloping lawn, well-manicured gardens and a large pond.

"You picked your home site well," Will remarked.

"Thank you." Flynn gave Maeve's hand a squeeze. "My wife wanted lots of green to look at. I don't think she cared much for Boston."

"You know I'm content wherever I am as long as

you're there," Maeve answered. Then she gave an impish grin. "But I do admit to liking this home better than the one we left behind in Boston."

Then Flynn spread his arms wide. "We hope you will enjoy yourselves. Our home is completely open to you. Walk around the place, inside or out, to your heart's content. There's a croquet set on the lawn for any of you who might be interested in playing and a chess set in the study. The cook is preparing a nice meal of baked fish and roast leg of lamb. We'll eat here on the terrace in about an hour."

The group drifted apart in very short order. Will challenged Flynn to a game of chess. Maeve and Bridget, along with Gavin and Mollie, headed for the croquet set. Caleb and Olivia followed behind with cries of "can I play, too?" Esther moved inside and sat at the piano. Ben stood beside her, ready to turn the pages of her music, and James and Agnes sat nearby, ready to be entertained. Within minutes, the lovely strains of a waltz floated through the open doorway.

Nora was content to sit on one of the terrace benches and hold Grace as she watched her sisters. She smiled when she saw Maeve and Bridget each take one of the twins and let them "help" hit the croquet ball with the mallets.

"Your sister has a beautiful home."

Startled at the sound of Cam's voice so close, Nora looked up just as he took a seat on the other end of her bench. "Yes, it is," she agreed.

"It gives your other sister's home some competition for the largest house in town."

Nora smiled. "I'm quite sure Maeve and Bridget don't feel any sort of competition on the matter." Now their husbands might be a different matter, but there was no need to voice *that* thought.

"And you?" he asked. "Do you wish you had a big fine house like your sisters have?"

"I'm quite content with my cottage." Nora meant that with all her heart. "I have no use for six bedrooms, I can't play any instruments so a music room would be useless and I have no books so I have no need for a library."

"Isn't there anything you would change?"

I'd like a large family to fill it. But she couldn't say that aloud. Instead she gave an answer that she knew he would appreciate. "A larger kitchen with two ovens would be nice."

He smiled. "I hear your baking business is doing really well."

Nora nodded, wondering why he'd sat down beside her. It was the first time he'd deliberately sought her out since that evening on the beach. Was he trying to make amends? Or was he merely at loose ends?

They sat in a not uncomfortable silence for a while, until Maeve and Bridget climbed the steps to the terrace, arms linked, smiles on their faces. Nora felt a momentary twinge of jealousy as she recognized they had a common bond that she lacked. But she was able to release it without a qualm a second later.

"Game through already?" she asked when they drew close.

Bridget laughed. "Caleb and Olivia got tired of it. Caleb decided he'd prefer to see if there were any turtles around the pond, and Olivia refused to be left behind. Mollie offered to keep an eye on them."

Maeve laughed. "And Gavin is keeping an eye on

Mollie." Then she held out her hands toward Grace. "May I?"

Nora reluctantly handed the baby off. She watched her youngest sister's face as she cooed down at the infant and saw a banked longing there. She guessed it wouldn't be long before Maeve and Flynn announced they were starting a family of their own.

Feeling suddenly restless, Nora stood and moved across the terrace to lean against the stone wall. She could feel the heat from the sun-warmed stones through her dress, but it was more soothing than uncomfortable.

Less than three months ago she had been desperate, destitute and uncertain of her future. Today she had a comfortable, snug home that no one could ever evict her from, lots of new friends who would drop everything to help her and a baby who'd touched her heart deeply. Also she was well on her way to having a thriving business of her own.

So why couldn't she be content?

Father above, I know I'm being impatient and prideful, but I'm trying to do better. I know I should be content with whatever lot in life is mine, but I also know that You want us to come to You with our longings. So I'm coming to You with mine. Please—

Cam joined her at the wall and rested his elbows next to hers. But before he could say anything, a child's scream rent the air. In a flash Cam was gone from her side and sprinting across the lawn. Nora lifted her skirts and was right behind him. What had happened?

Oh, dear Jesus, I'm sorry for my selfish prayer of a moment ago. Just let the children be okay.

She arrived at the pond a few heartbeats behind Cam. To her relief, both of the children were safely on the bank, though Caleb was soaking wet, and both he and Olivia were crying.

But Gavin and Mollie were in the pond, and Mollie seemed to be supporting an unconscious Gavin. Before she'd fully registered that fact, Cam had waded into the pond with them and lifted Gavin in his arms to carry him out. Concerned for Gavin, Nora tried to put aside her worries while she comforted Olivia and Caleb, and made certain they stayed safely away from the water.

Bridget came up behind her, breathless from running, and obviously concerned for her stepchildren.

"They're okay," Nora quickly assured her. "I think they just got a scare." She left Bridget to attend to the children and stepped forward to help Mollie out of the water, while Cam placed Gavin on the grass, well away from the edge of the pond.

"Is he going to be okay?" Nora asked, concerned by the fact that the boy hadn't yet opened his eyes.

Cam met her gaze without answering, his expression reflecting his own worry.

By this time, Maeve, Flynn and Will had also joined them, and Flynn had his medical bag at the ready. Flynn knelt down beside the much-too-still deputy and asked the others to give him some room. "Someone tell me what happened," he commanded in his strongest no-nonsense physician's voice.

It was Mollie who answered. "He slipped and fell backward into the water," she said, worry coloring her voice. "I think he must have hit his head on something because he sort of groaned and then went still." She wrung her hands, oblivious to the state of her own clothing. "I waded in and held his head up out of the water until Sheriff Long came, but I didn't know how else to help him."

"You did just as you should," Flynn reassured her. He gingerly felt along Gavin's scalp and suddenly the boy groaned and finally stirred. His eyes fluttered open and he looked around at them as if not quite certain what was going on. "What happened?"

"You took a fall and went in the water," Flynn said. "Now hold still while I examine you." His hands were busy, exploring Gavin's head and neck with practiced, efficient movements. "Tell me how you feel. Where does it hurt?"

Gavin grimaced. "My head feels like it's been hit with one of those croquet mallets, I'm soaking wet and I have water in my boots, but other than that I'm okay."

Flynn slid his hand under Gavin's back. "Can you sit up?"

"I think so." Gavin put word to action and in moments was sitting up and answering Flynn's questions in an intelligible manner. From his responses, it was obvious his confidence and sense of humor had survived intact.

Now that the concern for Gavin had abated, Mollie turned to face Bridget. "I'm so sorry, Mrs. Black. This is all my fault. I know I was supposed to be watching your little boy and girl, but I only took my eyes off Caleb for a minute."

"Tell us what happened." There was a hardness in Will's voice that commanded attention. He had stooped down to check on his children but this in no way diminished his presence.

Nora wondered if Mollie was about to face the considerable force of a father's anger. Instinctively she moved closer to the girl to lend her moral support.

But Mollie, obviously distraught over what had happened, kept her attention focused on Will and Bridget.

"The ribbons on Olivia's shoe came undone and I stooped down to tie them up again because I didn't want her to trip on them. I told Caleb to stay close, but he saw a lizard and went chasing after it before I could stop him. He tripped and fell into the pond." She glanced toward the deputy. "Gavin was lightning quick, though—he went right in and plucked Caleb out. But then *he* slipped on the wet bank and fell backward." Mollie pushed her hair off her forehead. "I made sure both children stayed sitting down away from the pond while I was helping Gavin." She took a deep breath. "Like I said, this was all my fault, I should have been watching more closely. I can only say again how deeply sorry I am."

Nora's heart warmed with pride for Mollie. Yes, a near disaster had happened under her watch, but children had a way of slipping past even the most watchful of caretakers. The important thing was, Mollie had taken responsibility for her actions, had kept her wits about her when it counted and hadn't tried to run away. The girl had definitely come a long way in the past few weeks.

"It wasn't her fault." Gavin stared past Flynn to Will and Bridget. "She *was* watching the twins real close like she said. And Caleb wasn't in any real danger. The pond only comes up to his waist on this end."

Caleb threw his arms around his father. "I'm sorry I didn't mind Miss Mollie, Papa. Please don't be angry."

Will's face softened as he stroked his little boy's head. "I'm not angry, Caleb." He glanced Mollie's way. "Not at anyone."

Then he looked back at Caleb, tilting the boy's head up to meet his gaze. "But now you see what can happen when you don't mind what you're told. You must promise me you will do better in the future."

The little boy nodded contritely. "Oh, I will, Papa." Then he qualified his promise. "At least I will *try*."

Nora hid a smile at the toddler's innocent honesty.

Flynn closed his bag, reclaiming everyone's attention. "I don't think Gavin has a concussion but he's going to have a whale of a headache for the rest of the day. Just to be safe, someone should keep a close eye on him for the next twenty-four hours." He turned to Gavin. "You shouldn't make any sudden, jarring movements or do any heavy lifting for the next few days. And if you have any dizzy spells you come back to see me right away. Understand?"

Gavin started to nod then winced and thought better of it. "Yes, sir."

Flynn stood and turned to Mollie. "It's a good thing you acted so promptly, young lady. You most likely saved Gavin from drowning."

Gavin looked at Mollie, a new appreciation gleaming in his eyes. "Seems I owe you my life."

Mollie blushed.

Nora wondered, was she embarrassed by being the center of everyone's attention? Or was it just Gavin's approving smile that put the pink in her cheeks?

Will rose and moved to help Flynn stand Gavin up, thanking the boy for rescuing Caleb from his dunking. As everyone began to make their way back toward the house, Nora looked around for Cam. She finally spotted him, standing with his back to the trunk of a nearby oak tree.

When had he moved away from them? More importantly, *why* had he moved away from them? She saw the strained look on his face, the clenched fists at his sides and headed his way without further hesitation.

She stopped in front of him and it seemed to take a moment for him to register her presence. Even then he didn't meet her gaze directly.

She said the first thing that popped into her head. "You should change into some dry clothes."

His lips barely curved as he smiled. "I will in a minute."

"Is something the matter?"

"I know how she feels." His voice was hoarse, ragged.

Something was definitely the matter. "What do you mean?"

"I know how Mollie feels. The awful feeling of things going out of control caused by one moment of inattention, the helplessness to turn back time and fix it."

There was an underlying meaning to his words that she wanted desperately to understand. "But everything turned out okay."

His gaze locked on hers and he seemed to really see her for the first time since he'd started talking. "Yes. This time it did."

"Cam, does this have something to do with your own troubles?" She held her breath, wondering if he would push her away again.

He held his peace for a long moment and she braced herself for the forthcoming rebuff. But then he let out a long breath and nodded. "You're right. You deserve the whole story. And then you'll finally understand." He muttered something under his breath that sounded suspiciously like "then it'll be over."

"I'm listening." Nora's heart pounded in her chest,

sending her pulse scurrying through her veins. She sensed that everything between them would change after this. And she wasn't certain she would like where it went.

Cam indicated they should walk and Nora fell into step beside him, following the edge of the pond. "After my mother died," he began, "and I left my father's house, I was on my own for a while. I worked in one of the factories in Boston, earning just enough to keep myself fed. One of the ways I survived was by finding a second job. When I wasn't working in the factory, I helped a lady I'd met there by watching her little boy in the evenings when she went out to work *her* second job. She didn't have very much, so she couldn't pay me, but she let me sleep in her apartment so I had a roof over my head."

Nora's gut clenched in sympathy for the harsh childhood he'd had. It was a wonder he'd grown into such a good, even-tempered man.

"The apartment she had was just a tiny garret room in a four-story tenement, but it was better than sleeping on the street. Her little boy, Tommy, was three years old—just about Caleb's age. I didn't mind watching him—he was a sweet kid, full of curiosity and energy. After a while, it was almost like having a little brother."

She smiled, picturing what a great big brother he would have made to such a child.

Cam raked a shaky hand through his hair and she knew he was getting close to the difficult part of his story. "But then one hot July evening a moth flew in the open window and Tommy tried to catch it. I didn't realize what was happening until it was too late.

Tommy followed that moth right out of that fourth-story window."

Nora couldn't stop the gasp that sprang from her lips and her hand flew to her throat. "Oh, Cam, how awful."

He didn't seem to hear her, his gaze was focused on something in the far distance. "I raced down the stairs, hoping, praying that somehow there'd been something there to cushion his fall, that he'd be okay."

She knew instinctively that that had not been the case.

"His mother found him before I did. She was kneeling on that grimy sidewalk, holding the broken, bloody body of her only child." He swallowed hard. "When she saw me she started screaming, telling me it was all my fault, that I had killed her baby."

Nora grabbed his hand and squeezed it, the need to touch him, to console him, overwhelming her. "Oh, Cam, she had to have been out of her mind with grief. But no matter what she said, it *wasn't* your fault."

"Tommy died while under my care, because I didn't watch him closely enough." His face hardened. "Don't you understand? My dad was a mean drunk and a miserable human being, but as far as I know, he was never responsible for anyone's death." He grimaced. "I can't say the same about me."

What a terrible burden he'd carried all these years. "You were just a boy—"

His eyes blazed at her, but she knew his anger was all directed inward. "Don't try to sugarcoat this, Nora. I was twelve years old. Old enough to be on my own, old enough to hold down a man's job and old enough to know exactly what my responsibilities to Tommy and his mother were."

He pulled his hand out of her grasp. "Now, if you'll

excuse me, I think it's time I changed out of these wet clothes. Give my regrets to your sister and Dr. Gallagher. I'll see you at your place this evening."

And with that he marched off toward the town square without so much as a backward glance.

Chapter Twenty-Two

Nora took her time returning to the house. She ached for Cam, for the lonely, guilt-ridden boy he'd been, for the torments that still haunted him as a man. So much about him was clearer now. And so much had become clearer about her own feelings for him.

Quite simply, she loved him. She loved his courage and his honesty, his generous spirit and his ability to feel the pain of others. She loved his stubborn determination, even when it was misdirected, and his maddening tendency to hold himself to a higher standard than those around him. And she loved the quiet, unobtrusive way he had of helping others while allowing them to maintain their dignity.

For good or ill, she was totally, achingly, deeply in love with Sheriff Cameron Long. She wasn't nearly as certain how he felt about her.

But one thing was certain, no matter how long it took, and no matter how much he rebuffed her efforts, she would make it her mission to help him see his own character.

She climbed the shallow stairs to the terrace to find

everyone gathered there, including Gavin, who now seemed to be wearing some of Flynn's clothes. A quick glance Mollie's way showed her to be wearing one of Maeve's dresses. It seemed the Gallaghers went the extra mile when it came to the comfort of their guests.

Nora let everyone know about Cam's departure, giving his need to change clothes as an excuse. If anyone thought it odd for him to leave without saying goodbye to his hosts, they didn't say anything.

Later, as they sat around the outdoor table enjoying their meal, Maeve turned to Gavin. "I have a surprise for you. Your brothers will be at the open house tomorrow."

Gavin's face split in a wide grin. "Sean and Emmett? That's terrific. It seems like forever since I saw them."

"You have brothers?" Mollie asked from her seat between Gavin and Nora.

"Yep. In fact they were the two boys who spotted you that day you nearly ran me over with the sheriff's horse out at Miss Nora's place."

"Well, glory be." Mollie smiled wistfully. "I always wished I'd had siblings. Where have they been staying?"

"In Boston. A woman we met on the ship coming over here took us all under her wing and she's been taking care of my brothers since we got here."

"That's right," Maeve interjected. "Mrs. Fitzwilliam and the boys plan to stay overnight with us so you'll be able to have a nice long visit."

"Mrs. Fitzwilliam!" Mollie popped up from her seat and Nora saw her face drain of color. "Mrs. *Elizabeth* Fitzwilliam?"

"Why yes, dear." Maeve stared at Mollie in concern. "Do you know her?"

Mollie nodded and sank back into her seat as if afraid her legs would buckle. "She's my grandmother."

"Your grandmother!" The three sisters stared at each other, starting to put the pieces of the puzzle together.

Nora felt excitement bubble up inside her at the realization of what this meant. God's ways really were mysterious—and magnificent.

Gavin, however, still didn't seem convinced. "But her granddaughter's name is Mary."

Mollie's nose wrinkled. "Mary is my real name, but I go by Mollie—it's what my parents always called me. But grandmother never would. She said Mollie was too common." She seemed truly distraught now. "That's how it always was between us. Please, she can't know I'm here."

Gavin stared at her earnestly. "But, Mollie, she's been looking for you. That's why she came to this country. She thought you were already here and wanted to find you and make certain you're okay."

"But, I thought—surely she was happy to see the last of me? We didn't get along at all and she was constantly berating me and telling me what a hoyden I was."

Gavin's brow came down. "I know she can be gruff and unbending at times, but in the short time me and my brothers have been with her I've seen below that to a very lonely and well-intentioned woman. She's been very good to all three of us, boys who were strangers to her before we boarded the *Annie McGee* and who were far from genteel. And she's mentioned you often, how she wishes the two of you had been able to get along better and how she hopes you haven't run into difficult situations."

Mollie didn't appear at all convinced. "She may have been nice to you, but she wasn't like that with me. If she's been looking for me, it's only because she wants to tell me again what a disappointment I am to her. I just couldn't bear to go through that again."

Nora touched Mollie's arm, claiming her attention. "Don't you think *everyone* deserves a second chance?" she asked gently.

Mollie stared at her for a long moment, then slowly nodded. "Of course." She swallowed hard. "I'll meet with her tomorrow."

"Good." It was Nora's turn to put on a brave face. "And you can introduce her to her new great-grand-daughter."

That evening, dusk was settling in before Cam showed up. He seemed to have recovered from his earlier dark mood and conversed easily with everyone around the supper table. He listened to the news about Mollie's relationship with Mrs. Fitzwilliam with suitable interest and even added his own reassurances to the still-nervous girl.

But Nora wasn't fooled. Without being able to put her finger on exactly what had changed, she sensed that he'd somehow distanced himself from the rest of them.

Or was it just from her?

Later, before Nora could pull him aside for a few words in private, he excused himself, declaring his intention to turn in early.

Nora watched him exit through the kitchen door, feeling her heart grow heavy. Was he so afraid to spend time alone with her? Or rather did he now resent her for having forced his story out of him?

Mollie was apparently unaware of any undercurrents. She was full of nervous, bubbly chatter that she seemed determined to share with Nora. She talked about the beautiful home the Gallaghers had built, declaring it to be finer than even her grandmother's. She talked about the incident at the pond, about how quick and gallant Gavin had been in his rescue of Caleb. And about how scared she'd been for both Caleb and Gavin. But mostly she talked about her nervousness around facing her grandmother the next day.

Nora, whose mind was still on Cam, only half followed the girl's conversation until she mentioned Grace's name. She immediately gave the girl her full attention. "I'm sorry, what was that?"

"I said, I know the transgression my grandmother will have the most trouble with is the fact that I had a baby out of wedlock. I just don't want her to look down her nose at Grace the way she did with me. Grace is the one good, innocent thing that came from all my wickedness."

Nora smiled reassuringly. "I don't think you need to worry about that." At least she hoped this was true. "She's been very fond of Grace, ever since she spent time with all of us on the *Annie McGee*. And look at how your grandmother has behaved toward the McCorkle brothers. It's obvious Gavin cares for her. Doesn't that speak of a softer side of her?"

Mollie shook her head. "That sure doesn't sound like the grandmother I left behind in Ireland. I half expect to see a stranger who happens to have the same name as my grandmother show up at the Gallaghers' tomorrow."

Nora gave Mollie a pointed half smile. "People change."

Mollie grimaced. "All the same, I'd prefer to see how she reacts to the rest of my story before I tell her about Grace."

"That's up to you, of course," Nora said diffidently, "but I think you'll be pleasantly surprised."

With a skeptical nod, Mollie excused herself and then bustled off to make certain her dress for tomorrow was immaculately clean and perfectly pressed.

Nora turned and stared at the door Cam had disappeared through earlier. Could he change, as well? Or at least his understanding of who he was?

Please, God, he's helped me in so many ways. Let me be the one to help him now.

The next morning Nora and Bridget waited with a very nervous Mollie in Maeve's parlor. It had been decided that Maeve, Flynn and Gavin would greet Mrs. Fitzwilliam and the two younger McCorkle brothers when they arrived. Then Flynn would take charge of Sean and Emmett, enticing them outdoors with the promise of fishing in the pond, while Gavin and Maeve accompanied Mrs. Fitzwilliam here to view a "little surprise."

The carriage had arrived a few minutes ago, so the moment of truth was upon them.

"I don't know if I can go through with this," Mollie said for what must be the twentieth time.

And just as she had the other nineteen times, Nora reassured her. "Of course you can. Just remain calm, trust in the Lord to guide you and let your grandmother see your heart." She patted Grace's back, glad the waiting would be over soon.

"You've both changed a great deal since you last saw each other," Bridget added. "She'll probably be every bit as nervous as you when she sees you."

Mollie looked skeptical, then her expression turned to panic as the door swung open.

Mrs. Fitzwilliam was the first to enter the room and her smile turned to shock as she recognized the girl standing before her. "Mary?" She took hold of Gavin's arm, as if she needed the added support. "Praise God, is that really you?"

"Yes, Grandmother, it's me."

"But how did you come to be here?" The matron allowed Gavin to lead her across the room. "I've been scouring all of Boston for you."

Mollie gave a tremulous smile. "It's a long story." She took her grandmother's hand and gave her a peck on the cheek. "But first, I must know why you've been looking for me."

"Why?" Mrs. Fitzwilliam appeared affronted by the question. "Because you're my granddaughter, of course. I was concerned for your well-being. And," she cleared her throat in an almost-apologetic manner, "I was afraid that there were some misunderstandings between us that we needed to clear up."

"Misunderstandings?" Mollie's lips pinched defensively, then she shot a look Nora's way and took a deep breath. "Please sit down so we can talk more comfortably."

Mollie had elicited promises from the Murphy sisters and Gavin that they not leave her alone with her grandmother, so it had been decided that Nora, along with Grace, would remain for as long as Mollie needed the support. Mrs. Fitzwilliam took a seat in a throne-like wingback chair while Nora and Mollie sat on a love seat across from her. Maeve, Bridget and Gavin quietly excused themselves.

Now that the initial surprise was over, Mrs. Fitzwilliam's demeanor took on a hint of imperiousness. "So, tell me this long story that ends with you being here in Maeve's parlor."

Mollie reached for Nora's hand, and Nora gave it a comforting squeeze, adding a silent prayer that this would go well.

Then, taking a deep breath, Mollie launched into her story, telling her grandmother all of the unpleasant, unsavory details without excuses, leaving out only the parts that involved Grace.

Mrs. Fitzwilliam let her speak without interruption, but her expression grew sterner with each confession.

When Mollie finished, she sat back and there was a long moment of complete silence.

Nora could sense Mollie holding her breath, waiting for her grandmother's response. She gave the girl's hand another squeeze, not surprised to feel a slight trembling.

Finally Mrs. Fitzwilliam straightened. "It seems you were lucky that your foolish acts were discovered by such charitable people as Nora and Sheriff Long." The woman's tone was stern, disapproving.

Mollie nodded. "It is something I have thanked God for every day since the moment I was arrested." She took a long, steadying breath and lifted her chin. "I know that I was willful and disobedient, Grandmother, and that I've done terrible things. I'm truly sorry for all of that, and am trying to make reparations. But I will understand if you can't find it in your heart to forgive me."

Still Mrs. Fitzwilliam's frown did not soften.

Nora tried to keep her expression even, but she felt a surge of disappointment. *Please, God, don't let her pride get in the way of a second chance for her and her granddaughter. Show me a way to help them reconcile.*

Grace started fussing and Nora suddenly smiled. "Mollie, I believe there is one more very important thing you have to say to your grandmother." She cut her eyes toward Grace purposefully.

Mollie's gaze shot to Nora and she gave a slight shake of her head. But Nora wouldn't allow her to drop her gaze and finally the girl nodded.

Taking a deep breath Mollie turned to Mrs. Fitzwilliam. "Grandmother," she said with obvious trepidation, "I would like you to meet your great-granddaughter, Grace Abigail Kerrigan Murphy."

Nora was both surprised and touched that Mollie had given the Murphy surname the place of honor in Grace's name.

Mrs. Fitzwilliam, for once, seemed struck speechless.

Then she turned to Nora. "Is this true?"

Nora nodded. "Mollie was aboard the *Annie McGee* and had the baby there. Grace is her daughter all right." That admission was still difficult for her to make.

The woman's expression had softened at last, glowing with a dawning sense of wonder. She held out her arms. "May I hold her?"

"Of course." Nora stood and placed the baby in her arms.

"What a sweet little bairn you are." Mrs. Fitzwilliam's smile and tone were doting. There was no doubt Grace, at least, had won a place in her heart.

Then Mollie stood and took Grace from her, handing the baby back to Nora. "We still need to settle matters between us," Mollie said to her grandmother. "And until we do, I'd prefer we not expose Grace to our bickering."

Mrs. Fitzwilliam nodded. "I see you have a mother's love for her child." She folded her hands in her lap. "If I seemed harsh to you it is because I felt you were not being totally honest with me. Now that I understand what you were holding back, and why, I want to apologize."

There was a great deal more discussion between the two women—explanations, admissions and tears as well as assertions of changed outlooks, forbearance and deeper tolerance. But in the end, grandmother and granddaughter hugged with genuine affection and promises to start fresh.

"Now, my dear," Mrs. Fitzwilliam said happily. "You must pack up your and Grace's things so that you may return with me to Boston tomorrow."

The words hit Nora like a punch in the stomach and her hands tightened reflexively around Grace.

But Mollie was already shaking her head. "I can't do that. I belong here."

"Nonsense!" Mrs. Fitzwilliam sat up ramrod straight, some of her imperiousness returning. "You belong with your family."

"Grandmother, I still owe money to a lot of people here, debts I'm working to pay off." Mollie cast a shy glance Nora's way. "And I have friends here." She raised her head determinedly. "I'm sorry if that makes you unhappy, but this is where my life is now."

Mrs. Fitzwilliam lifted her chin. "I can take care of those debts for you. As for your friends—" she smiled magnanimously "—you can come back to visit in Faith Glen as often as you like. Just as Emmett and Sean come to visit Gavin."

"Those are *my* debts, not yours," Mollie insisted. "And I promised Sheriff Long and Nora that if they gave me the chance to make things right, I would work until I paid off every last one of them. It wouldn't be right for me to just let you snap your fingers and make them go away."

Nora wanted to cheer. Mollie was turning into a fine young woman, one with backbone and character.

Mrs. Fitzwilliam eyed the stubborn tilt of Mollie's chin. "You can't be so selfish as to think only of yourself. What about Grace?"

Some of Mollie's confidence seemed to crumble and she glanced quickly at Grace. "What do you mean?"

"If you stay here what will your daughter's future be like? A poor washerwoman's daughter with no prospects? On the other hand, think of the advantages I can provide for her. She can have the best care, pretty clothes and a proper education. She can mingle with the cream of society."

Mollie shook her head. "I'm sorry, but while being able to provide fine things would be wonderful, I don't think it is the most important thing in a child's upbringing." Then she squeezed Nora's hand. "Besides, it's not for me to say whether Grace stays or goes. She belongs with Nora."

"What foolishness is this?" Mrs. Fitzwilliam turned to Nora, her smile taking an almost cajoling aspect. "Nora, you know I've grown quite fond of you and your sisters. And of course it was generous beyond measure for you to take both Grace and Mary in and care for them as you have." She spread her hands. "But you must agree that a child's place is with her mother."

Nora started to say something, she wasn't quite sure what, when she felt Mollie's hand press firmly on hers.

"Grandmother," Mollie said with great deliberation, "this is between Nora and me and we will do whatever is best for Grace. It's not something I will allow you to interfere in."

Mrs. Fitzwilliam sat back, obviously disconcerted by her granddaughter's forceful words.

Then Mollie softened. "Please, let's not allow this difference to put a wedge between us again. Can't we still be friends at least, even if I stay in Faith Glen?" Her hands trembled slightly. "Just like you and Gavin."

Mrs. Fitzwilliam rose from her chair and marched toward her granddaughter. Mollie stood, as well, and the two women faced each other, neither saying a word. Then the older woman reached over and gave Mollie a hug. "We can be more than friends, my dear. We are family."

Once her surprise receded, Mollie returned the hug with a fierce abandon. "Thank you, Grandmother."

Nora felt tears well in her eyes. She was so happy for the two of them that she felt ready to burst with it.

Thank You, Father Almighty, for letting me witness this beautiful reconciliation.

Mrs. Fitzwilliam stepped back and briskly brushed the wrinkles from her skirt. "I suppose I will need to follow Dr. Gallagher's example," she said severely, "and build a residence here in Faith Glen. What a great bother that will be."

Nora hid a smile. The woman was trying to sound disgruntled but it was obvious she was quite taken with the idea.

"Do you mean it?" Mollie asked.

The woman huffed. "I wouldn't say it if I didn't. It's the sensible thing to do. After all, there's nothing to keep me in Boston save the theater, and I can travel back when the fancy takes me. Sean and Emmett will, of course, be happy to be closer to their brother, and moving here is apparently the only way I'll be able to spend much time with my granddaughter and great-granddaughter."

She lifted her chin and turned toward the door. "Now, I must go at once and speak to Mr. Black and Dr. Gallagher to learn the best way to go about procuring land and constructing a home."

Once the reinvigorated woman had left the room, Nora turned to Mollie. "What you said about Grace—"

Mollie stopped her with an upraised palm. "I meant what I said. Both Grace and I owe our lives to you. That's a debt we can't easily repay." She smiled. "Now, shall we go see how your sisters' husbands are reacting to my grandmother's barrage of questions?"

Mollie took Grace from her as she made to rise, and Nora didn't try to take her back once she was standing. Instead she led the way from the room.

I'm not losing Grace, she told herself. *Mollie can continue to live with me and together we can raise Grace.*

She would just have to do her best to ignore the little niggling doubts that were creeping into her heart.

Chapter Twenty-Three

Nora leaned on her spade, wiping her forehead with the back of her hand. She glanced at her two sisters, working beside her in the cottage garden, Colleen's Garden, and smiled. Maeve had been living in Faith Glen for two weeks now and while the three sisters didn't get together every day, they made time to see each other two to three times a week.

Today they had decided to do some work in the garden.

The sound of children's laughter caught her attention and she glanced toward the nearby lawn where Caleb and Olivia were playing. Mollie was watching Grace this morning and Gavin was watching Mollie.

As for Cam, that distance she'd first noticed after he'd told her his terrible secret remained firmly in place. And the realization that she had no idea how to break through it was killing her.

"Nora."

At Bridget's hail, Nora brought her focus back to the present. "Yes?"

"You looked like you were miles away." Bridget's

voice had a teasing edge to it. "I was asking where we should plant this last rosebush."

"It's your garden," Maeve added, "so we need you to select the spot."

Her garden. That sounded good. She pointed to an area between the bench and the tree and walked toward it. "How about over there?"

Both sisters nodded approval and they strolled forward, tools in hand.

"It's really quite beautiful and peaceful out here," Bridget mused.

Nora agreed. The garden was now almost fully restored to its former glory. The weeds were gone, the beds were neatly planted and bordered, and the fall flowers were beginning to bloom. There was even a new stone birdbath in the center, a gift from Mrs. Fitzgerald.

As she speared the ground with her spade, Nora's thoughts turned back to Cam. To be honest, he was never far from her thoughts these days. She missed the easy camaraderie they'd shared, the way she'd been able to seek his counsel when she needed it, even his high-handed way of making decisions when he wanted to help her out in some way. If only—

Her spade struck something hard, sending a jarring wrench up her arm.

"Sounds like you hit another rock," Maeve said. "I hope it's not a big one this time."

Nora tapped it again. "I don't think it's a rock." The three sisters stared at each other for a minute, then eagerly went to work on the hole. Finally they unearthed a metal box about the size of a loaf of bread.

"Pull it out," Maeve urged.

Bridget peered into the hole. "Whatever can it be? Do you think Laird put it there?"

Remembering Agnes's story about the supposed treasure Laird O'Malley had buried out here, Nora didn't waste time on words. She got down on her knees and tugged the box out of the hole, her curiosity growing by the minute.

The sisters moved to the nearby bench and Nora placed the dirt-covered box on its seat. "There's no lock," she said after a quick check.

"Should we open it?" Maeve asked.

Bridget obviously had no reservations. "Of course we should open it, goose."

Maeve nudged Bridget away from the box. "You do it, Nora. You're the oldest and you found it."

With a nod, Nora reached down and tugged on the lid. It resisted at first, and then, with a low groaning of rusty hinges, it flipped open.

Inside was a bundle of letters, tied with a yellow ribbon, and addressed to Laird O'Malley. "That's Mother's handwriting," Nora whispered.

"Laird kept her letters." Romantically minded Bridget sighed. "But why would he bury them out here where he couldn't read them?"

"Perhaps he did it when he knew he was dying," Maeve offered. "So no one else would have them."

"Then perhaps we shouldn't read them." Nora closed the box. She wasn't entirely sure she wanted to know what her mother had said to this man who had loved her so deeply.

Bridget placed a hand on the lid. "But if he truly didn't want anyone to find these letters, wouldn't he have burned them? Perhaps he left them here, hoping his Colleen would come, or her descendents, and would see how much he still cared at the end."

She lifted the lid and handed them each a letter. "We *have* to read them, or his efforts would have been for nothing."

Nora slowly opened the one Bridget had handed her. It was short but eloquent, full of hope and promise. She glanced at the date penned in her mother's hand and breathed a sigh of relief. "This one was written before she married Da."

"Mine, as well," Maeve replied.

"This one, too," Bridget added.

Both of her sisters sounded as relieved as she felt. Nora thumbed through the remaining half-dozen letters. "All of them are." Then she paused over the last one. "Listen to this. It's dated just before Mother married Da." She began reading aloud to her sisters.

My dear sweet Laird,
I wanted to tell you this in person but your mother tells me you will be gone for some time. I have decided to marry Jack. I know that is not the answer you wanted, but I must follow my heart. He is a good man who loves me deeply and I know that we will be happy together.

While I will always have a special place in my heart for you, as we have discussed time and again, I cannot marry a man who does not share my love for Jesus. I wish you well, my darling, and pray you will find much happiness. I hope in time you will find your way to accepting the abundant joy of what our Heavenly Father offers so that I will see you again someday in heaven.
With much affection,
Colleen

Nora put the letter down and looked at her sisters, seeing the same tears glistening in their eyes that she felt in hers.

"So that was why she never married him," Bridget whispered.

"That poor man." Maeve swallowed. "I hope, in the end, he came to know Jesus."

"I think perhaps he did," Nora said slowly. "I saw his headstone in the churchyard. It had John 14:6 engraved on it."

Maeve nodded, quoting the familiar scripture. "Jesus saith unto him, I am the way, the truth, and the life: no man cometh unto the Father, but by me."

"Oh, I wish Mother could have known." Bridget's eyes were gleaming with unshed tears again. "That would have made her so happy."

"She knows now," Nora said softly. She set the letter back in the box and closed the lid. "I think we should put this right back where we found it. I can plant that bush a few feet to the left."

Bridget and Maeve both nodded agreement.

As they placed the box back in the hole and Nora began scooping dirt back on top, Bridget leaned against the handle of her hoe and looked around.

"This is so beautiful," she said. "Not just in the way it looks but in the sweet spirit that resides here. Mother would have loved it."

Nora nodded. "It's more than just that," she said. "*I* love it here, and not only because it is the refuge we ran to when we were turned out back in Castleville. I love this garden. I love the new family I've found—both the ones you two married into and the Coulters. I love this town and its generous people who welcomed us so wonderfully."

And, whether he's willing to accept it or not, I love Cameron Long. But she didn't say that out loud.

The trio made quick work of planting the last rosebush then decided it was time to have a bit of light refreshment. As they headed back to the house, Maeve and Bridget paused to talk to the twins and admire the miniature structures they'd constructed of twigs and vines. Nora proceeded on to the house, mentally planning what she would serve her guests. When she stepped onto the back porch, however, she stopped short. Gavin and Mollie sat on the porch swing, and both were radiating happiness and cooing over Grace who lay gurgling happily in Mollie's lap.

It was the perfect picture of a happy family. And it broke a small piece of her heart.

Gavin spied her first and scrambled to his feet, his face flushing guiltily. "Miss Nora. Hello. I, uh, I was just…"

Mollie rose more gracefully and stood beside him, intertwining her hand with his. "Gavin just proposed to me," she said, her joy obvious. "And I accepted."

Chapter Twenty-Four

That afternoon, Nora sat on the same grassy dune she and Cam had once shared, but today she shared it with Grace. The little girl lay on a blanket beside her, gurgling happily and whisking at the air with her hands and feet.

She smiled down at the child's vigorous play. Grace was getting so big. Soon she would be rolling over on her own and then later learning to crawl. There'd be no stopping her then.

Nora leaned back on her hands, listening to the seabirds and staring out over the ocean. So vast, so majestic, so timeless—a metaphor for God himself.

After a time, she smiled back down at Grace. "Thank you, little one, for coming into my life when you did, for adding sunshine and unconditional love and purpose to my world when I was struggling to find all three. You've given me a sweet taste of motherhood and a fathomless joy. I will always, *always* love you, no matter what."

The distant sound of footsteps intruded but she didn't look up. She didn't have to.

"I figured I'd find you out here." Cam plopped down beside her, sandwiching her between himself and Grace.

"I like the sound of the ocean waves."

"I heard Gavin proposed to Mollie."

Nora nodded. "Mollie is over the moon. And I'm very happy for them."

"You don't think it's too soon? It wasn't very long ago that he wanted me to lock her up."

Nora shrugged. "Who's to say how long it takes someone to fall in love?" She tried not to think of her own experience with romantic love. "It looks like there'll be two weddings this month." She hoped her tone was as light as she intended. "I assume Ben's wedding will come first so Gavin can have a place to move his bride into."

"That's the plan. Which means Mollie will be moving out of your house soon."

"Yes." She kept her eyes focused on the ocean, not trusting herself to meet his gaze just yet. "Which I guess also means there's no need for you to spend your nights out here anymore either." They both knew there'd been no need for quite some time.

She reached over and tickled Grace's toes, smiling when the baby laughed. "And Grace will be going with Mollie of course." Her traitorous lip betrayed her, trembling on the last word.

"Ah, Nora honey." He pulled her close against him and stroked her hair. She couldn't bring herself to pull away. "You know you don't have to do this."

"Yes, I do. Cam, it's okay, really." She rested a palm against his shirt, right over the spot that protected his heart. Her own pulse responded to the strong, warm beat beneath her hand.

He placed his own hand over hers, his gesture comforting, protective. And something else she didn't dare dwell on.

"I've made my peace with it," she assured him. "Mollie has turned into a fine young woman and Gavin will make a terrific father. You only have to see how he is with his brothers to know that." She forced a smile. "And they'll be right here in Faith Glen where I can watch Grace grow up and maybe be a part of her life."

Cam brushed the hair off Nora's face, wishing he could brush away her pain as easily. She was hurting inside, but, being Nora, she wouldn't let it defeat her. "She'll be lucky to have you in her life." As would anyone. "It's okay to cry if you want to," he told her. Though her tears would be like daggers to him. "I won't tell anyone."

"I'm going to miss her, of course, more than I can say. And Mollie, too, truth be told. But I think I understand now, something of what God has been doing with my life."

She always seemed to look for lessons in her circumstances. "What do you mean?"

"For a long time I was angry with Him for all the people He's taken from me. I wouldn't admit it at the time, but the anger was there just the same. But what I've learned these past few weeks, since Mollie came along, is that I should instead be grateful for the time He allowed me to have with those special people."

Cam ached for the hurt she'd felt, and admired her ability to find joy in it.

She pulled slightly away from him and met his gaze with eyes that shone with her passion for this lesson she'd learned. "Imagine, for three months, I had the privilege of getting to be a mother to the most beautiful baby in the world, got to keep her safe while He worked in her mother's life to bring her back to His side. That privilege could have been given to anyone else on that ship, but God put Grace in *my* hands." She paused, staring out over the ocean again. "Who am I to be angry that He didn't leave her with me longer?"

Cam looked into her face and saw how deeply she believed every word of what she was saying. Her faith was amazing and beautifully submissive—it both astounded and humbled him.

Then she surprised him yet again by moving out of his embrace and sitting up with her hands clasped together on her knees. "Now, enough on that subject. The matter of Grace is settled and while it may feel bittersweet now, we will both resolve to be happy at the outcome."

He nodded. "Yes, ma'am. So what shall we discuss? The weather? Mrs. Fitzwilliam's building plans?"

She cut him a prim look of disapproval for his levity. "Actually, I do have some things I want to say to you, and you *will* sit there and listen to me."

Uh-oh. That statement didn't bode well for him.

"But first I want to ask you a question and I want you to be totally honest, no matter what you think I *want* to hear, because this is important. Promise?"

Seeing her earnestness, he nodded. "Of course—I promise."

"Do you think it's a mistake to hand Grace over to Mollie? Do you think that Mollie will be a bad mother, that she might not take proper care of Grace once she's on her own with her?"

She'd seemed so sure of her decision a moment ago. Was she having second thoughts now? Or was she just trying to get a different perspective? Well, she'd asked him to be honest. "No, of course I don't think she'll be a bad mother. Mollie loves Grace, it's as obvious as the sun in the sky. She'll put Grace's well-being above her own and no one could take better care of her." He tapped her nose. "Except you."

Nora gave him an approving smile. "So, just because her momentary inattention allowed that accident down by the pond, she shouldn't cut herself off from ever taking care of children again?"

He stiffened. Too late he realized where she was going. "What happened at the Gallaghers' is not the same as what happened all those years ago when I was supposed to be watching Tommy."

Her gaze never left his. "It's not?"

"No." Maybe if he was blunt enough she would drop the subject. "For one thing, nobody died."

To his surprise, she didn't back down. "But that's no thanks to Mollie. Her lapse of attention could quite easily have resulted in a much more tragic outcome. Maybe next time it will."

He clamped his lips shut, wanting to put an end to this discussion. He'd come out here to comfort her, not dredge his past up again.

But apparently Nora wasn't finished with him. "And what about me?" she asked. "My lapse had much more serious consequences. Maybe *I* shouldn't be left alone with a child again."

Now she was being just plain ridiculous. "Nora, you've been the most careful mother I have ever come across."

She shook her head and he saw the sadness creep into her eyes. "Have you already forgotten that it was my fault Grace was kidnapped?" She reached down to let Grace grab hold of her finger. "I left this sweet, helpless babe, who depended on me to keep her safe, all alone in the kitchen, knowing the outside door was wide open. Thanks to my negligence, a stranger walked right into my house and stole my baby. We got her back eventually, but only because the kidnapper returned her. If Mollie had decided to leave town with her, we might have never seen Grace again, might never have known what became of her."

She shuddered and Cam felt as if he'd been punched in the gut.

Had she really blamed herself for what happened? He should have realized what she was going through and reassured her. "Nora, honey, you couldn't have anticipated such a thing. And you were just in the next room. You can't be with her every second. No one blames you for what happened."

She raised a brow and he suddenly remembered the point she was trying to make.

"Exactly." She poked him in the chest. "So, if things had turned out differently, if we'd never seen Grace again, should I have vowed never to take on responsibility for a child ever again, have cut myself off from the possibility of having a family of my own someday?"

Everything inside him protested that vision. Nora was made to be a mother. She had so much love to give, so much warmth to share. To let that one lapse ruin her future was unthinkable. Especially since he knew that what she saw as a lapse would make her even more diligent in the future.

His own situation was entirely different.

Wasn't it?

Nora apparently tired of waiting for him to answer her. "You told me the dark secret from your past and put it forth as the reason why you will never let yourself be responsible for a child again. Now I'm going to explain to you why you are absolutely, positively, completely wrong in your thinking."

She stared earnestly into his eyes. "What happened was a tragic accident, but an accident nonetheless. I know you like to think you are somehow more capable of looking out for others than most people and so should be held to a higher standard than anyone else, but that kind of thinking is not only misguided, it's just plain prideful. And pride is a sin." Her lips curved slightly. "I should know."

He couldn't share her smile.

"You care about people," she continued. "You care deeply. It's why you became a sheriff, and why you're so good at it. It's why you keep a close eye on troublemakers and an even closer eye on folks like the Coulters who have no one else to care for them."

He tried to say something but she wasn't finished.

"When Grace was taken—" she shivered "—you were the first one out looking for her each day and the last one to come back in every evening. There was no doubt that you cared very deeply about Grace and would have been as devastated as I if we hadn't found her." She narrowed her eyes as if in accusation. "That's not a man who should think twice about the kind of father he would make."

She reached down and lifted Grace, blanket and all, then stood over him with her precious burden.

"God will forgive you for what happened if you ask Him to. You just need to learn to forgive yourself."

He saw some strong emotion flicker in her expression that he was afraid to identify.

"Do something for me," she said. "Sit here awhile,

stare out at God's marvelous creation and really think about what I've said." Then she turned and walked along the beach, back toward the cottage.

Cam, his heart weighted down by the sadness in her eyes, turned and stared out over the ocean as she'd requested.

He plucked a handful of rocks from the ground beside him and began flinging them, one at a time, toward the water.

Nora was a sweet, tender, generous person. She was facing the end of her role as mother to Grace and she was doing it with dignity and grace despite her heartache.

Yet in the midst of this turmoil, she had taken time to try to heal his hurts, as well. And it hadn't been a halfhearted attempt. His lips curved in a tender smile as he thought about her passionate defense of him.

He only wished things could be as simple as she tried to make them sound.

He flung one last rock and then leaned back, letting the peace of his surroundings flow over him. Despite his resolve to the contrary, her words kept coming back to him, over and over.

She'd said his problem was pride, but this didn't feel like pride. On the other hand, how did he feel about her own so-called negligence that had allowed Grace to be kidnapped? If that had been him, he knew that he'd never have forgiven himself, would have seen it as further proof of his failings. Yet it had never once occurred to him to blame Nora for her role in allowing Grace to be taken. And it still didn't. What she did was perfectly innocent, perfectly reasonable given the situation.

Was this "different standard," as she called it, that

he held himself to truly an outgrowth of the worst kind of pride?

For the first time since it had happened, he willingly recalled the events of that long-ago night. He felt again the stifling heat of that garret room, felt again the bone-deep weariness he experienced from working all day in the factory and trying to keep himself awake at night to watch Tommy. He crossed the room to get a dipper of tepid water from the bucket on the table. Tommy's laughter made him smile and he turned just in time to see the boy run to catch the moth. He could still feel the splash of the water as the dipper fell from his hands, could hear his voice yelling for Tommy to stop, could still feel the pounding of his pulse as he tried to get across the room in time. But Tommy was too enthralled to listen and Cam's own reflexes were too slow for him to stop what was happening.

Cam shook his head, trying to push the nightmare away, but his brain refused to let him. And suddenly he pictured Nora in that same scene. He stood in the corner of the room and watched as she took his place. He saw her face twist in horror and grief as the final scene played out and what he felt for her was compassion and a soul-deep desire to comfort her and wipe away her tears. There was no trace of condemnation or recrimination for her.

He pictured that twelve-year-old boy as someone else and his perception of what had happened shifted, changed. No one could be everywhere at once. Sometimes terrible things happened without being anyone's fault.

Tommy's death had been horrifying and tragic, yes. But it had also been an accident. He would carry the painful memory of what had happened with him all of his life, he knew that. And that was as it should be. It was the burden he had to bear for his part in what had happened.

But that memory had lost its power over him. It was no longer a poison that was killing any chance he had at true joy. It had become more of a warning beacon, a reminder of what could happen when he dropped his vigilance.

Cam closed his eyes and offered up a silent prayer of thanksgiving. He felt freer, lighter than he had in a very long time.

Then he stood and headed down the beach. There was something very important that he had to do.

Chapter Twenty-Five

Nora stepped off the back porch and headed for the garden. Mollie was giving Grace her bottle and Nora was feeling restless. Had she done the right thing by confronting Cam the way she had? It was so hard to know how much to push and how much to let him work out on his own.

But she'd never been the patient type.

She paused in front of the bench, running a hand across the now smooth, sturdy arm of the thing. Cam had put so much of himself into this place. She could barely look around without seeing evidence of his handiwork.

"Hello again."

Nora whirled around to see Cam watching her, a strangely intense light in his eyes. She swallowed, trying to moisten her suddenly dry throat. "You seem to have made it your mission to come upon me unawares today."

"I did as you asked."

"Oh?" Something about the way he was looking at her was making her pulse flutter.

"Yes." His lips curved in a crooked half smile. "I find it's often in my best interest to heed your advice."

She smiled back at him, wondering at his strange mood.

"Oh, yes. I looked out over the ocean and thought about all your nonsense talk of sinful pride and different standards, and I finally came to one very important conclusion."

"What was that?" She was finding it difficult to breathe normally.

He stepped forward and took her hands in his. "That it was not nonsense talk after all."

She searched his face, trying to discern his meaning. Could he really have taken her words to heart?

"I'm ready to put it behind me now. And I have you to thank for that."

She squeezed his hands, heart swelling with happiness for him. "Oh, Cam, that's wonderful. But all I did was show you the truth that was already in front of you."

"You did so much more than that. You are amazing and generous and beautiful. And I love you."

Her heart actually stuttered at those words. But she didn't hesitate. "Oh, Cam, I love you, too. I have for quite some time."

He led her to the bench and sat down next to her. "I want to build a life with you, Nora honey. I can't give you a big fine house like Will and Flynn gave your sisters, but I can love you with every fiber of my being, every day of my life. Say you'll marry me and I promise to do my best to see that you never have cause to regret it."

She loved it when he called her "Nora honey" in that tender way he seemed to reserve just for her. "Oh, Cam,

I don't need a big house, I just need you by my side. Yes, yes, yes, I'll marry you and count myself blessed to do it."

Cam pulled her into a fierce embrace. "Nora honey," he said, his voice low and husky, "unless you have any serious objections, I'm going to give you the kiss I've wanted to give you since you first came into my life and this time I intend to do it proper."

He'd wanted to kiss her even then? She smiled and raised her face. "I thought you'd never ask."

With a strangled laugh, Cam did just as he'd promised.

Epilogue

Faith Glen, Massachusetts, June 1851

Nora and Cam stepped out on the ribbon-bedecked terrace at Mrs. Fitzwilliam's home. Nora's eyes immediately locked on the adorable toddler with the golden curls and sparkling blue eyes who was holding court at the far end of the terrace.

The little girl spotted Nora at about the same time and her face lit up. She lifted her arms and took a few shaky steps forward. "Na-wa!"

"Grace." Nora took a few quick steps, then halted when a familiar arm looped around her waist.

"Whoa there, Mrs. Long. No mad dashes for you, remember?"

She rolled her eyes as she turned to face her husband. "That was *not* a mad dash."

He tucked her hand on his arm. "No point taking any chances. Now, let's not keep Ladybug waiting."

Together they crossed the terrace at a much-too-sedate pace for Nora's liking. Finally reaching her target, she stooped to give Grace a hug. "Happy birthday, sweetheart. You're looking so pretty today."

Grace returned Nora's hug and gave her a loud, sloppy kiss. Then she turned to Mollie who was seated at her side, snatched something from her lap, and held it out to Nora. "Bee-bee"

Nora admired the rag doll. "Yes, baby. Very nice."

Grace giggled and snatched back her doll, then toddled over to Gavin, demanding he pick her up.

Before Nora could rise, she felt Cam's hand under her elbow. She allowed him to help her up, then put her fists on her hips. "Cam, you're hovering. Why don't you go join that group of men over there while I find Maeve and Bridget?"

"Maybe I should stay—"

"I want a word alone with my sisters," she said firmly.

He nodded reluctantly. "Of course. I know you've been fair to bursting to talk to them, but promise me you won't go haring off and that you'll be careful on the stairs."

Nora rolled her eyes again. If he was going to be like this for the next seven months it would drive her plumb crazy. Then again, it was nice to have someone who cared this much about her. More than nice. "I promise."

Cam dropped a lingering kiss on her cheek, then stepped back. "I'll be right over there with Will and Flynn if you need me."

She smiled. "I will always need you."

His eyes darkened at that and she laughed. "Now run on so I can find Maeve and Bridget."

But before she'd taken more than two steps, Mrs. Fitzwilliam found her. "Nora, I'm so glad you could come."

Nora smiled. The woman had softened considerably

over the past year. "Thanks for inviting me. Everything looks lovely."

"Goodness, we couldn't have Grace's party without her Aunt Nora. Oh, and that birthday cake you made for her is marvelous. Thank you for sending it."

"It was my pleasure."

Mrs. Fitzwilliam patted Nora's arm. "You just run along and enjoy yourself. I believe I saw your sisters strolling on the lawn."

"Thank you." Nora descended the terrace steps, stopping to greet a number of friends and neighbors, trying not to let her impatience show. Where *were* Maeve and Bridget?

She finally spotted them sitting on a stone bench in the formal garden. No doubt their current state had them tiring more easily then normal.

She moved toward them, reined into a walk by her promise to Cam.

"Nora." Bridget saw her first and started to get up.

Nora waved her back down. "Please don't get up on my account." To her amusement, Maeve didn't even attempt to stand.

She came to a halt in front of the bench and smiled down at them. Both sisters were glowing with health and happiness, and both sisters were very obviously with child. Maeve was due to deliver next month and Bridget two months later.

"We were wondering when you'd get here," Bridget said. "It's not like you to be late, especially when Grace is involved."

Nora hugged her secret close for a few more minutes. "Cam and I had something to take care of first."

Maeve sighed. "Can you believe it—Grace is one year old today."

Nora smiled fondly. "It seems like she's learned something new each time I see her."

"You know what this birthday means, don't you?" Bridget asked.

Nora nodded. "It's an anniversary of sorts for us, as well. One year ago today we were just setting out on our voyage to this country."

Maeve rubbed her very round tummy. "How could we have ever imagined what this past year would bring? New homes, wonderful husbands, loving families."

"Blessings beyond measure," Nora agreed. Then she clasped her hands in front of her. "I have a question for the two of you. Have your husbands been treating you with a ridiculous amount of extra care since you each found out you were going to have a baby?"

Bridget laughed. "Oh my goodness, yes. Will wanted to move us into a bedchamber on the first floor so I wouldn't have to climb the stairs."

Maeve shook her head. "My normally pragmatic husband has decided he will only take emergency cases from now until the time I deliver so that he can watch over me. I'm surprised he isn't here with us now." She shifted as if trying to get more comfortable. "I do believe every husband on the planet turns into a mother hen when his wife is expecting."

Bridget patted her little sister's hand. "True, but I find it can be quite nice to be so cherished." She laughed. "When it's not annoyingly smothering."

Nora smiled. "It's good to know that Cam is not the only one who is taking the news that way."

Maeve understood the implication of her words first and let out a loud squeal. "Oh my goodness, Nora, you're expecting, too!"

"What!" Bridget did stand now. "Nora, why didn't

you say something when you first walked up? When are you due?"

"We're thinking we'll have a Christmas baby."

She sat down next to Maeve, and Bridget sat beside her. Nora put an arm around both of her sisters and let the joy of the moment wash over her. "As I said, blessings beyond measure."

* * * * *

Dear Reader,

Thank you so much for taking the time to read Nora and Cam's story. I was honored and excited when my editor invited me to participate in this continuity series. Not only is this my first continuity but it is my first book set in this time period and this setting. The research was fascinating and I learned so many amazing tidbits about this time in the history of our country.

It was also great to be able to work closely with the two other authors involved in this project. Both Renee and Cheryl are great writers and amazingly generous women. Brainstorming different aspects of the three sisters' stories with them was a real joy.

I love to hear from readers and would be interested in hearing what you think of this particular book. If you've a mind to comment, please contact me via email at winnie@winniegriggs.com, or you can write to me at P.O. Box 14, Plain Dealing, LA 71064.

Wishing you a life filled with love and blessings,
Winnie

Questions for Discussion

1. In the opening line of the book we see Nora feeling an unwanted touch of jealousy at her sisters' good fortune. Did this make her seem selfish to you? Do you think this was a natural reaction?

2. What do you think of Nora's refusal to move in with one of her sisters when they genuinely wanted to take care of her and Grace?

3. What do you think was Nora's primary motivation in her decision to start a bakery business? Do you find this motivation admirable? Why or why not?

4. How do you feel about the way Cam manipulated Nora into agreeing to buy a means of transportation and then later convinced her to buy a horse and wagon rather than a pony and cart?

5. Cam believed his upbringing had a strong influence in shaping the kind of father he would become. How do you feel about that in "real life" situations?

6. Was Cam's gradual warming toward Grace believable to you or did it seem contrived?

7. How did you feel about Nora's attack against Cam when he came home without Grace the night of the kidnapping?

8. What did you think about Nora's decision to take Mollie in? What do you think you would have done had you been in her situation?

9. How did you feel about Mollie when she announced she was Grace's mother? How did that feeling change after she revealed the circumstances that led up to her current situation? After she had lived with Nora for a while?

10. Why do you think it took so long for Gavin to forgive Mollie?

11. Did your feelings about Cam change after he revealed the dark secret from his past? If so, in what way?

12. Was Nora's ultimate decision to release Grace into Mollie's keeping believable? How did it make you feel? Do you believe it was the best thing for Grace?

INSPIRATIONAL

HISTORICAL

celebrating
15
YEARS

COMING NEXT MONTH
AVAILABLE JULY 2, 2012

WOOING THE SCHOOLMARM
Pinewood Weddings
Dorothy Clark
Schoolteacher Willa Wright has given up on romance—
until Reverend Matthew Calvert sneaks his way into
her heart.

THE CAPTAIN'S COURTSHIP
The Everard Legacy
Regina Scott
London's whirlwind season would seem manageable to
Captain Richard Everard...if it hadn't reunited him with the
lady he'd once loved.

THE RUNAWAY BRIDE
Noelle Marchand
Childhood rejection closed Lorelei Wilkins's heart to Sean
O'Brien. Is a forced engagement love's chance to finally
conquer them both?

HEARTS IN HIDING
Patty Smith Hall
Beau Daniels is captivated by Edie Michaels, but can love
withstand the ultimate test of loyalty when he discovers
her family ties to Nazi Germany?

LIHCNM0612

REQUEST YOUR FREE BOOKS!

2 FREE INSPIRATIONAL NOVELS
PLUS 2
FREE
MYSTERY GIFTS

Love Inspired.
HISTORICAL
INSPIRATIONAL HISTORICAL ROMANCE

YES! Please send me 2 FREE Love Inspired® Historical novels and my 2 FREE mystery gifts (gifts are worth about $10). After receiving them, if I don't wish to receive any more books, I can return the shipping statement marked "cancel". If I don't cancel, I will receive 4 brand-new novels every month and be billed just $4.49 per book in the U.S. or $4.99 per book in Canada. That's a saving of at least 22% off the cover price. It's quite a bargain! Shipping and handling is just 50¢ per book in the U.S. and 75¢ per book in Canada.* I understand that accepting the 2 free books and gifts places me under no obligation to buy anything. I can always return a shipment and cancel at any time. Even if I never buy another book, the two free books and gifts are mine to keep forever.

102/302 IDN FEHF

Name	(PLEASE PRINT)	
Address		Apt. #
City	State/Prov.	Zip/Postal Code

Signature (if under 18, a parent or guardian must sign)

Mail to the **Reader Service:**
IN U.S.A.: P.O. Box 1867, Buffalo, NY 14240-1867
IN CANADA: P.O. Box 609, Fort Erie, Ontario L2A 5X3

Not valid for current subscribers to Love Inspired Historical books.

Want to try two free books from another series?
Call 1-800-873-8635 or visit www.ReaderService.com.

* Terms and prices subject to change without notice. Prices do not include applicable taxes. Sales tax applicable in N.Y. Canadian residents will be charged applicable taxes. Offer not valid in Quebec. This offer is limited to one order per household. All orders subject to credit approval. Credit or debit balances in a customer's account(s) may be offset by any other outstanding balance owed by or to the customer. Please allow 4 to 6 weeks for delivery. Offer available while quantities last.

Your Privacy—The Reader Service is committed to protecting your privacy. Our Privacy Policy is available online at www.ReaderService.com or upon request from the Reader Service.

We make a portion of our mailing list available to reputable third parties that offer products we believe may interest you. If you prefer that we not exchange your name with third parties, or if you wish to clarify or modify your communication preferences, please visit us at www.ReaderService.com/consumerschoice or write to us at Reader Service Preference Service, P.O. Box 9062, Buffalo, NY 14269. Include your complete name and address.

LIH11B

DOROTHY CLARK

brings you another story from

PINEWOOD WEDDINGS

When Willa Wright's fiancé abandoned her three days before the wedding, he ended all her hopes for romance. Now she dedicates herself to teaching Pinewood's children, including the new pastor's young wards. If she didn't know better, Reverend Calvert's kindness could almost fool Willa into caring again. Almost.

Wooing the Schoolmarm

Available July wherever books are sold.

Violet Colby's life is about to get turned upside down by a twin sister she's never met.

Read on for a preview of HER SURPRISE SISTER by Marta Perry from Love Inspired Books.

Violet Colby looked around the Fort Worth coffee shop. She didn't belong here, any more than the sophisticated-looking guy in the corner would belong on the ranch. Expensive suit and tie, a Stetson with not a smudge to mar its perfection—he was big city Texas.

That man's head turned, as if he felt her stare, and she caught the full impact of a pair of icy green eyes before she could look away. She stared down at her coffee.

She heard approaching footsteps.

"What are you doing here?"

Violet looked up, surprised. "What?"

"I said what are you doing here?" He pulled out the chair opposite her and sat down. "I told you I'd be at your apartment in five minutes. So why are you in the coffee shop instead?"

Okay, he was crazy. She started to rise.

"The least you can do is talk to me about it. I still want to marry you." He sounded impatient. "Maddie, why are you acting this way?"

Relief made her limp for an instant. He wasn't crazy.

"I think you've mistaken me for someone else."

He studied her, letting his gaze move from her hair to a face that was bare of makeup, to her Western shirt and well-worn jeans.

Finally he shook his head. "You're not Maddie Wallace, are you?"

"No. Now that we have that straight, I'll be going."

"Wait. It's uncanny." A line formed between his eyebrows. "Look, my name is Landon Derringer. If you'll be patient for a few minutes, I think you'll find it worthwhile." He flipped open his cell phone.

"Maddie? This is Landon. I'm over at the Coffee Stop, and there's someone here you have to meet.

"Okay," he said finally. "Right. We'll be here."

Violet glanced at her watch. "I'll give you five minutes, no more."

"Good." He rose. "I'll get you a refill."

"That's not—"

But he'd already gone to the counter. She glanced at her watch again as he came back with the coffee.

He glanced at the door. "You won't have long to wait. She's here."

The door swung open, and a woman stepped inside. Slim, chic, sophisticated. And other than that, Violet's exact double.

To unravel the mystery, pick up HER SURPRISE SISTER,
the first of the TEXAS TWINS series
from Love Inspired Books.

Available July 2012